ALL THAT GLITTERS

KATHRYN SCARBOROUGH

Copyright © 2020 Kathryn Scarborough

All rights reserved. No part of this book may be reproduced, stored, or transmitted by any means—whether auditory, graphic, mechanical, or electronic—without written permission of both publisher and author, except in the case of brief excerpts used in critical articles and reviews. Unauthorized reproduction of any part of this work is illegal and is punishable by law.

For:

Doris Dix Caruso, Brenda Wilson, Liz Salazzo, Jan Sady, and all "The Story Sisters."

"A wise and frugal government, which shall leave men free to regulate their own pursuits of industry and improvement and shall not take from the mouth of labor the bread it has earned — this is the sum of good government."

Thomas Jefferson

I used to think of myself as a decent man; not St. Francis, mind you, but the kind of man who generally tries to avoid pissing anyone off; to do good. But tonight, I'd walked away from a man who needed my help. His head bled slowly into the rain soaked gravel and yet I'd walked away.

But I didn't wonder what side of that precarious balance of saint or sinner I was on now. The man I'd become; the harsh, shoot now and ask questions later, infuriated by anyone that was in my way, side of my personality, was who I was now. Since that night in Carrboro when I'd seen that murder from so long ago, I'd been on a merry-go-round; the centrifugal force so great that jumping off was impossible. I left that man because in order to solve that murder, I had to steer clear of the cops, the federal agents, and everything but the truth.

All THAT GliTTeRS

Chapter One

32 days earlier
Infinite Hypnosis Clinic
Carrboro, NC

The sound edged toward me like a thing hiding in the fog. I was afraid, but leaned forward to listen.

I watched the gleam of lights in the distance. It was a car speeding toward me and transfixed, I stared, knowing the next moment would be my last.

"Breathe deeply. You are surrounded by white light. No harm can come to you."

My eyes shot open and I wiped away the sweat on my face with the back of my hand. Slowly, I remembered where I was. No one paid me the slightest attention, but still I tried to contain the shivers of fear coursing through me.

With my sleeve, I wiped the cold sweat from my face as my heart hammered painfully.

The young woman brought everyone around out of their collective trances. All twelve stood and buzzed around the hypnotist like worker bees in a flower garden.

"Wasn't that neat?" Monica's voice ratcheted up an octave and her round face glowed. "What did you see?" She gave me a little poke in the ribs, her signal that she meant business.

"What did *you* see?" I had to figure out exactly what I had seen.

"I saw these beautiful silky curtains, and they were blowing around. And then I saw a beautiful table that was so big it could seat just scads of people, and it had big, round, gold plates on it. And then I saw me, and I was wearing this billowing gown that floated all around my legs. But my legs were bare and I had weird looking sandals on and…"

Monica chattered away and I hit my 'off switch' effectively tuning her out.

Had I been in an actual trance? Had it really happened? My heart still squeezed painfully; could I have been that person run down?

"Now," the hypnotist said. "Sit down, please, close your eyes and breathe deeply. I will instruct you to get messages about your vision to receive more information about your past."

A chill ran down my back. I did not want to revisit the fog, the glaring lights, and the terror.

"Ooh, honey, are you okay?" Monica put a solicitous hand on my arm.

"Yeah, sure, no problem."

"Let's go up there. She's answering people's individual questions."

"Monica, let's call it a night. She gave out her cards. Maybe you can get a private session with her."

"Wow, that sounds great." Monica's round face beamed. "Yeah, let's go, you're looking a little peaked, honey."

When I reached my apartment, I threw my keys on the counter, moved into the kitchen and yanked open the fridge. The shaft of light from the opened door, rushed across the floor and up the opposite wall. A sliver of anxiety crowded at the back of my throat. I clamped it down as I grabbed a beer. I turned on every light in my entire apartment before standing in the middle of my living room and turning once, 360°.

I looked at each object in the room while I sipped my beer. Why was I in such a weird, fearful mood?

I thought about what I had heard during the trance. That noise might be the engine sound of an antique car. Cars in the Hercule Poirot television series might've sounded like the one in the dream. Deciding to double check my theory, I popped in a

DVD, an old Agatha Christie mystery, and picked an episode at random.

In the opening scene of the show, a man walked down a lonely, country lane. The fog, a swirl of gray and white wisps, lay like a blanket over everything; and the only sounds were a subtle wind and gravel crunching beneath the actor's feet.

In the distance, an engine started and its hum grew. The sound came and then lights that grew brighter as the engine drew nearer. The character shielded his eyes and tried to leap out of the way, but the car hit the man with a sickening thud. A terrible scream rang out. I stopped breathing and then gasped with the dreaded certainty, that I was the one who had screamed. The bottle fell from my fingers with a thud, the liquid slowly puddled onto the rug.

Over the next few days, I was plagued by nightmares, and those dreams raised even more questions. What had happened to this man in my dream. Was the man me? And as though my mother and Monica could sense that something was wrong, they called me only to be met by my one-syllable answers. Even conversations at work became strained and distracted.

My detailed, meticulous work began to suffer. I had to check and re-check everything I did in the lab. I was terrified that I'd make a mistake and hours, perhaps days of research would go down the drain. Just yesterday, I'd caught a colossal mistake before it had gone past my desk; I'd misplaced a zero in front of a decimal point.

Every night I'd return home and drink beer until I nodded off into a stupor, but wake once again to the sound of an engine racing toward me. In the dream, I always found myself standing in the middle of a foggy road, or was it someone else standing there? I didn't know; I was in this strange, unrecognizable place, as twin round lights sped towards me., I could do nothing but shade my eyes against the glare and wait for the end.

Staring into the darkness, with my heart pounding loudly in my ears, I knew this dream wasn't simply a dream anymore. Someone had run me over. Hit me with a damn car, and kept going. Only now as I stared into those twin bright lights, I began to realize it had been deliberate. That the man I'd kept seeing over and over again in my dreams hadn't simply been run over, he'd been murdered.

Chapter Two

What was there in my dream that I could reconcile with reality? Some annoying, 'know it all' part of my brain nudged at me, prodded me to find the reason behind it.

My mind worked over every detail of the dream, like a tape loop that never moved forward or back. There was simply no explanation for any of it. Did I believe in reincarnation? Was I the man run over, or was there a deeper, more complex reason for my 'waking dreams?'

I was a microbiologist and had worked in that capacity for more than a dozen years. I had never sought advancement in the medical school, although my credentials were better than most. I'd always thought the less controversial my behavior was, the better. Why, exactly? That was something I hadn't chosen to think about.

Working in the lab could be tedious. For the drug discovery now in play, I was the 'mouse wrangler': the keeper of the dozens of mice the medical school used for the drug trials, and I documented each and every detail about each and every experiment.

I shut the cage door on the group of the little, pink-eyed mice, my charges for the interim, and made a notation on the clipboard attached to the cage. I closed my eyes and rested my forehead on the cage door feeling the cold bite of the metal. I felt lightheaded and a little nauseous.

My gaze drew to the mechanical pencil I held in my hand as it began to change. The clear orange plastic, thickened, grew darker, then black, into a gold and ebony fountain pen. I stood very still staring at this unfamiliar pen held by an unfamiliar hand. The pencil and the hand morphed back to the way they'd been 10 seconds before. I put the pencil down and sat heavily in a chair against the wall. How was any of this scientifically, logically possible?

I had to find out what had happened in this dream, or trance, or whatever it was, and most importantly, what it had to do with me. If I found out why that other man had been murdered, I could put all this to rest and get back to my life. Surely, that was the only way. I had to approach this as I would any scientific research. I would start with an abstract, then the hypothesis, then…

I made a quick and unprecedented decision.

Doctor Lu the lab director and my boss, was a small, wiry, reticent woman of Chinese descent. The staff at the lab had a betting pool during the last clinical trial on how many times she would smile during the six-month duration. She never did, and consequently, everyone lost. She'd just returned to her office when I knocked on the doorjamb twice and entered. The doctor was looking through a pile of computer readouts and didn't look up as I came into the office.

"Doctor Lu, I need to ask you a favor."

"Yes, Eric, what is it."

"I need to take a leave of absence."

It was vital I understood why I was drinking myself into a stupor every night, only to wake up with a jolt after being run over once again in my dreams.

Doctor Lu looked up from her computer printouts, took her glasses off, and stared at me. "A leave of absence? Do you mind telling me exactly what this pertains to? We are at a significant point in this study. I need my best people on the job 100%."

"It's a personal matter."

The doctor cleared her throat roughly and stared at everything in the room before she again looked up at me. "A personal matter? Eric, this is not a good time. This is not a good time at all. The data we are working on is at a critical juncture. You know this. I know you know this. You're one of the most competent people I have."

"I'm sorry, Doctor Lu, but I have to get this done. I'm at a critical juncture in my life too, and if I don't do this now, I will be no good for you, for the lab, I won't be good for anybody. I'd like to say it's a matter of life and death, but that sounds a bit melodramatic," I said feeling at once shy and forceful. I looked at the doctor candidly meeting her stare head on. "Let me just say that it's, well… if I don't get it resolved I'll be in a bad way."

The doctor let out a huge breath, put her glasses back on, and looked down again at the computer printout. Her annoyance radiated from her as she leafed stridently through her desk calendar.

"All right, Eric. You can start a 14 day leave at the end of the week," she said jabbing her pen at the pad. "I hope that will be enough time for you to resolve whatever you need to do. You can always call me." She looked at me then, up through her glasses with concern, showing in her deep, brown eyes. "Just call me, okay?"

"Doctor Lu, thank you, thank you for this…" I left the office and returned to my station in the lab. If I was going to leave for 14 days, I'd better get things cleaned up and organized in case somebody needed to look over my notes.

I began an almost mindless tidying and cleaning. Beakers, spoons, feeding trays, syringes, all went into a sudsy bath. I wiped down the inside of the cages and all the lab tables and sinks. The numbing memorized tasks allowed my mind to work the problem of finding out about the dreams and getting my life back.

I'd best get in touch with the hypnotist from Carrboro, that is, if I really believed that getting in touch with that person, that new age, tie-dyed hippy… no, I couldn't afford to think that way. I'd have to explore every avenue open to me. Maybe she could help me get started. After all, data collection, research, that was my forte. I could research, this "past life" and find out all these

All THAT GliTTeRS

missing pieces of the puzzle. The first thing after work I'd go see that hypnotist. I still didn't know if I believed in all that stuff, but what other avenue was there open for me? I signed off my workstation and laptop, and gave the mice a two-finger wave, and left.

Chapter Three

Bone-wrenching fatigue washed over me, but I ignored it as I put my car in gear and turned down Manning. Instead of turning onto Columbia, I headed down East Franklin toward Carrboro.

The traffic was slow going, stop and start, and the glare of the sun, even in early spring, baked the hood and the driver's side of the car. I gave my mind over to avoiding other vehicles as I crept along Main Street in five o'clock traffic.

At 5:04, I reached Carr-Mill villages, a collection of organic food, tie dyed clothing, and trinket shops on Main Street. Perhaps the fates were with me, because a parking spot was open in front of the "Infinite Hypnosis Clinic."

I stopped the car and looked out the passenger side. "Smoking, weight loss, anxiety, depression, and past life regression," read the block letters painted on the plate glass window. I sighed. I'd never find out anything if I turned into BBQ sitting in the hot car.

I walked to the shade of the building, thinking, I hadn't called. What if she was busy? I reached for my wallet and took out the business card I'd carried around since that fate filled evening some weeks before. "Miss Margaret E. Dickinson, MCS, CHT, experienced Hypnotist." Hum, what the hell was an 'MCS' or a 'CHT' for that matter? No sense waiting around; no guts, no glory.

A tiny bell chimed from the back as I pushed open the door. The quiet music of sitars and high yodeling singers played through speakers strategically placed around the room. Cheap plastic chairs and tables cluttered with dog-eared magazines, abandoned Styrofoam cups, and soda cans lay crumpled on a frayed outdoor

All THAT GliTTeRS

carpet. A large fish tank dominated one wall of the waiting area and gurgled happily in the musty, stale gloom. I stood for just a moment, taking in the seedy and decidedly non-medical waiting room. *God, what am I thinking? I'm not doing this.*

I turned to leave just as the door to the inner office opened.

"Hello, may I help you?"

I recognized the woman as the practitioner from the group party I attended days before. She was probably near 30, brown hair, devoid of makeup, and wearing a T-shirt and jeans. I was sure her smile was genuine.

"Yes, I attended the group session you gave about two weeks ago? If you have time, I'd like to talk with you about it."

"I charge $50 an hour," she said. "And that includes a tape of the session. If you need an additional session about the same topic, those are $35 an hour."

I didn't speak, but glanced around the shabby office, pulling my thoughts together. If I could get my sanity back for $50.00, I was on it. "Would you take a credit card?"

"Absolutely. I have some time now, or when would you like to have your session?"

It took just a moment for me to decide. There was nothing waiting for me at home except beer in long neck bottles, my couch, and more nightmares. "Yes, let's start now. I need, well, to be able to start sleeping again. I've been having some problems since the last session, and recurring dreams... you can help me with that, right?"

She nodded as she led me through to her inner office. The practitioner's desk crammed against the wall was littered with magazines and post-it- notes stuck on the lampshade, the edges of the desk, desk drawers, and on top of each other to create a flowing wave of yellow.

A shabby red recliner sat against one corner of the room.

"Please sit here."

I sat in the chair, surprised at how comfortable it was. Miss Dickinson dimmed the lights and started a CD. The sound of tiny wind chimes swirled around the room.

"Please put your feet up. I want you to tell me precisely why you are here, don't leave out any details; try to be as specific as possible."

"During the last session I had a vision of being run over by a car, or I saw a man being run over; it was not clear. I did some research, and found out it was a car made in the early 1930s. I keep having this vision, or maybe it's a dream, maybe one of those waking dreams." I took a deep breath and closed my eyes for a moment to gather my thoughts. "I can't understand it at all. What does this have to do with me in 2017? Now, I'm having a lot of trouble sleeping, and my day-to-day life is suffering. I'm part of a research team. I work at the medical university in Chapel Hill, and I really need my wits to avoid making colossal mistakes. I wondered if you could help me find out more about this, then I could lay it all to rest." I looked down at my hands, and was appalled to see them tremble. The pit of my stomach surged upward and I swallowed hard past it.

I looked up at the hypnotist. "I'm not sure I believe in reincarnation. But, as a scientist, I'm ready to get all the data I can about it."

Miss Dickinson sat back in her chair with a little smile on her face and put her folded hands in her lap. "This is the way it works, I help you open up the doors, but you have to walk through them. I will lead you, or guide you, into this past life. I will give you all the information that we can find together. Then, you will have to do
some searching on your own. Is that acceptable to
you?" I nodded.

"What you have to do is to keep your mind open, and your heart open to what might be happening."

"Yes, I completely understand."

"I want you to push the chair back, put your hands on each armrest, tilt your head back and close your eyes. Breathe deeply in through your nose and out through your mouth," she said as she demonstrated. "Do the breathing five or six times. Just, slowly, slowly, slowly. That's right; breathe in and out, in and out. A white light will surround you and nothing can come in through the light to harm you. Breathe." Her voice was melodic and soothing. I was surprised because I actually began to relax.

"Now, I want you to go back, go back. Take your mind back to the first time you saw the car. I want you to look around. Tell me what you see."

I felt weightless, almost floating, deeply relaxed. I was surprised at how free I felt, how at peace. Slowly, the scene unfolded as if I were watching a movie, as if I were there, yet not there.

"I see a road. It isn't cement, it isn't tarmac, it's like gravel and dirt."

"What else do you see?"

The fog and a wet soaked air surrounded me and made me shiver. "It's very dark. I don't see any lights. It's foggy, and it's cold."

"I want you to look down at your shoes and tell me what you see."

"I see, what are they-- wingtip shoes. They have little indentations like alligator."

"Look at your hands."

I could feel myself look down; I was looking at someone's hands that were not mine. I was surprised to see a wedding ring on the left hand. "They are big hands with squared off fingers. The man has on a white shirt with gold cufflinks and wearing a suit. It looks like it's tailored, dark wool, maybe with a pin stripe."

"I want you to see if you can find a wallet."

"But what about the car? "

"The car hasn't come yet, not yet we're going to find out who this person is, first. Now, see if you can find a wallet."

"In the breast pocket, I feel a wallet, I'm opening it. I see… I see a license of some kind." I actually saw the license. It surprised me so that I almost dropped the square bit of velum. "It says the man is a journalist, for the Chicago Tribune. And- and—his name, his name is Albert James White."

I recognized that I was in the throes of the trance. I looked down the road. The hair on my neck stood on end and my hands shook so that the license fell onto the gravel at my feet. I turned and began to run. "Oh, I hear the car."

"Eric, it can't hurt you, you are surrounded by the white light. No harm will come to you. Now tell me, why, why the car?"

I ran, ran mindlessly, stumbling, falling forward, standing again, and still I ran. The white light be damned, they were going to kill me. My breath came in great gulps. I ran. I knew my life depended

on it. "It's because, it's because I found something out. Somebody's out to get me because I found something out and they don't want me to tell."

"Nothing can harm you," said the voice, the soothing hypnotic voice. "The white light surrounds you. Don't be afraid. Imagine yourself detached and as only an observer. You are only watching. Nothing can harm you."

My head swam with images: the car, the road, the fog, the license lying crumpled in the gravel at my feet. Then, I realized I was looking down at the road from a height. I was an observer. I breathed slowly, smoothly, and I was no longer afraid.

"Tell me what year it is."

"It's, it's, it's October, no September 1933."

"And where are you?"

"I'm someplace near, uh, near Chicago. Near Lake Michigan, no, maybe not, There are train trestles and train cars, and…."

"Okay, Eric, I want you to remember everything you've learned. Remember, no harm can come to you, this was another time, and no harm can come to you. I'm going to count from 12 to 1. At each number, you will find yourself more and more awake, now 12, 11, 10…"

All THAT GliTTeRS

I sat for a moment, letting my eyes adjust to the light in Miss Dickinson's office. I looked around, feeling groggy, my body and my mind out of touch. I glanced at the clock over the desk and saw that I'd been remembering this man and his death for almost two hours.

I felt like I'd been in the chair just a few minutes.

I tried to remember everything I'd discovered, every detail.

"It's important that you hear me out," Miss Dickinson said after I'd regained some of my composure and she'd given me a glass of water. "After listening to you now, during your session, and by what you've been telling me, I feel you've been chosen to right a wrong. Whether or not you are Jimmy White reincarnated will be revealed sometime later. Here's what I think, Jimmy White was killed. His killer was never found, his body was never found. I hope this doesn't creep you out, but he may be calling for you to resolve this matter, to lay him to rest, so to speak."

"Miss Dickinson, that does creep me out."

"Mr. Douglass, I can count on one hand the times I've heard stories like these, and I've been in this business more than 15 years. The universe, heaven, hell, where we are right now, all are on different planes of existence. It's the people that are shortsighted that think something like this could never happen, that occurrences like this only happen in comic books. Do you remember that quote from Hamlet, "there are more things in heaven and earth, than are dreamt of in your philosophy." My professional opinion is that you should pursue this, that you should do what you can to find out what happened to this man whose death you've seen. If you can lay him to rest, then you can get on with the rest of your life. But this is really important, so think about what I have said to you; finding out about this man and the way he died may be the only way to recapture your life. If you need any further help, I'm always here."

I thought about everything Miss Dickinson told me as I drove away from Carrboro and returned to Chapel Hill. Jimmy White was reaching out. Trying to get me to find out why he died, and where he was. The idea gave me chills up my backbone. My life usually was, and had been, so quiet, so what could I say, boring. I had always taken the least controversial path to anything. But I put my self-criticism on the back burner as I thought through what I had learned about Jimmy White during this last session with Miss Dickinson. And the detail, the one I could not seem to escape, was that someone had murdered this man, this Albert James White in 1933. Because he'd known too much.

Chapter Four

July 1933
Washington, D.C.

"Listen Joey, I can give you enough to pay your rent for the next month. Just think how proud your mother will be if you can stop mooching off her for a while."

"Well, I don't know, Mr. White. Those big wigs in there could have me for breakfast if they found out I was spilling information to you about what they're sayin'. Everyone knows who you are Mr. White; 'A. J. White, always gets his story.' Isn't that your motto?" The boy's open face, so frank and young, gave Jimmy pause. He was paying the kid, that was true, but Jimmy was most likely taking the kid's innocence, too. Joey, the busboy, had never in his young life considered that there might be senators and congressmen so crooked that they would steal candy from a baby. Jimmy hated to enlighten the kid, but the American public had a right to know what was going on, whatever that was, and he'd damn well find out.

"Yeah, Bub, that's my motto, but I can't get the story without your help. I know they're in there planning something big. All you've got to do is listen a little while you're serving their dinner. Act like one of them English butlers, ya know, 'serve from the right, take from the left.' Then clean up a little around the room so you can take a few more minutes and just listen. Now all you have to do is breathe deep, keep a clear head and listen hard. You meet me in my room, that's number 221, and spill it. That's $35.00 for four minutes work. Now, see you in a bit. Don't forget," he said as he placed a conciliatory hand on Joey's shoulder. "Breathe deep, don't get rattled, try to remember everything you hear, and I'll see you in 221."

Albert James White, Jimmy to his friends, paced the room. He hoped the kid wouldn't chicken out. Two senators and a few congressmen were in that smoke filled suite planning something that Jimmy couldn't figure. But the most telling part of the scenario was that they had a first rate gangster 'visiting' in the suite. No one would have guessed about Giovanni Aiello, "The Hammer" the Chicago gangster who had earned his nickname by beating his enemies with a ball-peen hammer, would be hanging out, and hanging onto, the gruesome group of government officials in the suite on the 10th floor.

Joey was nineteen years old, and an avid follower of detective stories and any newspaper article about current gangsters. It was just by chance he'd seen Aiello some yards away, there in the lobby, and decided to follow him up to the 10th floor. He'd peeked around the corner of the freight elevator and watched Aiello enter the maid's workstation two doors down from the room. The maid's room had ceiling high shelves of linens and glassware, a sink, and an ironing board. Joey knew that the room/closet led to the suite. When the gangster did not reappear from the maid's room, Joey knew he could only have gone through the short hallway that led into the suite. Joey had told Jimmy right away.

Jimmy White had almost rubbed his hands together with glee, sure that he was on the brink of a monumental discovery and a story that would win him the accolades of his colleagues and adoring public. As an investigative reporter for the Chicago Tribune, he'd made quite a name for himself exposing the crooks in the offices of the state government and utilities division and even more corrupt politicians. Nobody liked Jimmy. Politicians were actually frightened of him. Well, leery might be a better word. They sure scattered like cockroaches when he entered the room. Too bad.

A knock at the door brought Jimmy and his musings up short. "Yeah," he said to the closed door.

"Mr. White, it's me."

All THAT GliTTeRS

Jimmy opened the door a crack and Joey pushed in. The kid was red in the face and breathing hard. He had run for the elevator.

with his two shelved cart. Dirty cups and saucers, and a silver coffee carafe scattered across the top of the cart. Joey kept trash and supplies discreetly covered by a tablecloth hanging down from the top shelf.

"Well?"

"You're not going to believe this."

"Okay, spill it."

"This is what happened," he said as he recounted the scene.

Joey had cleared the coffee table littered with ashtrays filled to overflowing, and discarded items of clothing, pencils and wads of paper. All the while, he listened, his mind pulling in the information, while his hands completed their familiar tasks. He dumped the ashtrays into one waste can and the wadded paper in the other and set down a tray containing a carafe of coffee, cups, a pitcher of cream, and a sugar bowl. He lay down a second tray of condiments, bread, cheeses, and deli meats. Let them make their own sandwiches.

The men said nothing to him, nor did they acknowledge that he was in the room as they carried on their conversation. Joey was, after all, one of the faceless minions, workers never looked at or considered, at their beck and call. He'd gone into the bath and gathered the towels lying in sodden heaps on the floor, wiped down the sink, and straightened up. He returned to the suite area, taking surreptitious glances, trying to remember what each man looked like as he bent to pick up wadded paper from the floor, and more ashtrays. He committed to memory, words and phrases he'd heard repeated. He straightened shoes and picked up discarded clothing.

He made sure that the trash can, and linens were hidden from view, all the while making a show of ignoring the men. Being there, in that room, terrified him. But he listened, listened, sure that at any minute Aiello would whip out a ball peen hammer and bash his head in.

Anxiety lurched up from the pit of his stomach as he opened the door and pushed himself and the cart into the hall, and to safety.

"Hey boy," one of the men called. Joey's heart jumped into his throat lodging fleetingly around the bile from his stomach.

"Yes, sir." Joey put on a façade forcing himself to look open, pleasant, and just a little stupid.

"Hey, you did a good job in here, kid. What's your name? We'll call for you again if we need anything."

"I'm Joey, Sir. Glad to be of service."

"Well, that's fine, Joey. Here, you did a good job." The man tossed a coin and Joey caught it neatly with one hand.

Joey recognized the man. He'd seen a picture just last week of Senator Abrams of Massachusetts. He looked into his open palm; fifty cents. He'd struck it rich. "Thanks, sir. You just call for Joey and I'll be here, quick as can be." He nodded, and smiled, and gave a salute to the man as he backed his cart completely out of the room.

He pushed the cart to the elevator and rang the button. He hopped nervously from one foot to the other. He had to remember, remember, all he'd heard. Mr. White was right. These guys sounded like trouble, like they were going to take over the country and the 'average Joe' would be none the wiser. And the way they talked about the president—Joey thought FDR was about as great a guy as he'd ever heard about. The president was going to help the country and what had he said, 'we have nothing to fear but fear itself?' Man, that's the cat's pajamas. But these men didn't sound like they cared about the country or the people or FDR. Yeah, the men in the suite sounded like big trouble.

Joey rocked nervously from one foot to the other waiting impatiently for the elevator, glancing furtively at the door to the suite. He was half-sure that the gangster would come out and pound him to a pulp without batting an eye. The elevator ground to a halt and the doors swooshed open.

"Hey, Joey."

A shaft of light from the ceiling of the elevator spilled over the shoulder and chest of the operator's red uniform. In his mind, the light turned to blood; blood flowing across the operator's body. Joey shivered and turned his head to one side to keep from looking at the operator straight on. He swallowed hard past the lump in his throat. It was all in his mind. He knew it, all in his mind.

"Hi Fred, hey, take me to the second floor."

"How come you're not taking the freight?"

"Look, just take me, okay? I gotta see a guest on two."

"Sure, sure, gee willakers. Keep your pants on, will 'ya?

"Hey Fred, don't take it the wrong way, I just got a lot on my mind," he said as the elevator began its laborious decent.

"Yeah, yeah, no harm done, well, here we are 'my lord' second floor."

"Thanks, Fred, see 'ya." Joey pushed the rattling cart down the hallway to the room trying to forget the vision of blood covering Fred. He took a deep breath, just as Mr. White had instructed, and knocked on the door twice, two knocks in rapid succession. He heard the lock turn. The door opened a few inches and Albert James White's one blue eye showed through the crack.

Chapter Five

"Mr. White, it's me."

"Come in, come in."

Joey held up his hand. "Quick, get out your pad. Ready? They said something about a shipment, something about trains and then he said, Abrams did, that they had to get a guy they knew to replace the driver. They were going to hide whatever it was in the storage place under a train trestle. And they had a piece of paper that Abrams drew on. Either it was a diagram or maybe it was a map. And they said something about… wait… I'll try to remember."

"Yeah, yeah," said Jimmy, glancing up from his tablet. "Go on, before you forget anything."

"Okay, well, like I was saying there's a storage area under a train trestle somewhere."

Joey sat heavily in the chair, clutching his head in his hands. He tried to remember everything. "They said something about two guys, one named Costello and the other O'Brien. They couldn't decide on which. But I saw Aiello this morning on the 10th floor. You know who he is right? He went into the maid's room, but I know for a fact that the maid's room has a hallway into the suite. He could have entered the suite that way and no one would be the wiser." Joey snapped his fingers. "Say, Mr. White, you know, one of the things I just happened to pick up was lots and lots of wadded up paper from the floor."

Jimmy blinked. After a split second, he snapped his fingers. "Joey, you're a genius."

The boy looked embarrassed. "I guess I wouldn't be trying so hard if they hadn't been saying such bad stuff about the president."

Jimmy blinked when he recognized the level of Joey's naïveté. He wasn't accustomed to it. Knocking the president, huh? Maybe

Jimmy had best shelve his thoughts about the president for a later meeting with this enterprising young man. He didn't want to put Joey off; the kid was a great informant.

Joey brought out the wads of paper on the bottom shelf and in the trash cans. He tried to extricate ashes, cigarette butts, pieces of cold cuts, and blobs of mustard from the other trash. He began flattening the pages out and putting them into stacks. Jimmy grabbed another handful and within a few minutes, there were three piles of crinkled, but flat sheets. Jimmy's eyes gleamed with delight.

"You've done me a great service Joey. Here." Jimmy took his wallet from the inside of his jacket and rifled through taking out slips of paper, coat checks, and receipts. He slipped his fingers into a compartment behind his journalist's license and extricated two $20 bills. "Here, kid. You've earned it."

"Wow, $40.00, Mr. White, wow." Joey had never seen that much money in one place. He blinked hard and tried to swallow. The money was all well and good, BUT he had to make Mr. White understand the traitorous talk he'd heard. He had to.

"It's not just the money. You have to tell on those monkeys. I don't know what they're moving or when, but they said just awful things about the president and I know they're trying to have a, what a 'ya call it, oh yeah," he said snapping his fingers, "a coup. I mean Mr. White, this is America."

The boy was so candid and his face so honest that Jimmy couldn't stand to be the one to burst his bubble. He knew plenty about the president, plenty, but he wasn't about to knock FDR off the pedestal the boy had him on.

"And it always will be America to everyone who stands up for what our country believes in, everyone just like you. So you go ahead, pay your rent, and then go buy yourself a steak dinner. You deserve it."

"Thanks, Mr. White. Say, they asked my name and told me they'd ask for me again. You want me to try to get some more information?"

All THAT GliTTeRS

"No, I think it will be too dangerous. You let someone else take the call. And here, here is my card. It has my work number and address at the Tribune. You can call me there and reverse the charges. The hotel switchboard can get through easily. And you can leave a message with my secretary if I'm not there, her name is Gladys Mahoney. Just tell her your name and where you're from and a return number and we'll get hooked up."

"Well, Mr. White," the boy looked up at him then, his face so open that Jimmy regretted lying to the kid. "You call me again if you need anything. And I'll make sure to get in touch if anything else happens."

"Right-o."

The boy took the cart and left the room. Jimmy was alone with his notes and flattened bits of paper. He didn't know who was in the suite of that penthouse holding private meetings besides the "Honorable Gentleman from Massachusetts" and Aiello. Who exactly was up there? He couldn't camp outside the room to see who went in and out. They could spot him a mile away. He was proud that senators and congressmen considered him the greatest thorn in their side since the British in 1776.

His one good source at the House of Representatives had written him a confidential wire. They'd come up with a self-styled cipher, because a confidential wire was only so confidential. The informant said there were four men; Joey had said that one was Abrams the other he knew was Justice Bergman. That left two. What were they planning? Something that had to do with a commodity they were shipping somewhere? Something they were stealing from the American people, or was the commodity something from overseas?

Jimmy felt deep in his journalist's bones that he would find out the particulars and expose them. And if the Democrats and FDR went down after the plan was exposed, then so be it.

He knew the name O'Brien. The O'Brien's were a small-time gang in Chicago. He'd written some articles about them, exposés, op-ed pieces, the stories they hadn't liked. They'd run liquor from

Canada a few years back and had just enough clean real-estate dealings that the district attorney basically left them alone. But not Jimmy, oh no; he'd expose all of them and send all of them straight to prison— or to hell. Nealy O'Brien, the little punk, had loose ties with the family organization and sometimes worked for his big uncle, twice removed or some such, Seamus O'Brien. But Nealy was a mouse; just a little annoying mouse and Seamus usually kept him at a distance so his actions wouldn't hurt the family.

Jimmy had seen Nealy talking to Congressman Gillespie on J Street, right on the corner like they were discussing the weather. Bunch of pompous asses.

The big crooks weren't in on this; just the crooks that were expendable, the kind that could disappear and no one would bother to come looking for them. Unless Aiello stuck around. But even Aiello was small potatoes compared to Costello or Nelson or Bugsy Siegel. He'd expose all of them, the whole dirty bunch, politicians, and mobsters alike.

Jimmy lit a match and for a moment, watched it glow, just remembering. He stared at the flame:

It was dark, so dark it felt like a damp blanket wrapped itself around him, wrapped around him like a shroud. He shivered, making himself think of other things, brighter things.

Jimmy White tried to gather his wits. He must do his job and report on the war, this seemingly endless war.

He was crammed in a trench with several dozen others. The mud oozed up and soaked into his boots and socks. He shivered from the cold, the wet, and the fear. Some Brits, some Americans, some French, all huddled together, trying to indifferently share their body heat. The terrible smells, blood, feces, sweat, and fear permeated the fog of the trench. But it was so very, very dark, a black-on-black dark. There was an order, no lights, nothing that could be seen by the Germans. The sun had gone down hours ago and he couldn't see his hands in front of his face. He wanted to check the time, but he probably wouldn't be able to see his pocket watch either.

All THAT GliTTeRS

He settled for a cigarette instead and fumbled in the dark until he found his matches and case.

The match flared to life, and for a brief second, he saw the rows of soldiers packed together like sardines along the sides of the trench.

The soldiers were British, Americans, French, a few Poles, and a Belgian. They were all dirty, hungry, with hollow, staring eyes.

The match went out, but he could still see the shapes of the soldiers, like the negative of a film pressed on his optic nerve all around him.

The ghostly shapes made him shudder. He shuddered again when he realized that the odds were excellent that many of them might be dead tomorrow.

"Excuse me? Might I have one?"

The very polite English voice broke the silence and made Jimmy jump up—in surprise. It took a few seconds, but he decided the voice was addressing him. Without responding, Jimmy took out another cigarette and moved it toward the direction of the voice. The man sat next to him, near enough to smell his sweat and his wool gabardine.

He saw him, a British soldier, blonde hair and a well-kept mustache appeared as the spark gleamed briefly from the flare of the match. Jimmy handed the man a cigarette and struck a match. The match died before he could light it. Jimmy struck another, and it died too.

The Brit chuckled, "Good God, man, are you an hourly wage earner? One would think so; it takes so long for you to light one bloody cigarette."

Jimmy smiled in the darkness. "Actually, the Chicago Tribune pays me by the word."

The two men chuckled, relishing in the rare and lighthearted camaraderie. The third match flared, the tiny flame standing straight and resolute and finally did its job.

Chapter Six

Chapel Hill, NC
Present Day

I typed *Albert James White, Chicago Tribune,* into the Google search bar. Multiple articles came up from the Tribune and I scrolled through three pages before I found an image of Albert James White. He was a middle-aged man with brown, silver streaked hair, maybe 40 or 45. He posed for the camera, leaning forward so that a dark gray shadow outlined his upper body from behind. He had a strong, almost hard face with an angular jaw and heavy brows, and a pencil thin mustache. He looked like he wouldn't yield, like a bulldog snapping his jaws over something and never letting go until he was damn good and ready. The suit jacket had wide lapels and a black silk handkerchief peeking out of the breast pocket. I stopped staring at the man's picture. I got nothing, no glimmer of recognition, no goose bumps, nothing from the digital dots of black and white that made up his face and form. I read the obituary from the archives of the Chicago Tribune.

Albert James, "Jimmy", White 1889-1933. A major contributor and investigative journalist for this newspaper, 'Jimmy White always got his story.'

The obituary went on for another four paragraphs. During his twenty years at the paper, Jimmy had earned many awards.

Surviving Jimmy are his wife Clarisse, daughter Jenny, aged 14, and son Al Jr. aged 17. Memorial Service at Saint Barnard's 2 pm Wednesday with a reception at the home immediately following.

I sat back and wiped the sweat from my face with a paper towel from the kitchen. Reading the obituary was just so surreal. I didn't recognize any of the names or the face of the man taking front and center on the computer screen. The man whose life I was embroiled in through no fault of my own. My closest flirtation with the 30s had always been my love of old black and white movies, crime dramas, with gangsters portrayed by Edward G. Robinson or George Raft, and of course my favorite, Humphrey Bogart.

Just past the obituary was a front-page article.

"Jimmy White, disappeared." The article went on for a few columns leading to little information.

I researched court records just past the new year, 1934. Clarisse White had gone to the courts in February 1934 to have her husband declared dead, and Jimmy's editor had backed her up. He had asked that the court grant the request so that the widow could obtain the insurance money of $5000.00 immediately. There was no more information so I filled in the blanks with what I suspected might have happened. Jimmy was murdered and whoever had done it had gotten rid of the body. Thinking of it made me shiver, so I determined not to think of it.

I logged off the computer and closed my apartment for the night. I started deep breathing exercises and sat quietly in a relaxed posture as Miss Dickinson had instructed. I covered my eyes with a cloth to block out any ambient light, and all too soon, images began to swim through my head.

I saw a tall, slender blonde woman with skin like white porcelain; a girl, not yet a woman, brown haired and brown eyed with a winsome smile; and a young man with a wide lapel jacket and tie. The faces were so familiar in some way, and yet the where's and why's escaped me.

The faces of the three, the woman, the girl, and the boy, crowded through my mind as I ended the 'session' and got cleaned up for bed. Maybe tonight I'd dream, and the dreams would lead to a resolution.

I lay down on my bed and continued the deep breathing and slowly, my mind cleared, and I began to relax. I was in a stupor, almost sleeping, and the closest thing I could equate with the numbness in my limbs, was to being drugged. Tiny bits of thought, fragments of phrases, and pictures flitted through my mind. I heard voices off in the distance. Jimmy was there, I was sure of it— but to whom was he speaking?

"Listen, Mike, this story is gonna break wide open. I got my best informant from the Congress on this—He's sent me quite a few wires about it. Roosevelt thinks he can get away with murder. He's gonna take everybody's —." The voices faded, and I wondered what Roosevelt going to take?

"The guy is not a king, he's an elected official, you know; like a dogcatcher. Executive Order my ass."

"Yeah, Jimmy, but these government guys are tough nuts. You, me, and the Tribune is going to have to make sure that we don't get caught in even a tiny exaggeration of the facts."

"Yeah, I know, Mike, but my informant at the House has collected some pretty damning evidence. And the information I collected at the hotel in Washington connects Bergman, Abrams, and two others, in a scheme to…"

The information floated beyond my reach, and despite listening intently, I only caught the back end of more voices emerging from the dark.

"The shipment they kept talking about was coming out of Chicago. And this guy, Nealy O'Brien. He's the nephew twice removed of the big time Irish Chicago mobster, Seamus I think. Abrams thinks O'Brien is expendable. The little mug is supposed to help them hijack it."

The dream finally began to recede and break apart and when I woke up, I realized I was staring at the ceiling of my bedroom. The two men in my dream were so real, so definable, that it felt like I could've reached out and touched them.

I took a tablet and pen and wrote down everything I could remember from the dream. Then I drew a sketch of the room marking where each man stood. There'd been a man named Mike, and Jimmy, who Mike had been speaking with, and then there'd been all this talk about a shipment, hijacking, Indianapolis, Chicago, O'Brien, Abrams, and some guy whose name started with a B or had it been a G.

I moved to my computer and logged on. I typed in the name O'Brien and Chicago and 1930. Google only recognized five articles with all of those keywords.

All THAT GliTTeRS

I looked at my watch. Two o'clock in the morning. Typical. Maybe I'd sleep when I was dead. I wrote down everything as well as bookmarked information I found about the O'Brien Family, an Irish mob from Chicago, who'd smuggled Canadian whiskey during prohibition. O'Brien's son, Patrick was born in 1908 and had been convicted of murder and died in jail in the late 50's. Abrams was another matter. Jonathan Abrams was the two term Senator from Massachusetts from 1928 to 1940. So, what would a senator from Massachusetts be doing with a gangster from Chicago? And what was this about Roosevelt and an executive order?

I researched for another hour, thanking God for computers and the Internet, until I began to get a sense of what had been happening in 1933 with Jimmy White. I found an empty notebook and began writing all the information that I remembered from my dreams. I looked at the words, *executive order* and underlined them in red twice. There was something about those words that sent a chill up my spine. But I didn't know what exactly.

Several hours later, I stopped, showered, grabbed a cup of instant coffee, and made a mad dash for the University and work.

I muddled through the rest of the day trying to decide my next move. It was Friday, and I had 14 days of leave to decide what, if anything, I could do about the dreams, and Jimmy White.

Could I really be, as Miss Dickinson had said, a conduit between the past and the future. For some reason, the universe wanted me to solve this eighty-year-old mystery and bring peace to those involved; those that were already dead, she meant. That was as easy to swallow as the reincarnation crap. But, I was a man of science, and felt compelled to research and to solve this puzzle. I re-read the notebook again at lunch, and decided that there were way too many holes in the story to make any logical conclusions.

Chapter Seven

Wollaston Beach near Quincy, MA
Present day

For more than a decade the house had been boarded up. Urban decline in a neighborhood of this caliber rarely happened. This area near Quincy had once been exclusive homes for those with old but only moderate amounts of money. He'd been searching through the buildings, making his unceremonious entrance with the use of a crowbar. He'd been doing it for months. His searches yielded journals, account books, and bundles of letters yellowed with age. These he threw in a corner without so much as a glance. He was looking for something solid, something he could take to his fence that would translate into dollars. He supposed he could do something more productive, but the solitude of the abandoned places appealed to him.

The man hung around the courthouse and found out which of the old places were up for demo and when exactly they'd be demolished. The city fathers didn't want any of the abandoned homes to turn into meth houses and vagrant hotels. Not around Quincy.

The man had found an old watch, a little better than a costume jewelry necklace, and a teapot that had been worth around $100.00. He wasn't going to get rich fast doing this. And yet, it appealed to him. He'd been working on this place for two days and it had yielded little. The dilapidated chandelier in the dining room hung askew from the Victorian style shell molding, the large, high-ceilinged room, had at one time been resplendent. He idly shoved debris away from the walls with his feet to get to the old sideboard.

All THAT GliTTeRS

He leaned his hip against the 'Junque', his word for antiques so beat up they were worthless, and began to push. The sideboard made a terrific screeching sound as it moved by centimeters away from the wall. An old notebook fell out and spilled a folded square of paper onto the floor. This looked like it might be something. He picked it up and slowly unfolded what looked like a map. But to what? The notebook yielded page after page of names, and manifest numbers. This was way more interesting. A column on the left side of the notebook contained a list of names and numbers in two rows of neat block print under the heading, *Federal Marshals*. He took off his coat and wadded it up to make a pillow where he could sit and read. The notebook was precise and detailed, but without a reference, a starting point, it was like reading Swahili. The guy Abrams, the author of this tome, knew what he was talking about, but neglected to include a subject for the reader. The last several pages of the notebook contained information about trains, timetables, and destinations.

He scratched his head thinking. He might be a lazy thief, but he did have a brain. He understood that whatever this Abrams character was getting, stealing, or lifting was recorded in this notebook, and it had something to do with Federal Marshals, trains, and September 1933.

He studied the map carefully. It was brittle with age and exposure but managed to stay together. The map had two pages. The first laid out the route by rail from Indianapolis to Pittsburg, all the stops, the times, everything. The second was a detailed map of the rail yard in Pittsburg. Pittsburg had been one of the steel centers in the 1930s and the mass of intersecting tracks, bridges, cement abutments, and outbuildings, translated into a bewildering jumble of words on the page. But one item on the map stood out like a sore thumb. It was a giant red X, meticulously drawn over a bridge in the center of the yard.

It stood to reason that whatever the items these characters stole had been put there, no doubt to be picked up by Abrams at a future date.

All THAT GliTTeRS

He'd take this little 'treasure map' and go get a cup of coffee at the internet café. Maybe he could figure this out and find out what was stolen. Maybe the item was still in Pittsburg just waiting for Benedict Gillespie, direct descendent of Congressman Gillespie of Arkansas, to pick up.

Chapter Eight

Doctor Lu would probably be glad to get rid of me before I made a catastrophic mistake, so I left work early. I logged on to my computer at home and worked for several hours. I got information about Roosevelt's executive orders, there'd been about 30 for just 1933 related to Jimmy White, Chicago, O'Brien, and Abrams. By 9 o'clock, I had gathered all the information I could from secondary sources. Time to make phone calls. I called the Chicago Tribune, certain that I would only get a voicemail at this time of the night, but the information switchboard was open.

"Ah yes, I was trying to find some articles written by an investigative reporter named Jimmy White in the 1930s. Could you put me through to your archives? Do you have an historian?"

"Sure, we have an archivist and I think she's in her office now. Would you like me to put you through?"

"Yes, thanks."

"Archives," a cheery voice said over the line.

"Yes, I'm doing some research on a reporter that worked for the Tribune in the 1930s. I haven't been able to locate any of his articles online. I'm especially interested in anything he wrote about Roosevelt's executive orders during that time. Do you have any of those articles?"

"Well, I'll need to look through our digital file. Can you give me more specifics?"

"No, I'm really just looking around to see what I can find."

"Well, give me your email and your cell number, and I'll shoot you some information. I'm going to be off for the weekend in another few minutes. If you were in Chicago, I could just set you up in the room with the computer and the digital files. Are you in Chicago?"

"No, I'm in North Carolina. But you can do that? You can give people the digital files, and just let them look?"

"Oh yes, it's one of the services we offer the public. You never know what kind of information you might need, so we try to be as helpful as we can with what we have on file."

"That's terrific." Some of the pieces of the puzzle began to coalesce in my mind. How was I going to find out this information? You go to the primary source. The primary source, the files, the articles, and even Jimmy White's notes. Maybe I could right a wrong. If Jimmy White was murdered, maybe I could find out why. Then the dreams would stop and I could get back to my life. Maybe. There was no going back. I could do this, and then I'd be better for it, way better. It took me only seconds to make a decision. "Listen, I'm going to be in Chicago on Monday. Would it be okay if I came over to your office and spoke to you about this?" No guts no glory.

"Sure, that's why we're here. Just go to the main information desk in the lobby and ask for Melissa in archives, and they'll direct you to the office."

"Okay, I'll be there sometime during the day on Monday. I'll see you then. Oh, by the way, my name is Eric Douglass, and I'm from
Chapel Hill, North Carolina."

"Well, great Eric Douglass, I'll see you then."

Chapter Nine

I made a trip to my mother's on Saturday. I chose not to tell her about all the craziness of the past, just that I needed to get away for a bit. She gave me a quizzical frown, but did not ply me with questions. Since my mom had lost my dad almost twenty-five years before, she had been mom and dad to me. For a time, she had to work two jobs, but still found time to help me with my homework, have a hot meal on the table for me every night, and make it to many of my high school ball games. On my way out the door, she hugged me gently, and slipped a $100 bill into my back pocket.

"Just for goodies from the vending machine, okay?"

"Okay, Mom, thanks, you're the best mom ever, and not just because you give me money." I kissed her on the forehead. She was a big softie and I loved her to death.

"Just find out what's bothering you and come on home."

"I will, now I have to go see Monica."

"Don't worry, you have a core of steel just like your dad. You may not know that you do, but you do."

I stopped for a moment, the memories of my dad and the hole in my heart from his death came flooding over me, sucking me down, like the sand when the tide went out. I looked up at her and gave her a quick hug. I'd think about my dad later. "Thanks, Mom, I'll call you from Chicago."

I brought a bag of sandwiches and chips from my favorite deli, hoping the gesture would soften Monica up. My avoidance of confrontations with her was a learned behavior. And the whole convoluted, unhealthy behavior would stay that way until I changed it. She took the bag I proffered, took out the sandwich and turned it over, frowning at the grease the grilled cheese had left behind.

"This hasn't been cut in half," she whined, and I felt myself wince. "But thanks anyway," she grumbled.

I ignored the snipe and plunged on with my story.

"Monica, I've taken a leave of absence from work. I have to go to Chicago on Monday."

"What do you mean, you've taken a leave of absence? Why are you going to Chicago? Come on, Eric, you have been so distant lately. What's going on?" She pouted prettily. In the not too distant past, I would have tried to kiss that pout away, but this time, I didn't cave.

"I have to go, it's personal, something I'm not ready to talk about yet. But I'll call you when I get there." I thought for a moment. Better a clean break, knowing Monica the way I did. I walked to the door.

"Look Monica, I'm coming to a crossroads here and I think it's best if we don't see each other for a while. I'm sorry, but I have lots of things going on right now. I hope you understand, but even if you don't, there's nothing I can do about it." My little speech surprised Monica and it surprised me, as well. For some reason that I'd yet to figure out, being open and direct was not usually how I operated. Monica was not an easy person to be around with her endless "neediness". If she was an animal at the lab, I'd say she was high maintenance. In the past, she'd been able to make me squirm just by looking at me sideways. But then again, it was probably because I spent a good deal of time with white mice, my clipboard, and the various critters I saw under the microscope. None of those little suckers talked back or argued or whined, and during working hours, there was rarely a need to even speak. And then again, Monica was the last person anyone would practice being confrontational with.

Monica took a breath and opened her mouth to speak, but I cut her off. "I'm sorry Monica, I'll call you from Chicago, and maybe we can talk then. Right now, I have lots to do, so I'm going, bye."

I closed the door, and as I made it down the steps to my car, I heard,

"EEEERRRRRRIIIIICCCCCCC!!!"

Chapter Ten

There were several flights leaving from the Raleigh Durham Airport for Chicago each day, so I booked my flight and made a reservation at a convenient Ramada Inn accessible to the local transit system. It was my intention to get all the information I could about 1933, Jimmy White, Roosevelt and that damned car, and any other stray bits of that 'other life', before I made my return flight to RDU. With that data, I damn well better figure out what was going on and resolve it.

My Dell computer was three years old, but still ran very well, and the Ramada website informed me that each room came with Wi-Fi at no charge. I needed to be able to log on and do research when I wasn't at the Tribune looking through Jimmy's old articles and whatever else was on hand for 'civilians.'

Standing in the middle of Franklin Street and announcing to my lifelong friends that I was going to chase a murderer that had killed someone, maybe me, eighty years before, gave me chills. I shook away the fog settling over me. I was not sure if I believed any of it, but how could I reconcile the dreams if I didn't know if something had happened to me? Maybe I'd end up just having a grand old-time exploring Chicago.

Making the 6 am departure from RDU was a hassle. No one, except my mother and Monica knew that I was leaving town.

After the frenetic hustle to get to the airport on time and finding a parking spot in the multi-level car park, my annoyance grew exponentially by the inevitable backup at the TSA station. The line of sleepy people stopped and started, stopped and started, and was as slow as proverbial molasses in winter.

While I waited, thoughts of whining Monica lumbered through my brain. She was another problem. How had I put up with her for so long? It had probably been just plain lack of minutia. Maybe our relationship was the result of finding the safest, least controversial path. A mode of behavior, it now occurred to me, had become a part of my life since my dad had died all those years ago. Hindsight was always 20/20.

I looked up at the line of people moving from one 'pen' or another, herded by the government minions acting like overzealous border collies. At another time, I might have balked at the treatment. Right now, I just wanted answers to the questions about Jimmy White, how they related to me, and to get back home.

The TSA agent wiped some odorless, colorless substance across my palm. Then I put my bags on the conveyor belt and stepped into a semicircular box.

"Raise your arms over your head please."

I mimicked the picture inside the box and waited for the machine to rotate once around my body for all of a half second. Maybe the TSA guys were porn producers who took the best x-ray shots and spliced them together into a feature film. Ha!

Two and a half hours later, the JCS 190 jolted, lurched and eventually touched down at O'Hare International. I collected my things and moved down the long jet way. I stood in the center of the expansive lobby, a single entity, as a sea of humanity rushed past me.

The Ramada Inn on the west side of the city was convenient to the elevated subway, and I took the next train to the stop closest to the Chicago Tribune. The huge granite tower was a massive structure that looked like a medieval cathedral. I walked slowly toward the main entrance, taking in every sight and smell. Grinning gargoyles looked down from the granite façade of the Tribune Tower; not just the medieval kind, but silly, satirical creatures designed by some mason who had his tongue firmly in his cheek. The inside of the Tribune Tower lobby was amazing. It was resplendent with marble, wood, shining brass door knobs, bannisters and about a thousand people coming and going. All along the thirty-plus-foot high walls were quotes etched into the marble. I read the lines about free speech, good government, and freedom of the press. The atmosphere felt like a foreign country to this North Carolina boy.

"Can you tell me where the archives are?" I asked the man at the information desk.

"Yes, sir, it's a few streets over on Grant. It's where they print the papers. Just follow this map, two blocks away, easy to find."

"Great, thanks." I left, map in hand, and arrived at the auxiliary building within a few minutes and followed the signs to the archives. The large, cavernous room was a surprise. It was airy, spacious and well lit. A young petite, brown-haired woman stood behind the long lobby desk that spanned most of the width of the room.

"May I help you?"

"Is Melissa here? I spoke with her Friday evening." I cleared my throat, trying hard not to sound like a science geek. "I'm here to see some of your archived papers from 1933."

"I'm Melissa, glad you made it. But 1933? That's 365 days' worth of newspapers. Do you have a date or a journalist?"

"Yes. Jimmy White and I think June or July 1933?"

"Sure. All of that information is on microfiche, but I can get you started."

"Great!"

Chapter Eleven

A stately Victorian home built just prior to the Civil War was still occupied by the family that had 'bought it' by gunpoint from the first owner. The house in the Canaryville section of Chicago was one of the few that had escaped the Great Fire of 1871. The house was filled with the ghosts of Irish bosses, enforcers and crooked politicians. The descendants of the O'Briens still lived in the home. This 'family' had kept the south west of the city free of Italian and Lithuanian mobsters. Instead, they'd kept that area of the city for the Irish, and particularly, the O'Briens, the family that had lived in the house on Halsted for so many years. Few knew of its vague past and its initial owners. Kathleen O'Brien, the heir apparent to the O'Brien wealth and power, was a lithesome, willowy blonde; a real knock out at age 36. Her oval face and moss green eyes were more reminiscent of her mother than her rough and tumble great-grandfather, Seamus O'Brien.

Seamus's empire started with a gang of toughs who he'd talked into following him at age 16. He'd been in the United States only two years.

His mother had died on the voyage from County Cork, and his father, always a mean drunk, but still a wily old fox, had started a numbers racket after he and his two sons had settled in Chicago. The father died fifteen years later, stabbed in a drunken brawl. Seamus had sent his younger brother, Patrick, to seminary and he, Seamus, settled down to a business just nibbling on the edges of civility and the law.

His business exploded into an empire during prohibition. He thought the Italians, the gangs with the real power in Chicago, was the plague of the city, and he was always careful to avoid them. He stayed in his little corner of the city; the "big fish in the little pond."

The 'G-men' always paid more avid attention to the Italian mobsters than they did to the more sedate Irish.

Seamus had developed a method of smuggling Canadian whisky from Ontario that was almost flawless. The operation started at Sault Ste. Marie, Michigan; that bit of America that jutted out into the St. Mary's River within sight of Canada. Cases of Canadian made liquor were offloaded onto innocuous-looking fishing boats and sent down the St. Mary's River, eventually ending up in Lake Michigan. There, the cargo passed through many hands, always-Irish hands, and several boats, and many steps ahead of the rarely suspecting federal agents. Seamus took and cajoled and finagled, and when prohibition ended, his finances were in such good shape, he had indeed created generational wealth.

In 1933, Seamus's son Patrick, then only 25-years-old, took over a great deal of the family business, leaning more and more toward legitimate enterprises.

Patrick shot one of the Costello gang in broad daylight some years later, and was sent to prison where he died before he could be released.

Thomas, Patrick's son was born in 1947. He had some of his great-grandfather's mean, drunk, but wily personality. He pushed the boundary with his grandfather, always wanting to go back to the 'old ways'; to take things by coercion and force rather than by any legitimate means.

Thomas's bravado ended when his wife, Patsy, died when their only child, Kathleen, was four-years-old. After that, Thomas withdrew from society, the family and from life itself.

Nealy O'Brien, a 'shirttail' relation, if there ever was one, had never proved himself to the family. He was too brash, too shortsighted, and always in trouble. Seamus thought the kid was nothing but a thug, and Nealy's actions too often brought shame on the name O'Brien. But there just wasn't much the old man could do about it.

"Ms. Kathleen?"

Kathleen didn't recognize the old, dry-as-parchment voice, but she did recognize the number. It was a number that the 'family' had been paying Ma Bell for the past fifty years. The bill came on the same date of the month and was paid on that date, month after month and year after year.

"Yes, this is Kathleen O'Brien, who is this?"

"It's Ralph, Ralph Gunderson. Your grandfather gave my father this house back in the thirties and he had his people put this here phone in then and paid for it all this time. Hardly use the thing. Call out for pizza or my medication every now and again, but…"

"Mr. Gunderson, why are you calling?" Kathleen would be respectful, but she didn't want a blow by blow on what he took on his pizza.

"Oh yes ma'am, well, it's like this here. I found this here box out in the shed. Just lying there up on them cross beams near the roof tree. Hadn't seen the box in about, well gosh, now let's see—well, anyway…"

Kathleen tried not to roll her eyes. She had the sneaking suspicion that old Gunderson, would never get to the point.

"Your grandpa set it up," he droned on. "Set it up sos we'd keep some of the records your old great-grandpa wouldn't keep in the house. Not sure what it's all about, ya know. Lots of things going on in '32 and '33, what with prohibition comin' to an end an all. Anyways, we were to keep some of' those…"

Kathleen had heard all about the turmoil and all the lambasting her great-grandfather had taken from some journalist at the Tribune. There was a file around in that dusty, old attic about the journalist and the events that went on then. Things she just didn't know about because it was just like the files: old, dusty, brittle and just not important.

She tried to remain unhurried, and the tone of her voice soft and coaxing. But her impatience came through anyway. "Mr. Gunderson, I'm sure this is all very important if Seamus asked your father to keep these records for him; so could you tell me exactly what this is all about? I must confess, I haven't a clue." She asked the old man as sweetly as she could, hoping not to rattle him.

"Well, you see, Patrick your grandpa, don't cha know, he told my father and my father had me take up the torch, sos to speak, to keep the box of papers. Quite honestly, I hadn't thought about that box your great-grandfather gave us for a mighty long time. This was when the real estate side of the business just started. Maybe the box has lists of Canadian suppliers when they was runnin' booze out of Canada. I looked through it, but couldn't make head nor tail of it."

Kathleen paused as she tapped impatiently on the desk blotter. Was it important enough to get over there and pick up the box? Maybe she could make a determination after she'd dug around upstairs in the attic to find out exactly what was so important. That would be like finding a needle in a haystack. She felt herself sigh, loath to think of the research, elbow deep in the files, all handwritten in fading ink. Maybe she'd take a glass up with her and crack open one of those bottles of Canadian whisky to ease the tedium.

"All right, you've called, so where are the records now?"

"Well, it's like I was saying, there's some old newspapers in there from June, 1933. There are articles by that journalist, Jimmy White, that really slam your great-grandfather Seamus." "Yes, go on." God, ancient history.

"Well, my daddy was there when ol' Patrick was takin' it on the chin from that journalist, and I never forgot it. When he started the real estate business, my granddaddy did lots of things helpin' him with that."

Kathleen stopped again, her pen hovering over the page. Journalist, Tribune; nothing rang a bell. She could remember nothing about some muckraker in the family's past. After prohibition and way after the gambling and numbers running, and all the other gruesome gangster activities, they started their legitimate businesses that included, fishing and oil. Inwardly, she sighed; she wouldn't scare the old boy, put him off or more importantly, ignore him. If her grandfather had set his father up in a house with a permanent phone, more than a half century before then he had a reason, a very, very good reason. Old, wily Patrick was a shrewd character. "Mr. Gunderson, let me send someone over to take the information from you. You've done a wonderful job doing what was asked of you so many years ago. We are immensely in your debt. I'll send someone over for the information, and by the way, what do you take on your pizza? One of the guys will bring you an extra-large for doing such a wonderful job."

"Ah, now Miss Kathleen, just doin' my job," the man said with great humility. "I take anchovies and extra sausage, by the way."

"We'll be in touch, and thanks again."

Chapter Twelve

July, 1933
Washington, D.C.

Jimmy scrounged around DC for 10 days, sweltering and suffering in the heat and humidity. Like a bulldog, he never let go of a story until it was on the presses of the Tribune. He listened to the conversations of justices, senators and congressmen in posh restaurants. He'd order a cup of coffee and a sandwich, just so the management wouldn't throw him out while he sat with his back to the men on whom he was eavesdropping. Very few of these 'sandwich trips' yielded any information. The guys he wanted to eavesdrop on were not usually where he could find them. What he was hoping to hear, proof of collusion and treason, was spoken of in back alleys and whore houses. He had his suspicions about which man was doing what. When he saw any of them look like they needed to wash their hands, he'd hurry into the washrooms. Jimmy then would park himself in a stall with his feet against the wall and listen. He'd heard lots of tidbits and snippets of facts. Only a few of the loose ends could be tied together to form a pattern. He knew Abrams and Gillespie were meeting with a thug from Chicago. He kept hearing, 'the gentleman from Chicago,' most likely a code word for some mobster. Who, he didn't know. Several crime families ruled booze smuggling: Al Capone, the Aiellos, and the Gennas. There was also the Irish gang; the O'Briens on the west side. They had illegal and legitimate business dealings. Capone wouldn't have anything to do with anything that he hadn't thought of himself; neither would the others, except maybe the O'Briens. So, who exactly was it, and what exactly did they want from the guy, the 'gentleman' from Chicago'?

"Hey Mr. White."

Joey, the busboy, his regular informant, was Jimmy's insurance policy. He figured he was one-step ahead of the bad guys, Abrams and his little band of thieves, with the information Joey brought to him. Joey was a smart kid, and obviously smitten with crime novels and movies about G-men. He regularly visited the room on the 10th floor and covertly listened intently to everything said while he picked up the trash and brought it to Jimmy's room.

Jimmy had not wanted Joey to go back to the 10th floor; it was dangerous. But the need for information outweighed the concern. No one like Abrams, who was convinced that the world was his oyster, would ever think that he was being spied upon; especially not by one of the many invisible minions serving the patrons at the hotel.

Joey's stroke of brilliance was taking out the trash, including the notes thrown out by Abrams. There were names, dates, lists and numbers for bills that were up for votes in the senate. The senator from the great Commonwealth of Massachusetts was so arrogant that it never occurred to him that anyone, especially a low-life busboy, would have the audacity to go through his trash and retrieve anything that might implicate him.

"Yeah, what have you got for me today?"

"Don't know, but they made an awful lot of trash. They're arguing to beat the band up there about who's going to do 'the job'. Say, Mr. White, you don't think they're anarchists, do you? They're sure talking about something against the government. And they keep bringing up some kind of order. Let's see, it sounded like an 'x' something?"

Jimmy's mouth popped open in surprise. He stopped rifling through the wads of papers, his hands still and his mind open. "Executive?"

"Yeah, that's it exactly. They were talking about an 'executive' order and what they could do to get… well it got a little confusing, I don't mind telling you. And here's the big thing, when they said it, they turned and looked right at me. I tell you I thought the floor was going to come up and swallow me whole," said the boy, exhaling with great exaggeration. "Sometimes, this Dick Tracy stuff is scary. Hey, the Tribune runs Dick Tracy, don't it?"

"Yeah, kid. Now, what did they say when they were looking at you, Joey?"

"They said there were going to meet their 'associate' in Arkansas at Gillespie's warehouse so's they could talk, 'in confidence'."

Jimmy legs gave way and he slumped onto the bed. Executive order, Chicago criminal, shipment, trains: what did it all mean? He had to find out. But first, he'd have to check in at the Tribune. And he'd have to see how his wife and kids were doing.

Chapter Thirteen

Kathleen made her way into the attic after changing into jeans and a sweatshirt. The attic was up a very steep, narrow flight of stairs that took a sharp bend to the right before ending on the landing. Despite her ridged exercise and excessively proper diet, Kathleen was winded when she got to the door. She paused and shoved it open with her hip. The place was resplendent with cobwebs and dust motes big enough to choke a horse. She'd thought about wearing a mask to cover her mouth and nose, nixed the idea, and now she was sorry she hadn't done it. She coughed and sneezed, metaphorically banging her head against a brick wall. Why exactly was she trying to 'die by dust'? The old guy had told her that her grandfather, or more pointedly the family funds, had been paying first, the elder Gunderson, and then the younger, for decades to keep an old box of documents and newspapers. The only thing Kathleen had ever heard about that in particular was that someone at the Tribune had given her grandfather grief, and then the guy had up and died in the early 30s. What possible reason was there to know all of this, some 80 years after the fact?

Kathleen muttered to herself as she pushed aside a very large and intricate cobweb.

"This is 288, two gross; get it? 144x2; jeez, I crack myself up."

There were short, squat windows on two sides of the vast, open room. That available light and the two large old-fashioned globe fixtures made all the corners of the musty place almost visible. Still, the attic was creepy, dirty and nasty. Kathleen hated having to come up here. Her father and grandfather always taught her the importance
of accomplishing family business with no outside help. It was good practice, excluding all but the family members on any information

that might be, or might have been, a little shady. *Might have been*, being the operative statement. The O'Briens' business practices in the past 50 years were completely on the up and up. All were well accounted for; again, accounted being the operative word. She could show the books to the IRS for the past 50 years and get a sterling rating. After her father's few brushes with the law in his younger days, he'd distanced himself from the more rash personalities of the family, and drilled into her the importance of being on the up and up. Few things, he'd said, were recoverable once they were lost; virginity and a good family name were among the most important.

Kathleen smiled to herself as she pushed aside a trunk. Her Pop preached at her all the time, and she took to heart most all the spiels, but not necessarily the one about virginity.

Behind the trunk was a line of old wooden filing cabinets. Kathleen had a sort of schematic of the items in the attic that she'd brought with her from her office. Some OCD member of the family had drawn the chart out chronologically. There was even a file on the name of the ship and the other passengers that had crossed from Ireland with Seamus, his brother Patrick, and their father Sean, *An sionnach d'aois*. The name in Gaelic meant 'the old fox'. Of all the things Kathleen had read about him, Sean the wily, Sean the always sneaky, Sean the 'I'll stab you in the back before I give an inch', lived up to his name. And to boot, the only picture that survived of him showed her great-great grandfather with distinctly pointed ears. To Sean, everyone but the Irish were English, and whatever he could do to them, they had coming. Not exactly made of the best moral fiber, was the patriarch of the family. Hopefully, four generations of marrying other Irish not descended from County Cork men had weakened that particular gene pool.

Ah, 1932. Kathleen grabbed the files for 1932, 33 and 34 and carried them into the center of the room. The files were coated with dust and all clipped together with rusting paper clips. Kathleen slapped them against her jeans, sneezed hugely for good measure, and then too disgusted with the attic as a whole, made her way down to her office.

This whole business had piqued her curiosity. Why would her grandfather have to stash a box filled with who-knew-what away from the family home? Too weird for words. What, or who, was he trying to protect?

All THAT GliTTeRS

Chapter Fourteen

Present Day
Office of the archives,
The Chicago Tribune

    I now realized as I consulted my watch just how tired I was. I'd been in Chicago for all of 26 hours. Reading Jimmy White's articles had answered no questions, but only created more. The people at the Tribune had been great helping me, and so far, I'd found little to confirm my assumption that Jimmy (or I) had been murdered. If I still believed in it, that is, this reincarnation thing. And no one seemed to know where or if any of White's notes were still around. The archivist, Melissa, had told me not to get my hopes up. Whatever Jimmy had been writing about, The Tribune had decided that it was not important enough to keep his notes or drafts. It was all just ancient history.
    I discovered that Jimmy was a terrific writer, after hours of wading through his articles. He kept his audience on the edge of their seats while giving out useful information peppered with innuendo and often indignation. Of course, most of the time, Jimmy was slamming some politician, state or federal, or law that some 'joe-schmoe' who was just trying to feed his kids, could have cared less about. And then the Irish mobster, O'Brien; Jimmy seemed to be particularly vehement about everything Seamus O'Brien did.
    If I had been Jimmy, that political passion had not transferred to me. I couldn't stomach politics. Too much damn drama. I voted sometimes for the most conservative person I could find on the ballot, and then promptly forgot about it. I always hoped I'd done the right thing, but I knew nothing was probably going to change in the

long run. What had Gertrude Stein said? 'If voting changed anything, it would be illegal.' I knew if there were enough votes against biological testing then I'd be out of a job. But the problems of the 21st century would have to wait because the first half of the 20th was my focus now.

In two of the articles, the name Senator Abrams came up, as well as a Congressman Gillespie, and more disturbingly, Bergman, a justice of the Supreme Court. That's where I'd start; a little research on those three to find out what they were up to in 1933 might help answer some questions. I assumed that Jimmy was murdered to keep him quiet about something. But that wasn't a fact; it was just an emotional response to the dreams.

"I'm going to go to lunch," I told Melissa, the archivist who'd helped me so much. "Would you like me to bring you back anything?"

"Where are you going?"

"I have no idea."

Melissa giggled a very uncharacteristic big-city girl, giggle. "If you like pizza, Roma's is on the next block. Go out the main entrance," she said, demonstrating as she turned her body. "And then left. Cross the next side street and Roma's will be in the middle of that block.
You could bring me a slice of pepperoni, that's my favorite."

"They'll do that, by the slice I mean?"

"Sure, it's ready to go all the time. It'll be the best pizza you've ever eaten, I guarantee."

"Okay, I'll be back after a while."

"You've got such a southern accent," said Melissa with a coy little tilt of her head. "It's so cute."

"Well, uh, thanks, I think," I said as I hurried out the door and down the hall. The door swooshed to a close and I took several long strides out of the building and onto the street.

The last thing you need to do, Eric, I told myself, *is get mixed up with another girl like Monica. 'Your accent is so cuuuuute,'* I mimicked and rolled my eyes.

After lunch, I dug up some more facts about the senator and congressman. I could make some educated guesses with that information. Gillespie and then O'Brien were in cahoots to steal something, but what? And I know this had to tie into Jimmy's murder. Is this why he, or was it me, was murdered? I knew that he'd been run over deliberately because he'd figured out something–but what exactly? Jimmy was like a bulldog when it came holding on to information and then spilling it to the public via his articles; he never let anything go. The innuendo-packed articles that he had written had given me some ideas, but too few to actually pinpoint a cause and relationship. Information from my dreams. But they were just ideas.

Chapter Fifteen

July 1933

Jimmy White gazed out the window of the Chicago-bound train. His mind felt numb, and the edges of exhaustion slowly curled around his body. He'd been in DC for two weeks. Two weeks of that southern hell of heat and humidity. His brain felt dead and his body worse. He gazed around quickly and didn't see any ladies nearby, so he took off his suit jacket and unbuttoned his vest. Sodden rings of sweat stained his shirt, but there was nothing he could do about it now. He settled back against the seat, hoping to catch a breeze from the window and a few moments of rest.

"Hey, look over there."

Someone seated near the front of the car stood and pointed out the window, and gestured to several dozen people: men, women, and children gathering around something.

Jimmy leaned against the window and half stood to get a better view.

"What are they doing?"

"Those are the ones that have it bad in Philly. There's nothing to eat and nowhere to go, so's they make their way out here to the country and pitch tents and then gather what they can in the fields."

Jimmy looked at the man with incredulity. "What on earth is there to eat in the fields?"

"Well, dandelions, sometimes they find nuts or bulbs or some such, wild things too, like berries."

"Good God." Jimmy sat with a plop. How sad, how horrible that Americans, any Americans, would have to resort to gleaning wild foods from a field to feed themselves and their children. He shook his head. There was nothing he could do for those folks.

He turned all business and pulled out his briefcase to read the notes for his exposé against Senator Abrams, Congressman Gillespie and the president himself. The man wasn't a king, he was an elected official, and this was the USA!

What was FDR's motivation? Manipulating world markets and governments? How could demanding that citizens fall in line with his dictates help feed and house the people he'd seen in that field? FDR had overstepped his bounds. He had to let the free market work. That's how jobs were created. People would go back to work and not have to eat squirrel food they'd wrestled from some wild animal. Build up the economy, don't tear down the Constitution. He'd do some more snooping, get some direct quotes, back up his sources, and the people would be in such an uproar that he'd bring the whole rotten mess down.

Chapter Sixteen

Present Day
Chicago, IL

I copied everything from the year 1933 written by Jimmy White. The few notes written in Jimmy's own hand were in a type of self-styled cypher. I took the sheaf of papers and stuffed them inside my briefcase before I grabbed the subway back to my hotel. I gazed out the dirty window of the train at the alien landscape. I lived in a city; Chapel Hill was a city, Raleigh was a city, but they sure didn't look like this. I turned that thought over, but there were other more pressing matters to think about, like O'Brien and Gillespie and Abrams and what did any of this have to do with why I/Jimmy was murdered. Jimmy had been hinting at something in his articles, and that may have been the something that got him killed. But who had done it and why? Because whoever it was getting too close to exposing someone? Someone like Abrams? Or was my first instinct correct, that a mobster like O'Brien was a more likely suspect for a 'hit' on an investigative journalist like Jimmy, who was taking serious shots at him from the 'fifth estate' and using the Tribune to hide behind.

I made my way to the elevated train stop near the Ramada. I am always good with directions, and I rarely get lost. I'd been born with an innate sense of always knowing where I was. Too bad I couldn't bottle that sense of direction and sell it to poor lost fools groping their way around. Monica couldn't find her way out of a paper sack. Now, why had she come to mind? And why, come to ponder, had it taken me eight long years to decide to break it off with her? Ah, well, I'd figure that one out later, after I'd laid poor Jimmy to rest.

I made my way to another area of the city called Canaryville, on the west side of the lake that was not right downtown but had been more of an old suburb since the turn of the last century.

After settling down in a coffee shop, I opened my laptop. As research was my forte, I started with the hardest thing to uncover, the man I'd seen multiple times in my dreams, Nealy O'Brien.

I looked up everything about Nealy O'Brien, the name that I kept hearing in my dreams. In my gut, I knew that the information was crucial to understanding what went on in 1933 with Jimmy White, and who murdered him.

I found several articles about the O'Briens, about Seamus, but not about Nealy. Since Nealy was a gangster and the O'Briens of Chicago were Irish gangsters, maybe Nealy was part of that family.

Jimmy had written several exposés about the O'Briens, the Irish crime family who plagued Chicago in the early part of the 1920s. I found the obits for Seamus and then one for James, born in 1947. Surviving James was one daughter, Kathleen, still living at the same address. If her father, James, was born in '47, I assumed Kathleen might be around my age. Maybe the old crime boss, Seamus, had gotten rid of Jimmy out of revenge for lambasting him in his articles. Maybe they'd run him down and then gotten rid of the body, and old Jimmy was somewhere pushing up daisies. Maybe I'd just wander on over to the O'Briens house and scope it out.

Chapter Seventeen

Home of Kathleen O'Brien
Chicago, ILL
Present day

"Miss Kathleen?"

Kathleen looked up from her seat on the floor amid the stacks of files she'd brought down from the attic, at Juan her houseman. There was a plethora of paper: folders, ledger books and pictures scattered all around her in a semi-circle. Kathleen sat back on her heels, and then shivered, thinking of the spiders that might still be in her hair from her sojourn in the attic. She shivered again as she unsuccessfully used a tissue to wipe the dust and grime from her face. She might need a real scrub brush instead. "What's up?"

"There's a guy that keeps walking up and down the block. I think he's checking out the house."

"What? How come?"

Juan shrugged his shoulders as he stepped further into the room. "You want me to help you with some of this stuff? Looks like it's making you pretty dirty."

Kathleen knew Juan considered her a neat freak to the point of obsession. He tried to hide his chuckle when he saw her covered in dust and cobwebs that clung to her ragged jeans and sweatshirt. Kathleen would never allow herself to leave the house without being 'dressed to the nines', including mascara and lipstick. She leaned forward and shook her hair. "Are there any creepy crawlies on my head?" Juan stepped forward and pushed a tentative finger around on the top of her scalp. "No, I think you're good."

Kathleen got to her feet, dusted off her jeans, and grimaced at the smudges of dirt all down her front.

"Naw, he'll have to just take me the way I am. Let's just figure out who our visitor is."

Kathleen and Juan walked into the wide foyer. Large multipaned windows placed on each side of the mahogany front door gave a clear view of several yards of the property's white picket fence and further down to the sidewalk.

There indeed was a man. He had brown, wavy hair cut short on the sides, but longer on the top, a high brow, square jaw, and ruddy cheeks. He wore an open jean jacket over a white T-shirt, jeans, brown loafers and aviator glasses. Kathleen wondered what color his eyes were. He certainly seemed handsome, although not as sophisticated as the men she usually dealt with. "And you say he's just walking up and down the block?"

"No, he's just walking to the end of the fence and then turning and walking back."

"Hum, well, I'd better go talk to him." She looked down at herself and grimaced again, but shrugged her shoulders and opened the front door and walked out onto the porch. The man saw her and stopped for just a moment and then continued on, coming toward her.

Kathleen walked down the wide portico steps and to the gate that faced the sidewalk. The man was almost adjacent to her when she spoke. "Can I help you? My houseman told me you've been walking up and down in front of the house for a while."

The man pushed his hand through his hair and smiled at her. He took off his sunglasses and extended his hand. He had the most remarkable pair of sapphire blue eyes Kathleen had ever seen. "Uh, I'm sorry. It was not my intention to intrude. I'm Eric Douglass. I'm here in Chicago doing some research, and this house came up in my search, so I thought I'd look it over. I hope you don't mind."

Not only was the man gorgeous, in an uncomplicated and kind of understated way, but he had a low, smooth voice with a southern
accent that washed over her like warm honey. Kathleen smiled before extending her hand. "I'm Kathleen O'Brien and I own this house."

"O'Brien? Are you related to Nealy O'Brien?"

Kathleen pulled a face. "We try not to acknowledge that he was once a distant part of the family. My father said he was a thug, but of course, he was dead even before my father was born. I think he died under mysterious circumstances in the early thirties, '33 or sometime around then. I don't suppose it was too mysterious though," she laughed. "From what I understand, someone stuck a knife in him while he was in DC," she shrugged her shoulders in dismissal. "It's so strange that you ask after Nealy; I was just reading an old file about him. I'm sure I wouldn't even have remembered the name, but I went into the attic just now and…" She looked down at herself ruefully. "Well, a lot of old, dusty files."

Eric laughed. "Yep, I can see that," he said as he reached over the fence and wiped a smudge of dirt off her cheek. "Oh, sorry."

Kathleen felt herself blush but pushed the feeling aside. She cleared her throat and looked away, but turned back to Eric with what she called her lawyers' dispassionate face.

"So, Mr. Douglass, what's your connection?"

"Who, me?" Eric played dumb. If he decided to come again to ask about the O'Briens' possible involvement with Jimmy's death and disappearance, he'd have to slowly ease into it. Slowly, and decisively after he'd found evidence that someone in the O'Brien gang had murdered and then did away with Jimmy. It would be very awkward to blurt out, "Was your great-grandfather a murderer?" That would not be a diplomatic approach. But he knew he didn't know, not the whole scenario. Just bits and pieces, just fragments of the story. The biggest problem was, if he did learn Jimmy was murdered by a disgruntled O'Brien, what could he do about it now?

All THAT GliTTeRS

"But it was a pleasure to meet you Miss O'Brien. Perhaps I'll be in touch." With that, Eric smiled and walked down the sidewalk backwards, never taking his eyes off her until he reached the end of the block, then he turned and disappeared from sight.

Did this man have something to do with all the mysterious papers old Ralph Gunderson had reported he'd found? Now, that would be a strange coincidence. Most importantly, was Eric Douglass here to throw around allegations about Seamus? Kathleen knew she was being over-dramatic. She had no control over what had happened eight decades ago. She knew she was being over-protective of the family, but that's how she'd always been. Ever since she'd found out about her family's gangster past, she'd done what she could to make sure no one else knew, especially not her colleagues in the courthouse. It was so embarrassing. All her life she'd glossed over what the family had done from the 1890s until the 1950s. She wanted no one to know, although, intellectually, she could see no possible reason why they'd even care. It was a knee jerk reaction, and she knew it. Kathleen frowned at the thought and then felt herself shiver. Rubbing her arms vigorously, she tried to belay the chill.

So, what was that all about? And did she have to worry about Mr. Douglass digging up something she'd rather stayed buried?"

KATHRYN SCARBOROUGH
Chapter Eighteen

Chicago, IL
Present day

Oh, man, I'm out of time,. I yawned as I consulted my watch and stretched, looking idly around the archives room. I'd accumulated a small mountain of data. I kept the information I'd gotten from my dreams on the left side of the pages in a notebook, and the information from Jimmy's articles and other sources on the right. I knew that Nealy O'Brien had existed because I'd found a birth certificate dated 1908. But that was the only 'hard fact' I'd been able to uncover about Nealy, a.k.a. 'wannabe a tough gangster' O'Brien. I'd dreamed about him enough times – if I could take those 'waking dreams' at face value, that is; and the thing was, those 'waking dreams' had never proven to be inaccurate. Other than the birth certificate, the trail was cold. I'd found plenty on Abrams and Gillespie, the creeps; public servants, 'my Aunt Fanny'. Abrams had been written about in several newspapers. The stories were ambiguous enough so that the papers could not be accused of libel. A record from the senate in 1934 had begun proceedings to have him sanctioned for tax evasion. And during his next term, he had resigned. I supposed qualitative assessments of those who have been dead for more than a generation was a big waste of time.

Abrams, Gillespie and O'Brien were in cahoots about something to do with an executive order. That's what I had heard more than a dozen times in my dreams. Of course, FDR had been quite busy during his first term, and there had been more than 30 executive orders issued during just the first eight months of 1933. Some of them could be dismissed easily, others not so much. I narrowed down the few, and I would bet my next paycheck that it had something to do with gold that was involuntarily taken from citizens in 1933. Citizens were required to turn in their gold coins and ingots to the government. The almighty Uncle Sam would haul the stuff off and eventually it would be transferred to Fort Knox when that facility was finished in 1936. Maybe, if I could get my hands on a few more of Jimmy's notes, I could figure this out. Maybe some of Jimmy's old notebooks were still in the house he'd lived in. It was a million-to-one shot, but I was out of options for the time being.

I still needed primary sources, but there were none left in print, unless of course... I sat up quickly, snapping my fingers. Just maybe there were some descendants of Jimmy White still here in Chicago. Just maybe they had some drafts of Jimmy's articles. It was a real long shot. Who kept stuff their grandfather or great-grandfather had written? Jimmy had been a prominent journalist, a somebody, so maybe there were notebooks somewhere in a cardboard box in some attic. I looked up the address I'd gotten from Jimmy White's obituary and found that the same house still existed on Google Maps. Well, things were looking up.

"Is there a way to look up who owns a house in the greater Chicago area?" The archivist, Melissa, looked up. She was mindlessly devouring a chocolate donut while reading one of the many files on her desk. She gave me a big, toothy, chocolate covered grin, before putting the donut down and wiping the crumbs from her fingers. I turned away, embarrassed for her, but my puerile emotions would just have to step aside for some real solid information about Jimmy White.

Melissa dodged around trolleys filled with newspapers, folders of large mock ups of pictures and photographs, and gestured for me to follow her into another room.

"Here," she said, as she held her arms out to encompass a wall filled with phone books. On the bottom of each spine, the books were numbered chronologically, etched in white paint.

"These are names, followed by addresses, like a regular phone book, and these
are by address, so each section of the city is numbered, like #1 Allison Street, and then the next street alphabetically and numerically. Do you know the address?"

"Yes," I said, looking down at my notes. "The address is 400 Pleasant Street, and I think that's in a neighborhood called "Oak Park".

"Well, let's see." Melissa retrieved a wheeled ladder kept for accessing books on high shelves and pulled it toward the end of the huge wall. She took down one of the books and leafed through it, shaking her head and muttering to herself. She re-shelved that book and reached for another, a little further down the wall. This one paid off. "Yep, here it is," she said as she climbed down the ladder. She managed to get as close, it seemed to me, as she could, without actually touching me. She even looked up at me shyly through her thick eyelashes. "Would you like me to go with you? I know which train to take; I mean you are going aren't you?"

I scanned the page Melissa handed to me as she rattled on, paying no heed to her fluttering eyelashes or the proximity of the breast she casually pressed against my forearm. I took a half step back and glanced up, willing myself not to blush, before staring again at the page. "Uh, no, that's okay. I think I can find it, I'm pretty good with directions."

Melissa audibly sighed as I spoke. I glanced up over my reading glasses at her. She wore a decidedly goofy look on her face.

"I just love the way you say your I's," she gushed.

I stared at her, forcing my jaw to stay closed and the word 'Huh' to stay inside my mouth. I shook my head a little and looked back down at the book. *Maybe I have more charisma than I realize.* Being attached to Monica since grad school had certainly put the kibosh on how I saw myself through the eyes of the fairer sex. Maybe I'd turned into a player. Now, that's a word I'd never coupled with the name, Eric Douglass. My life was becoming stranger and stranger.

"Really, that's okay. But thanks for the help." I backed out of the room, tripping on a trolley and dodging around a pile of books.

All THAT GliTTeRS

I couldn't think about women right now, I had a job to finish, and just a few days to finish it. I grabbed my jacket and my computer case and made for the subway entrance.

There was a White still living at the address. Maybe I'd meet Jimmy White's descendants, or were they my own descendants living in this house?

Chapter Nineteen

I took a local instead of an express; the elevated train took more than 45 minutes to reach Jimmy White's old stomping grounds. The neighborhood was to the west and about seven miles from Chicago. I'd found out Oak Park had been around since before the Civil War and the population had boomed after the Great Chicago Fire of 1871. When Jimmy lived there, the homes were lower-middle class. Now the homes, condos and apartments were selling for millions.

I pulled the collar of my jacket tighter around my neck and pushed against the wind gusting steadily, probably from Lake Michigan, a few miles to the east. My eyes teared furiously, soaking my face. I'd always thought the wind coming off the Atlantic at Nag's Head on the outer banks of North Carolina was vicious; I guessed I'd have to re-think that one.

The house was some blocks from the train station, and I walked down the broad avenues, which were nicely landscaped and surrounded by flower beds and trees. I rehearsed my story, mumbling out loud to myself. Hearing my voice helped to calm the jitters, but only a bit.

I knew I could be denied entry to the house, but maybe nothing of Jimmy's had been kept. If that was the case, I'd be right back to where I'd started. If I still lived in the same house my great-grandfather owned, there might be remnants of his life tucked away somewhere. *No guts, no glory; just get on with it, Eric,* I murmured.

I shook my head and wiped my wind-streaked face with my, what Monica called, old man's handkerchief, before I crossed the sidewalk and climbed the steps to 400 Pleasant Street. I looked around. The neighborhood was indeed 'pleasant', reminiscent of

All THAT GliTTeRS

Norman Rockwell and Thomas Kinkaid prints, but so different from southern neighborhoods, from the way the sidewalks were laid out, the areas to park, the front gardens; everything seemed uncomfortably alien. I took a final look around, and then faced the door to Jimmy's old house before I knocked. My stomach was doing a jig, but in my bravado, I pasted a good ol' southern-boy grin on my face. A middle-aged man wearing a V-neck sweater over a button-down shirt and slacks answered the door. He held an opened newspaper in hand and glared at me, obviously annoyed by the interruption.

"Yes?"

"Excuse me, sir, are you Mr. White?" The man's annoyance radiated with such vehemence that I took a half step back.

In the seconds before the door was sure to be slammed in my face, I tried hard to look but not stare. If the reincarnation idea was valid, then I was, or had been, related to this man in some way.

"Who wants to know?"

"I'm sorry to bother you, sir. I'm doing some research about Jimmy White, the reporter from the Tribune in the 1920s and 30s. I found that he'd lived in this house and that there are still members of the White family living here. I thought I'd take a chance and see if y'all have any information about him. Am I in the right place?" The man's face changed from annoyed to quizzical.

"Jimmy White was my grandfather and he died in the 30s."

A grandson? The information made my already madly beating heart beat a little faster. *No*, I told myself in no uncertain terms, *this man is not REALLY your grandson. Get that notion out of your mind. There are many facts you need to find and understand, and that family reunion stuff is not pertinent to what you HAVE to know.*

"Yes, sir, I know he did. The archivist at the Tribune thought you might have some old notebooks or something. She said nothing was at the paper. I'm doing research for a book I'm writing about FDR. Your grandfather was writing a story about

Roosevelt in the summer and fall of 1933, that might be very important to my research. Do you know if there are notebooks or scrapbooks tucked away somewhere? I sure would be much appreciative if I could see them." My story gushed out faster than I thought I could tell it.

The man put down his paper and opened the door wider. "Can I see a driver's license?" I pulled out my wallet and showed him my license and my UNC ID card, hoping that my thumb covered up the line on the bottom, about medical research. The university ID did it and Mr. White opened the door a little wider. "I guess you'd better come in."

"Thanks. I know this is a terrible imposition, but I would really like to see if you have anything of his."

The man stuck out his hand, "I'm Albert the III. My son is Albert the IV. We sometimes forget that we had a locally famous man in the family. I have no idea if there's anything left of Jimmy's. But I suppose it won't hurt for you to look. If there is anything, it's in the attic. No telling what you'll find up there." After shoving his paper under his arm, Albert III started up a wide staircase that rose with an elaborate sweep to the right of the front door. He stopped after a few steps and turned, looking down his nose through his reading glasses at me.

"Now, who did you say you worked for again?"

"Oh, I'm freelance. I'm writing a book about FDR, and I've found out some interesting things that Jimmy wrote about the president and some of his more controversial executive orders. I already have a publisher lined up and they advanced me the money to make this trip to dig up some more facts." *Probably should not have said anything about the publisher. That is easily checked.*

"Oh, okay, that's nice," he said with a smile. "Hope you'll let me read it when it's finished."

"Why sure, Mr. White."

Albert III stopped again on the first landing and turned. He was obviously embarrassed, and he looked at the floor, at the ceiling and finally, at me. "You know, he died before I was born. My father was a teenager when Jimmy died. I don't think my father liked him much, hum, don't know," he mumbled as he opened a door in the middle of the hall.

"I wonder why?"

Mr. White shrugged, but didn't look back at me. "I don't think Jimmy paid much attention to him. My father, on the other hand," he said over his shoulder with a proud smile, "lavished attention on us from the time we were born. He married when he was in his 40s. I don't think he had a happy childhood." Mr. White shook his head and turned again toward the attic staircase.

"I'm sorry to hear that. My father died when I was 12. Well, anyway," I mumbled and followed Albert up the steep staircase.

"When was the house built?" I wanted to change the subject. It wasn't pleasant to hear what a deadbeat Jimmy had been.

"In the 1890s. It wasn't in such a great location when Jimmy bought it, but it's gone up in value since then. Since Frank Lloyd Wright designed and built houses in the city of Oak Park in the 1950s, the neighborhood has taken off in value, God bless him."

The staircase was very steep and narrow, and Albert stopped in the middle to catch his breath. A single bulb hung from a black cord high up in the ceiling and cast a shaft of light down the center of the stairs. There was no railing, and I touched the wall for balance as I climbed. I searched for a flicker of recollection, a shimmer of déjà vu, something to tell me that I wasn't on a fool's errand in this strange, northern city. But nothing came to me. It was like everything I touched, I saw or I read about Jimmy, was a blank page. The only time I felt anything was during the dreams.

When we reached the landing, Albert turned on a lamp perched precariously on top of an old trunk. I turned around completely one time. The room was almost as spacious as the downstairs, but only a portion in the center was tall enough for a person of my height, five feet 11 inches, to stand upright. The sides of the room tilted with the slant of the roof. Floor space was limited, so boxes, trunks and suitcases, were shoved against the walls. There was one dormer set against the back wall with a wide window that offered additional light.

Was there something here? Something I could remember? I touched trunks, boxes and wiped the thick dust on my jeans.

All THaT GliTTeRS

Albert moved boxes, chairs and tables out of my way until I stood almost under the dormer window that faced the side of the house.

"Here," he said, "I think some of Jimmy's stuff might be here. If you'd like, you could take a look at some of these boxes I've moved toward the edge."

What should I feel, or not feel? I opened the first two boxes. With a cursory glance I saw notebooks and mounds of scrap paper. The third box was much the same. Something metal reflected off the ambient light from the window. I reached in and drew out a fountain pen. I held it between my fingers and a cold shiver raced down my spine. Was this the same fountain pen I'd seen in my hallucination in the lab a few weeks ago in Chapel Hill?

"Here," I said, holding it out to Albert without looking at him. "It might be a valuable antique."

I pushed past the knee-high boxes and made a path toward the back of the huge attic. Out of the corner of my eye, I caught a glimpse of a dresser. The piece of furniture was a vanity, with a centered mirror and drawers on each side. It had seen better days. I avoided looking at my reflection in the mirror. I was spooked enough as it was. But something, some memory, nagged at me. It not only nagged, but the memory almost screamed at me. I pulled out the righthand drawer and found cans of pomade, combs, hairpins, and hairnets. A small round box protruded from the back-left corner, and there was something; something that I recognized about that little round box. I pulled at it, but it felt like it was glued to the drawer bottom. I tugged, this time harder, and it came loose. The cold metal box lay in my hand. I'd held it before. I didn't know why or how, but I knew I'd held this box 'before'. I pulled and pried at the lid of the box until it came loose. Inside was a wad of money, there must have been five or six bills rolled together; a $5.00, a $1.00 and a few $10.00 bills. "Here," I said and handed the money to Albert. "I'll bet this is worth something." Albert took the bills and carefully unfolded them with a sharp intake of breath.

"This one is a $100 dollar bill, and it's a gold certificate, see?" he said, pointing to the words in the middle of the bill that required the government to pay the bill's face value in gold to whoever was in possession of it.

"Bet you couldn't get gold for that now, it would be such a tiny speck, anyway…"

"Tell me about it."

I looked down inside the round, metal box and my heart stopped. An image came to me, almost blinding in its clarity. Lying on the bottom wrapped in a piece of a handkerchief was a pair of silver cufflinks. I dumped the cufflinks out into my left palm and stared at them, afraid to look away. Suddenly, the floor of the attic felt like it was coming up to meet me. I grabbed for the edge of the dresser; sure I was going to fall dead in a faint at the feet of my… Albert White.

"Hey, are you all right?"

"Yeah, I guess so. I just felt a little dizzy. Maybe it's 'cause we're up here in the attic, heat, I don't know." I shoved the cufflinks back into the metal box, put the lid on quickly, and handed it to Albert. There was something quite surreal about all of this snooping around in this man's past. It was terrifying and then again, I felt like I was watching myself in a movie, but I wasn't watching the movie, I was actually in it. I took a breath, hoping to dispel the fear washing over me, and reminded myself why I was here. "Did you tell me that there were boxes of Jimmy's notebooks up here?"

"Yes, I'll have to rummage around," said Albert, turning almost completely around to look over his shoulder. "Oh, yes, I think those cardboard boxes that are directly behind you have some of Jimmy's notebooks. You may look through those as much as you like. If you'd like to take some back to your hotel room, I have no objection. If you would just please bring them to the house before you return to
North Carolina."

"Yes, I can do that. You just don't know how much I appreciate this." Truer words were never said. I just wanted to solve this mystery and get back to my life. I shook my head, forcing myself to focus on the task at hand. I made my feet move around and looked down. There were four or five cardboard boxes stacked on top of each other. I opened the first one, grabbed a handful of notebooks, and pulled them out. I gave a cursory look at each one but put a few to the side. I repeated the process with each of the boxes until I had a small stack of notebooks from 1933. When I turned back to Albert, the older man was examining the gold certificates and cufflinks that I had found.

"Well, if you don't mind, I'll go ahead and take these with me. I'll transcribe everything I can into my computer and then I'll bring them tomorrow before I go back to North Carolina. Here's my cell phone number and my email. If there's anything else you can think of, please get in touch with me. I transcribe quickly, so I don't think I'll need these notebooks past tomorrow evening. I can't thank you enough," I said, extending my hand to Albert, "for all of your help in this matter." I nodded to the bills in Albert's hand. "I think you can get a lot for those gold certificates from a coin dealer. I hope the guy gives you top dollar for them. I have no idea what they're worth, but I'm sure they're worth a lot. Again, thanks so much for all your help."

Albert and I made our way to the front door of the house where we again shook hands. I backed out of the door and raised my hand in a wave.

Chapter Twenty

Kathleen O'Brien scoured the folders she'd retrieved from her attic the day before. It was all well laid out information about the family's bootlegging operation from 1920-1933; real estate, fishing, everything that made the family money; listed in one of the folders was everything that they'd paid taxes on, and everything they hadn't paid taxes on. Every little slip of paper, every invoice, every tax bill, catalogued chronologically by some ancestor of meticulously detailed sensibilities. Twice she'd read the name Nealy O'Brien. Nothing definitive about him or his movements, just mentioned as an afterthought. In the margin of each sheet of paper was a strange notation doodled next to the entry that mentioned her distant cousin's name. She wasn't sure what the notation meant; what the doodle indicated was not explained. She continued to putter around in the folders, not really getting very far. If she was going to figure out what Eric Douglass had to do with Nealy, and she couldn't figure out for the life of her what that was, she'd have to read everything that Jimmy White had written about his accusations against Seamus and Patrick. Was there a connection in some way? And this business with that old man Gunderson calling, like a voice from the grave; she shivered.

She'd sent Juan over the day after the old man had called, to take his information. It amounted to exactly nothing. By the time Juan had traveled across town, Gunderson had misplaced the box with the files and old papers. Old Patrick, her grandfather, had set the house up for Gunderson's father. His wish was that he keep the papers that Patrick had entrusted to him, and that's when the story fell apart. Box or no box, documents or no documents, there was no real story, only conjecture. Perhaps Gunderson senior had done a very good deed for the family, and maybe Patrick had made the whole thing up. Could it get any more mysterious?

What was this weird squiggle next to the three or four notations about Nealy, and a few others from the 30s and 40s?

Kathleen leaned backwards, with her head resting on the back of her desk chair, pushing her toe against the floor, and idly moving slowly around in a circle. She stared at her wall calendar, letting her mind go blank. The calendar's picture was of one of the covered bridges of Pennsylvania. The photo showed the entrance to a one-lane wooden bridge, the dark interior stretching out, so that the other end was obscured. It looked just like a tunnel.

And then she remembered; there were tunnels, tunnels under the house. The entrance was through the back wall in the basement. She had lived her whole life in the house on South Halstead and thought she knew a lot about the structure, but now she remembered. The tunnels under the house connected most of the houses in the neighborhood. They'd been dug during the last quarter of the 19th century, connecting each house to the next in the long street of large Victorians. She wondered how many of her neighbors knew of their existence. The O'Briens had been in the house since 1918. A childhood cousin, who also knew of the tunnels' existence, had told Kathleen about them. But that cousin died years before when Kathleen was a teenager, and she hadn't thought about the mysterious underpinnings of her house since then. The tunnels had been used to store crates of whiskey during prohibition and to move the smugglers who the 'G' men were after, to waiting boats on Lake Michigan and escort them out of harm's way.

No one had been under the house for decades, so who knew what the condition was? The bottled whiskey was probably no good anyway, since it hadn't been left in the casks. No casks; lots of alcohol and no flavor. But who knew?

The tunnels were there before the O'Briens had even bought the house. Kathleen wasn't sure she could remember, or even if she'd ever been told what the tunnels had originally been for. So, if the notation referred to some other document that was stored in one of the tunnels, would it be important for her to find it? Could it shed any light on Nealy, Jimmy White, and maybe the reason the journalist had it in for her ancestors? She could be the one looking and finding whatever was there, to make sure nothing incriminated or besmirched her family name. There were things that those men from County Cork had done, bad things, grossly illegal things, but she wouldn't have to deal with the besmirching if she was the one that found the documents or letters or whatever was there.

She pondered all of this, trying to remember if one of her uncles or her father had told her to keep non family members away from the tunnels. Were there still casks of Canadian whiskey down there?

A knock at her office door brought her out of her reverie.

"Yes, come in."

"Miss Kathleen, that man, the one that was walking past the house yesterday, he's here to see you."

Kathleen felt her mouth pop open in surprise. Now, what was Mister Eric Douglass doing back here?

"All right, Juan, you can show him in. At least I'm a little cleaner than I was yesterday."

Kathleen stood with her hands folded at her waist. She waited for the door to open and admit Eric, then she'd find out why he was here. Before she was through, he'd tell her everything.

Chapter Twenty-one

August 1, 1933
Offices of the Chicago Tribune

    Jimmy thought he had it figured out; this plan of Abrams and Gillespie. He just had no solid proof… at the moment. According to the Executive Order 6102 issued in May, and just now being implemented, all persons were required to hand over their gold coins and bullion to a federal reserve bank in exchange for a slip of paper, a small handful of greenbacks of "equal" value. The handing over of personal property was not to be thought of as punitive. Really? How could anyone not think of handing over their gold double eagles, as well as $5.00 and $2.50 gold coins as anything but a punishment? The ruling was supposedly a move by FDR and his liberal cronies to forestall the hoarding of gold. According to the order, the government could reach into a private citizen's bank account and just take the gold. Then it would be taken to several pre-designated areas, put on trains, and sent to the NY Federal Reserve vaults in Manhattan. If his figures were even close to being correct, then the Chicago area would collect around 1% of the total amount, which would turn out to be millions of dollars in gold.

    One of the men that helped corral the congressional interns, Bill Jacobs, was his informant at the Congress. He'd told Jimmy information that was reported during committee meetings and House debates and then that information cover-up, went quickly. Public information was intended for taxpayers, but then again, it wasn't. The documents were kept from being easily accessible to the public.

With enough information of this type, Jimmy could blow FDR and his party sky high. The problem was… he had to get hold of the documents. And then he'd have to really figure out how they were doing it so that he could catch them red-handed.

Jimmy reached for his notebook, and then stuck his hands in his pockets, rocking back and forth, head down, deep in thought. Then he looked at his editor, and said, "Think I'll go to Arkansas. One of my informants sent me a wire. Seems our man, Gillespie and his counterpart Abrams are going to meet somewhere near the Mississippi River. With the walls having ears in Washington, I guess they think they can't get a private word in. I found out since the last time that Gillespie is the middleman for a shipping company that sends loads up and down the Mississippi. I'll find out which ones and see if I can get a line on what's up."

"Jimmy, be careful. If these guys are half as bad as you think they are, they will be a force to be reckoned with."

"Yep, I'll send you a wire when I get some information. May I get an advance on my expenses?"

"Yeah, yeah, tell Hilda in payroll I said to give you $75. And give some of it to that wife of yours. You being gone so often, I'll bet she has bills to pay. Make sure you sign for the $75."

"Oh, right, yeah, I guess she does. I'll check in with her and the kids before I go. There's a train tonight at 6:00. I'll be on it."

The Mississippi
Near Little Rock, Arkansas
August 28, 1933

Jimmy had to use a bigger portion of his expense money than he would have thought necessary. He had to grease the palms of the warehousemen and flat-boat pilots to get close to Gillespie's warehouse, some twenty miles due south of Little Rock.

He'd taken most of the money he had for these occasions from a hiding place in the attic in his home in Chicago. So far, just to get to this point, he'd used $42. He was glad he'd bought a round-trip ticket. It would be too bad if he'd had to wire Carlson for some train money. He thought he'd rather hoof it back to Chicago. He kept a little metal box in an old dresser, stuck far in a corner in a drawer. In it, he stowed the occasional silver dollar, green back and a pair of sterling silver cuff links that some politician had given him by way of a subtle bribe. Jimmy spilled the story about the man and kept the cuff links. Served him right. In his little corner of the attic, he kept boxes of notes, outlines and depositions from important court cases, and copies of the Tribune that had printed his most memorable stories.

A man with a flat-bottomed boat rowed him out to the warehouse and left him on the downwind side of the dock that jutted out into the Mississippi. Jimmy sidled up to the warehouse, making sure his back was to the river and in the cover of trees and shrubs, and far enough away from the entrance and watchful eyes. The boatman had informed him that three, and sometimes as many as five men had been hanging around the warehouse on and off for the past day. Jimmy quickly guessed who they were. He moved carefully through the brambles and weeds and put his eye to a crack in the back corner of the warehouse. The place had been abandoned ten years ago; the boatman had told him. Vegetation grew in the cracks, up the walls, and like a spongy mass, deadened the sound of his stealthy approach.

Jimmy almost gagged at the smell of rotting vegetation, hemp rope, and water-soaked wood that met him head on. A beetle, large as a half dollar, latched on and began to meander up his pant leg. Jimmy shook his leg violently, but the bug hung on. He reached down and flicked it off and then watched the round, brown body scramble over leaves and branches away from him. He looked through the crack; it wasn't hard to recognize Abrams, even though the senator was many feet away inside the darkened interior of the warehouse. He saw Abrams take off his white straw hat, and perch it on the knee bent over his leg. The senator took a drag from his cigar, stood and walked idly around the warehouse. A man walked in through the front. It was Gillespie, the congressman from this district of Arkansas, making as much noise as he possibly could. Jimmy watched avidly as Gillespie waltzed up to the senator and slapped him on the shoulder. "Abrams." Jimmy could just hear the men above the Mississippi lapping against the shoreline.

"'Bout time you got here. Wondering where you were."

"Sorry, we had a flat, and then O'Brien showed up late."

"Listen here, why are we having anything to do with that low-life?"

Jimmy saw Gillespie roll his eyes at the senator. "Because, senator, we need some muscle." Gillespie put his hands on his hips and leaned forward in an effort to get Abram's undivided attention. "We need someone to hire the men to move the shipment. We need someone to strong-arm the guards that are watching the shipment. We're in it if we can't get the memo to the Pinkerton's in time to stop the real guards from coming. If they show up with our guards standing around, can you imagine the mess? Got it?"

"Yes, I see." Abrams stepped on his cheroot as O'Brien strutted through the door.

"Well, well, looky who's here? I suspect you two honorable gentlemen are ready to get started with this little endeavor?"

"There's no need to be cocky, young man." Abrams sniffed at O'Brien like he smelled something a little off.

"Look here, Mac, I'll be any way I want to be, got it?" said O'Brien, pushing his face into the senator's.

"Okay, let's calm down. We have a lot to discuss," said Gillespie, pushing himself between the two men.

Jimmy watched as Abrams and O'Brien eyed one another before they went to opposite ends of the huge room. "Now O'Brien, we have to make sure you can get about six men, all very trusted men to help with this. We need that many because the shipment is quite heavy, and the whole project needs steady and reliable men." *Heavy*, Jimmy thought. *Heavy!*

"I need to know what it is we're lifting. I'm not going to let any of my men get mowed down for nothing."

"You are being paid handsomely for this. What do you need to know, aside from what we've already told you?" said Abrams with a sniff.

Jimmy watched as O'Brien flicked his fingers along the broad lapels of his jacket. The kid was as cool as a cucumber. It had to be 90° in that warehouse, but Nealy didn't sweat a drop.

Abrams frowned at Gillespie and then tuned a scowl on O'Brien.

"Listen, sen-a-tohr, me and my boys had better be paid handsomely for this. We're the ones that'll take the heat if something goes wrong. There are about a million things that could, and probably will go wrong, and we'll be sitting ducks, see? Now, I figure we have about two months to get all the parts of this shindig together before it comes off. Two months ain't a long time when you're making a plan to fight the government, know what I mean?"

O'Brien scratched his head dismissively as he turned and walked away. Jimmy heard Abrams sigh, and watched as he shrugged his shoulders. He supposed O'Brien wasn't behaving the way Abrahms thought he should. "Now look, my boy," Abrams said as he began drawing a diagram on the back of an envelope.

Jimmy craned forward but could see nothing. He had to get a hold of that envelope. That might be all the proof he needed to bring the bunch down.

"We know approximately how many pounds there will be, and we have a dummy document already printed up with altered information. You understand the word, altered?"

O'Brien growled at him and made to lunge, but Gillespie shot out an arm and stood successfully between them. Abrams shook out his coat and straightened his lapels and tie before he continued. Jimmy listened, but the low, mournful sound of a boat on the river covered the voices. Then Abrams turned his back and paced to the far end of the warehouse, O'Brien and Gillespie in tow. Their voices, deadened by the interior of the warehouse, became a mere rumble. Jimmy could hear nothing of what the men were saying. The man turned again, and Jimmy caught 'September 23, downtown Chicago'. The three men had almost walked the length of the warehouse, coming nearer and nearer to Jimmy, who strained to hear what was said. He saw O'Brien push his hat back on his head and put his hands on his hips. O'Brien walked up and down the warehouse for a few minutes, stopping almost in front of

Jimmy. The gangster looked over Abrams and Gillespie with disgust, but Jimmy noted a glimmer of interest as well. Jimmy watched carefully as a myriad of emotions crossed O'Brien's face. The man's face was an open book. And that particular trait, more than anything else, made him a terrible gangster. He obviously didn't like Abrams or Gillespie, but he probably needed this chore if he was to show his 'uncle' Seamus and the other Chicago gang bosses that he could handle an assignment, any assignment.

Once again, Jimmy had come up empty-handed. Would he ever find out what these men were up too?

Chapter Twenty-two

Present
Day
Chicago,
IL.

Eric transcribed all the notebooks into the Dell during the night. He made two backups; one on a CD he kept in the zippered cover of the briefcase, and another on a four-gigabyte thumb drive secured to his key chain. Yeah, geek city. He never created any kind of document without making a backup, several backups.

Earlier that day, he'd made another trip to Oak Park to return the notebooks to Albert. Having been to Jimmy's house twice now, seeing the steps leading up to the porch and that front door made his stomach feel like it would go through the floor. Maybe all of these notions about him being Jimmy in a past life were real. Why else would he have had such a weird reaction when he saw the small round metal box, the cufflinks and that fountain pen?

After listening to Albert's stories and then reading Jimmy's articles, it was only too evident that the journalist was self-absorbed and egotistical. The memories and the dreams were terrifying and so real, so detailed, and so exact; how could he NOT believe that he had been there? Were they really memories or just figments of his imagination? He still didn't know anything about Jimmy's murder, except that his body had never been found. He knew why he was at Kathleen O'Briens again; because Nealy was such a prominent fixture in his waking dreams. Was Seamus O'Brien, the head of Nealy's family, had been instrumental in Jimmy's death? Kathleen had been very friendly yesterday, maybe she'd loosen up and tell him more about her family history, the stuff he couldn't find on Google. Eric had found plenty in the public records of the Cook County District Attorney's office about the O'Briens illegal activities from 1929 to 1933; the convictions and the allegations. There was something about that name, Nealy, who he was certain had something to do with Jimmy's murder.

"Come in, would you like a cup of coffee?" Kathleen asked and turned to her houseman without waiting for confirmation from Eric. "Juan, please bring us some coffee and some sandwiches, and some of that fruit we had at breakfast. It was really good. It's so close to lunch, we might as well sit and eat."

Kathleen waited for the door to shut before she sat down on her side of the desk and looked intently at Eric. He looked like he hadn't slept all night, but nevertheless, he was neatly dressed in a pair of khaki slacks and a light blue button-down shirt. Eric pulled out his laptop.

"What do you have there?"

"I'm glad you agreed to see me. I know how weird this all is, but here's the thing; I have been doing a lot of research about Jimmy White, the Chicago Tribune journalist from the 1930s. I actually went to his home yesterday and his grandson let me transcribe some of Jimmy's notebooks. You live in the home of your great-grandfather, and so does Albert White III. That kind of thing, people living in the old family home, just doesn't happen as often in the south," Eric said with a short laugh, and saw Kathleen's genuine smile. "But I am off track here. After reading White's notes, I'll tell you, he used a strange sort of self-made shorthand. I suppose he wanted to keep his information secret prior to publication. Maybe he was afraid someone would steal his idea. I don't know, but what I've learned about the man is that he was so arrogant, so self-absorbed, all he thought about was the newspaper, and getting his story." Eric felt an uncharacteristic twinge of guilt, which surprised him. If Jimmy had neglected his family, it had nothing to do with him. Thinking of his own father gave a familiar tug at his heart. At times, he'd try to reconcile how he responded to the pressures in life relating to a causal effect; his dad died; he never grew emotionally complete. That was simplistic in the extreme. And finding out that Jimmy was such a caustic jerk; couldn't he have acted more responsibly to his family?

"Jimmy White has nothing directly to do with you now, in 2017, but some of the stuff he wrote about indicates he had it in for your family, your great-grandfather, and some of your uncles; it was practically yellow journalism. Jimmy took every accusation from the district attorney about the O'Briens, and each and every incident was overblown in his articles. I read them all and the corresponding notes. You told me yesterday that you'd been up in your attic looking for some information about that era, the 1930s, so I thought you might be interested in what I found. I told you I was going to write a paper about Jimmy's op-ed pieces; you'll get to hear it first. Are you game?"

"Well, yes." Kathleen sat back in her chair. This was a surprise. Of all the things she thought Eric Douglass might say, this certainly hadn't occurred to her. There had to be a reason Eric was here, why he was looking into all of this ancient history. He seemed much too bright and much too pragmatic to just fly off on a tangent.

"So, what have you found?"

"As I said, Jimmy's shorthand was a little hard to get used to. My field is research, not this of course, but the building blocks of the discipline are always the same, so I just messed with it long enough until I figured it out.

Juan knocked on the door and brought in a tray of sandwiches, fruit and coffee. She poured Eric a cup of coffee in a fine china cup. He took a moment and drank slowly before continuing.

"So, at the end of the 1920s and into the 30s, there were at least half a dozen articles that White wrote slamming your great-grandfather. I know I'm getting off the track here, but this is what you might want to know.

"It seems Nealy O'Brien was doing something for a senator from Massachusetts named Abrams, and this wasn't in any article, it was in some notebooks marked 1933. I haven't figured out yet what it was he was doing. But I know, just by looking at the death certificate, that Nealy, just like you said, was murdered by someone in Washington, DC. I'm just wondering if there's any connection. All I can think of is that Senator Abrams had some connection with Nealy's murder. Does Nealy's untimely demise tie in with Jimmy's murder? I know that Jimmy was killed around the same time period, maybe within a few days."

"Abrams… Abrams, I've read that name somewhere." Kathleen began leafing through a notebook that she'd transcribed into items, dates, people, from reading the files. "You know," she said as she looked up at Eric, "my people, all of them, took pains to write everything down. Seamus began the practice in the 1890s. He told my grandfather that the nuns had taught him rudimentary bookkeeping and how important it was to keep a journal, because the mind can't keep the details straight. It's true, of course."

"Oh yes, in my job, I notate everything."

"And what is it exactly that you do?" Kathleen asked as she kept her place in her notes with a pencil.

Crap, maybe I can skirt around the 'mouse wrangler' bit. "I'm a microbiologist and work for the medical school at the University of North Carolina. Our department has a grant right now and we're in the first stage of some clinical trials, drug discovery. Don't want to bore you with that," I said as I quickly looked back down at my computer screen.

Kathleen stood and walked around her desk. Miss O'Brien was smooth, sophisticated and stunning. My mouth watered just looking at her and I liked very much the way she looked at me. She was not just a 10, she was way beyond that; her number was in the stratosphere somewhere. She leaned her hip against the desktop, crossed one leg over the other and then folded her arms at her waist. Her facial expression was inscrutable. I couldn't tell what she was thinking. She had to be one good lawyer with that deadpan gaze.

I closed my eyes briefly, thinking about Monica, who always wore jeans so long that the hems near her heels had big gaping holes with threads following behind her. Never mind the grungy tops she wore on her more than ample bosom that showed off rolls of fat around her waist and midriff, no matter how often I'd made hints about how bad it looked. It wasn't that she was fat; plenty of folks couldn't help that. It was just that she didn't care enough for herself to do anything about her appearance.

I dismissed thoughts of Monica to gaze at Kathleen. She was so close; it was hard for me to keep my mind on Jimmy White's murder, let alone breathe. I hadn't thought about a woman's beauty in this way for longer than I could remember. I took another long look at Kathleen and mentally shrugged my shoulders. This was not the time for self-psychoanalysis.

"Tell me something, Mr. Douglass, what's your interest in this anyway? It seems unusual that a researcher working at a medical school would care about something that happened almost eighty years ago?"

I had figured someone was going to ask me that, and I'd have to give Kathleen a different answer than I'd given Albert III. I was just not comfortable yet with telling her about a past life that might have been mine.

"I am going to write the story I spoke of before. My curiosity was peaked when I came across a document that my great-grandfather had kept in the family Bible. The crux of it was that in 1933 FDR wrote an executive order stating that everyone, without exception, had to surrender their gold to the government in exchange for gold certificates. Here look at this; I found it on Wikipedia."

Kathleen came around the edge of her desk and took Eric's laptop and read the page with avid interest. He continued:

"The Douglass's turned in the few coins they had and never got them back. Instead, they got certificates worth $20 for each ounce of gold turned in. After the confiscation, the gold was set at $35 an ounce. Not exactly fair, but let's face it, most of the country was enamored with the president and there were only a few voices that nay-sayed him. One of them was Jimmy White. I had a few days off, so I thought I'd come see what I could find out. Supposedly, the gold was collected and then shipped off to the New York Federal Reserve underground vaults, and then to Fort Knox after its completion in 1936 - supposedly. I thought if I could get enough information, then maybe I could get the government to give the gold back to the people, the families that they'd confiscated it from, and at the same time write my story."

Kathleen stared at him; her face froze in surprise. Then she threw back her head and laughed

Chapter Twenty-three

Kathleen laughed so hard tears coursed down her face. "Give back, give back? You are kidding, right? Aren't we talking about the United States, bloated, too-big-for-itself government?"

Eric looked up sheepishly at her, as the color rose in his face. For the first time, Kathleen saw a dimple in his left cheek make a brief and splendid appearance.

"I know it sounds crazy, but in the notebooks, I found a note scratched on the back of an envelope written by Jimmy White, and for once, it wasn't in that weird shorthand. Here, I brought it with me." Eric reached into the front pocket of his computer case and drew out a folded wad of paper. With great care, he extracted an envelope from what looked like a mass of carefully folded tissue paper. Eric put his forefinger underneath the first item and drew it down, slowly reading as he spoke.

"White must've been copying this from something he heard while he was sitting in a restaurant or behind a corner. Everybody, all your ancestors and the politicians he wrote about, knew what he looked like, and were on the lookout for him. I know they never wanted to say anything in front of him, because he was known to expose everyone and anyone even without substantiated proof. It's really straightforward.

"Here's what it says; he has the points bulleted:
1. Shipment from central bank in Chicago.
2. Indianapolis rail hub, switch?
3. Where was the shipment sent, and where would the shipment be stowed until it could be picked up?
4. O'Brien to hire six men for the job.

5. How has he managed to pay off the federal marshals that are overseeing the gold pickup and delivery?

6. Find out where it is going.

7. Find out who O'Brien hired.

"See, he's getting redundant. Sometimes I can't make head or tail of his notes, and then sometimes it's as clear as a bell. Now, here's something that should be easier to find." Eric continued reading.

"8. Get the names of citizens that had been relieved of their gold.

"I know that wouldn't have been easy. The information must have been recorded somewhere. And what do you suppose Jimmy White would do with that information? That is, if he could get it?"

I shook my head. I had to assimilate all of this information if I was going to solve this mystery. How else was I going to return to the present and put my life back in order? I continued:

"9. Names may be recorded in the Central Federal Bank, check names."

I folded the envelope and returned it to its cocoon of wrapped tissue paper.

"So you see, it's all a big mystery. I have no way of knowing if any of these things on this envelope actually transpired. This is what I do know: there really was an Executive Order 6102 that gave Roosevelt the right to take away the average citizens' gold coins and ingots. There really were Senator Abrams, Congressman Gillespie and Nealy O'Brien. There really is a rail hub in Indianapolis, and there really is a direct route from Indianapolis to a dozen cities in its outlying areas; if indeed, that's where it was spirited away. I don't know enough about the rest of it to make good a qualitative decision. See, there are too many gaps, too many holes in the story. Maybe Jimmy just assumed that the gold was going to be lifted by the crooked politicians with Nealy's help. Were they going to steal a chunk of it? That's the only thing that makes sense. Why else would they align themselves with a known felon who they knew could recruit men for them? Too many gaps and I'm just not sure if it's important enough to pursue to find out if it's really so.."

I looked up at her, wondering what she thought of me. She probably thought I was a kook. Still, the more I read and the more I researched, I knew in my gut that Jimmy had been murdered, and the reason for his murder was something to do with the gold shipment from Chicago that supposedly had gone to New York City, and ultimately to Fort Knox.

"You know… if you get enough information and you really want to know where the gold is, you can go to DC and talk to the people in the Treasury Department, or maybe the National Archives. They probably won't tell you squat, but the thing is, it's such ancient history, maybe they will. There are time limits on declassifying different types of documents."

"Are you kidding me? Those guys would think I'm a bigger kook than you do." I tried to look competent and cool, but knew I fell short of the mark. I smiled, trying to lessen the unease in the room and get the frown lines between her eyes to smooth out. "They'd probably throw me into a federal penitentiary just to shut me up." It pleased me that she smiled and laughed a little at my comment.

"Look," Kathleen said, "I'm not a big proponent of the government, but there is some rule of law. They have to figure out what to charge you with and make sure it would stick before they did anything. I guess they could throw you in the dungeon," she said with a smile. "But who would they go after? What if there really was a gold shipment? What if it had never gotten to the New York Federal Reserve? Where do you think it could be?"

"Well, if it really did happen, I think it's someplace around one of the rail yards that connect to Indianapolis. It was heavy enough so that it would take several men pulling one of those long, low wagons with the steel wheels. It must have been put into boxes. No one would throw gold coins in a heap. They'd have to be tallied and then recorded. Whether or not the shipment made it out of the hands of the Federal Government, where it could have been stashed almost eighty years ago is another question. There are two more notebooks of Jimmy's that I haven't decoded as yet. What would Jimmy know about any of this? And the big question is; do I need to know? It's a great mystery, but, a; I don't have enough data to draw a conclusion, and b; I don't know what I'd do with the information if I did know."

"I like the way that analytical mind of yours thinks. You know, I just might have an idea." Kathleen walked back around to her desk and began leafing through the files. She picked one up with 1933 printed in black on the front. Kathleen leafed through the pages, put her forefinger on the margin and drew it down, slowly. "Every time I see this little symbol, see here," she turned to show Eric a small, neat doodle interspersed sporadically along the far-right margin of nearly every page in the file. "I've checked carefully and every symbol by the item has something to do with Nealy O'Brien. I'm trying to remember if anyone ever told me what the symbol signifies. There is one thing," she said as she sat down with a sigh and placed both of her hands flat on the desktop. She looked up at me and stared. Maybe she was wondering how gutsy both of us really were. "There is one thing; we can go down into the tunnels and see if there are any files with this symbol on the cover."

"The tunnels?" I queried. I felt my eyebrows rise in surprise. Had I heard correctly? There were secrets in a tunnel somewhere, secrets about the gold and Jimmy White. "Exactly what tunnels are we talking about?"

"When the houses in this neighborhood were built, there was a series of tunnels that went from house to house. I am not clear on what the purpose of the tunnels was. I don't think my great-grandfather was crazy about a tunnel leading into his house. If I remember correctly, someone told me that the far end of the adjoining tunnels had been blocked with rock. My great-grandfather certainly didn't want anyone to just waltz up into his basement and gain access to the house that way. I'm not sure if anybody's been down there in the last 75 years.

"Let's see, if Nealy O'Brien had access to the house, which I'm sure he did, would he have used the tunnel for anything? Nealy does not strike me as the literati; I have no way of knowing what he wrote or if he thought it was important to write anything down. But if this little doodle in the right-hand margin indicates something I was told about long ago – it's the tunnels. If anything, that makes sense, it may be that there are files down there." Kathleen stood slowly, her head still down, staring at the file, thinking. Methodically, she brushed her blouse down over her skirt, looked up at Eric and gave him a little smile.

"I know there's only one way to find out. We need to go down into the tunnels and look.

Chapter Twenty-four

August 1933

Jimmy returned from Arkansas with nothing. He rubbed his hands over his face as he looked over his notes again. He'd been back at his desk at the Tribune for the past day putting together everything he'd learned in DC and Arkansas. What exactly had he learned? The three; O'Brien, Gillespie and Abrams were in cahoots to defraud, and it had to do with an executive order. FDR had written many that year, but the only one that made sense was the one about the gold.

1. The executive order demanded that everyone in the country give up their gold coins and ingots to the government.
2. Abrams, Gillespie and that thug, O'Brien, had a plan to steal the gold that would be gathered in Chicago at the central bank downtown sometime in September.
3. If they did steal it, how would they get it out of the city and the state, and where could they put it until they could lay their hands on it?
4. Could a rail car with contraband be switched to another line before its ultimate destination of New York?
5. BUT would a part of it never arrive?
6. Could the gold be switched with concrete blocks painted gold. But that couldn't be right; that was too corny, even for Abrams. Could it be taken from the train and put somewhere around the rail yard? Again, he thought, *I'll have to*
do more digging on that. He was scheduled to visit the rail yard in two days to do some snooping.

7. The fake gold, if it was fake gold, would be taken, and the real stuff picked up at the convenience of Abrams and Gillespie. But that couldn't be right either. It just couldn't. Abrams and Gillespie were thieves, but they were also smart, and they wouldn't leave themselves open like that. Fake gold would be recognized in a second and then all the G-men would have to do was backtrack; no, that couldn't be it.

Jimmy mulled over his notes, trying to read the minds of the men he wanted so desperately to expose. This story had gotten right into his gut. He was consumed by it. It took every waking thought and breath. He might be able to put some bite into this story if he could put his hands on that envelope Abrams had doodled on.

"And another thing," Carlson, Jimmy's editor said. "I know your Constitutional sensibilities are out of whack on this one, and I do agree with you that these men must be exposed, but we've got to do it so that the accusations are rock solid. There can't be any 'reasonable doubt', not another op-ed piece by you just blasting away with no solid proof."

"Very well. I'll see what I can do."

"We need pictures, funds changing hands, the people they've hired to help them, all that and nothing less. If these hired officials are undermining the government for their own largesse, then the American people should and will know about it, and they'll know about it from us. We have to be the watchdog, the sentinel for the American people. High ideals, I know, but not too far reaching, I think."

All THAT GliTTeRS

"Mr. White, your wife is on 228," Jimmy's secretary said as she pushed open the door of his office.

"My wife? She never calls. Okay, thanks Gladys." Jimmy reached for the third phone from the left on his desktop. "Clarisse? What's the matter?" He supposed, if he thought about it for more than a second, he'd think of his wife in kindly terms. She was only semi-transparent in his thoughts. A concept he really couldn't quite put his finger on. They had no grand passion. But she took care of everything: the house, the children, the bills, making sure his collars were back from the laundry; she was a good sort.

"Jimmy, I want to know if you are coming home tonight. Your daughter has her recital and you haven't been home in months, not for anything more than to change clothes and give me a few dollars."

Clarisse was always such a good sort, but she sounded miffed, almost angry and tearful. Not like her at all.

"What's this all about? You never call here. You know I'm busy."

"I just told you. Your daughter has a recital tonight and... and," she stammered and sounded all stuffy like she'd been crying. This was not like Clarisse at all. She was seldom emotional, and never particularly demanding. "I expect you to be here, do you understand me?"

Jimmy pulled the phone away from his ear and looked at it quizzically; this did not sound like his very compliant wife at all. "Now listen, Clarisse..."

"No, now you listen. You are never home. We could be starving to death and evicted from this house, as if you ever cared about it. I've been to see your editor and told him that we're two mortgage payments behind. Mr. Carlson has agreed to have your salary put into our bank account and paid the bank what you owe them. Now, I will not have our children going without food or clothing because you have forgotten we exist." Jimmy thought he heard her stamp her foot over the phone.

"Gee, I'm sorry, honey, I had no idea..."

"Of course you had no idea!"

My God, she was really getting warmed up now. He'd never heard her raise her voice, never in 20 years of marriage... maybe he'd...

"Listen Clarisse, I'm sorry, honey. I'll try my darndest to get home tonight, I promise."

She took a big audible breath that he heard very clearly on his end of the line. "If you aren't home, I'm going to have the locks changed. It's a new world since the war, Jimmy. Women aren't chattel anymore. We have the vote!" And she slammed down the phone.

Quietly, Jimmy hung up. Images of the people he'd seen gleaning in the fields from the train crowded out the thoughts about Abrams and Gillespie.

"Gladys," he called.

His secretary, nice, reliable, middle-aged Gladys, wearing a purple print dress with a crocheted collar, pushed open the door to his office. She wore a headset around her neck, and Jimmy wondered if she'd heard any of the conversation he'd just had with his wife. "Yes, Mr. White?"

"Listen, call that florist on 12th and send a dozen roses over to my house, and get them to put in a big box of chocolates with it," he said, pulling a mound of bills from his wallet. God, were his children really hungry? He shivered thinking of the people he'd seen from the train. That image would be forever etched in his memory. What a lousy father he'd turned out to be.

Gladys raised her brows, but thankfully said nothing as she reached for the bills. "Sure Mr. White, I'll get right on it."

Jimmy scratched his head and sighed. He looked at his watch, 2:30, that didn't give him a lot of time. He looked back down at his notes, trying to fill in the gaps that he still didn't have solid information about?

When he looked at his watch again, it was 7:30.

Chapter Twenty-five

The busboy, Joey, put in a call to the Tribune, but Jimmy was on his way out the door. "Gladys, take a message for me, will you?" He sighed, thinking back on the 'final drama', with his wife earlier that evening. She'd had the nerve to replace the locks and after getting home, Jimmy stood outside forced to bang on the door to be admitted.

"Hello! Anyone here? Clarisse? Albert? Come-on, someone let me in, it's your father."

His son, Albert, finally opened the door and let him in.

The boy stood to one side as Jimmy came into the front hall. His wife walked through the kitchen, wiping her hands on a towel. When she saw Jimmy, she stopped.

"What are you doing here?"

"I live here, remember?"

"Oh no you don't, not anymore, you don't. We have discussed this Jimmy. I have talked to you about this until I'm blue. I am not going to let you continue to demoralize our children. And myself."

"Do you realize," she said, bending over from the waist, and practically snarling at him, "that there have been men here, pounding on the door demanding money that you owe. I went to your editor. He graciously paid the two months back mortgage payments and gave me extra for the light bill and some food. What is wrong with the man who would let his children go hungry?"

"What do you mean, hungry?" Jimmy stared at his 17-year-old son, the boy's face pale and pinched. He turned and looked at his daughter, who was sitting on the bottom step and crying quietly. "Have you been hungry, the two of you?"

"Oh, daddy…" his daughter said as she dissolved into near hysterics.

"Now, do you see? You have upset this household for the last time. I have packed your bag; it is sitting in the closet under the steps. Take it and get out."

"How will you manage if I'm not bringing home a paycheck?" "Paycheck– paycheck? Jimmy, you really have lost your mind. Since you started this story about FDR, not one bill has been paid, and not one dime has passed over this threshold for our use. I'm not sure how I will manage. But I know I will have enough, if you aren't using all of your salary to pay informants."

His daughter cried, not the great gulping sobs of a minute before, but more quietly now, the kind of tears that could break a man's heart. His son stared down at the floor and would not meet his eyes. His wife, his wife of 20 years stood in the foyer and glared. He scratched his head; he was really at a loss. When had he let things with his family get so out of control? Jimmy took three long steps across the foyer and stooped down to open the door of the under stairs closet. The door stuck, as usual. He kicked it, banged on the upper left-hand side, and finally managed to get it open. He pulled out the bag and stood for just a moment, looking at his family. His mind whirled with questions and very uncharacteristic self-incriminations. How had he let all of this happen? He reached down and pecked his daughter on the top of the head and slapped a reassuring hand on his son's shoulder. "I'll be back, you two. I'll be back and I'll make it up to you. I promise." He did not look back.

He'd have to take control of the family situation as soon as this story was put to bed. He'd make it up to all three of them. Clarissa was really a good egg; he was the one who'd messed up their marriage. He was the one who'd have to make amends.

Chapter Twenty-six

Present day Chicago, Ill.

Albert White III had taken the drawers in the little dresser in the attic out and turned them upside down. Eric had found the metal box containing the silver cufflinks and the hundred-dollar bill in that dresser, so he pried the bottoms off of the drawers with a screwdriver, looking for more treasure. He was anxious that he miss nothing. To think that, through all the hard times his family had had, there had been a hundred-dollar bill just sitting up in the attic. Those Ben Franklins could have paid for food, heat or doctor bills.

He took turns being enraged with his grandfather and excited about more finds. His father had told him only limited information about Jimmy White. Albert's father had suffered due to Jimmy's arrogance and nonchalant attitude he'd had for his family. After Albert had had his own children, and just before his father's death, the old man had told him that there had been long periods of time when the family went to bed hungry every night. He said he told the story not for his son to feel sorry for him, but as an admonition to Albert to take care of his own children. And to think there was a hundred-dollar bill just sitting up here in this stupid drawer that could have fed that entire family for who knew how long. Hell, it could've fed the whole block, the whole neighborhood back in 1933.

He made his way down to the kitchen and poured himself a cup of coffee. He stared out at the backyard, thoughtfully sipping the mug of Gevalia Breakfast Blend. Memories and stray disjointed thoughts about his father and his grandfather crowded through his mind vying for attention. And then he thought about the young man, Eric Douglass. Douglass had returned the notebooks he'd borrowed, bringing them back with gracious thanks. Albert had put the dusty tomes in his desk thinking that maybe he'd just look through them himself and find out what and why Jimmy White was so intense. Maybe he'd just do that. Maybe there was a clue about where more cash had been stored in the house. Maybe he'd just look through them himself.

All THAT GliTTeRS

Chapter Twenty-seven

Kathleen changed into jeans and a sweatshirt, and she and Eric were ready to go through the basement and down to the tunnels. Kathleen enlisted Juan's help, and the three carried several electric lanterns and dust mops. Eric raised an eyebrow at the dust mops.

"There are probably some gigantic spider webs down there, and I don't intend to walk through any." Kathleen shivered.

The basement access was through the kitchen at the back of the house. The kitchen was large and filled with modern stainless-steel equipment. Each and every gadget Eric saw was new and updated, except for an old-fashioned Formica-topped, red table, the kind every kitchen in America had in the 1950s. Eric looked at the table quizzically but said nothing.

"Oh," said Kathleen. "That table belonged to my mother, and I never wanted to get rid of it. I know it doesn't go with the rest of the kitchen, but I have very few things from her." *She's sentimental, who would've thought.*

The basement at 44th and Halston held all the usual accoutrements: freezer, washer, dryer, a drying rack, and shelves filled with old bottles and cans. On the far side of the basement, inset in the wall stood a wide, humming, back-lit built-in wine refrigerator. It was so large that it encompassed the entire wall. Eric stood very near the glassed-in doors and could read parts of the bottle labels. Even though his wine knowledge was iffy, Eric was aware that some of the bottles probably cost more than his salary for an entire year.

Generational wealth; ain't it grand.

They walked past the washer and dryer, and an old-fashioned furnace, further and further into the basement. Soon, they had to crouch down past the duct work and plumbing until they reached the far wall. Eric was sure it was the outer foundation of the house.

In the center of the wall was a heavy timber door with old-fashioned hinges and a latch pull. Juan held up the lantern and Kathleen vigorously used the dust mop to get rid of the multiple cobwebs that covered the door. She propped the dust mop against the wall, grasped the latch, and pulled. The door did not budge. She turned and looked at Eric and shrugged her shoulders. Eric handed her his lantern and tried the latch. It didn't budge. He looked over at Juan, "Do you have a crowbar?"

Juan turned back into the basement. After lots of clattering and banging noises, he reappeared with a crowbar and a cold chisel. He smiled and handed Eric the two tools.

"Great," Eric said. "This is great, now, you two hold up the lanterns so I can see what I'm doing." Eric began gingerly rocking the crowbar back and forth along the top edge of the door. Then he did the same on both sides of the door. He put down the tools and again tried the latch. The door began to move, but it was still stuck at the bottom. Eric kneeled down, and using the cold chisel, pried the bottom of the door up from the jam. After many minutes of jostling, prying and hammering, Eric tried the latch again. This time the door opened slowly, jerking and protesting with a high-pitched screech.

"Sounds like an old Bela Lugosi movie."

Juan and Kathleen held up their lanterns as the aperture in the wall opened, revealing a door frame draped in cobwebs. A cloud of dust rushed out to mix heavily through the breathable air.

"Yuck!" Kathleen said. "This is 288, two gross."

"What," Eric said, grinning, "the lady can make a mathematical joke? Nice to know."

Kathleen smiled. She used her sleeve and wiped under her nose, oblivious to the black streak left behind, looking like a mustache. Eric coughed hard trying to cleanse his lungs then turned his head and coughed some more as he made short work of the cobwebs covering the door to the tunnel. Kathleen moved ahead down the darkened passageway with Juan and Eric holding lanterns, the light throwing the walls into stark relief. All three coughed and sputtered as they moved further down and then at angles away from the house. The top and sides of the tunnel opened up after about 50 feet and the air was almost fresh.

"There must be several vents from the outside of some kind down here," said Eric. "Otherwise, the air wouldn't be so much better."

"Oh yes, I think so. I don't really remember who told me, but someone around the turn-of-the-century, that's the 20th I mean, drilled some air holes up to the surface. I suppose they knew what they were doing because so far the tunnel hasn't collapsed in on itself."

Eric looked around with the available light from the three lanterns. They were in a room about 20 feet across and 10 feet high. The room extended past the reach of the lanterns glow. On the right side, were a series of shelves from floor to ceiling. They were made of wood and each was about 16 inches high by 14 inches wide, like cubby-holes for students at a primary school. Some of the shelves held bottles of whiskey, while others held notebook paper, leather files stuffed with, who knew what, and even cups with pencils.

"Okay, where do we start?" Eric asked.

"Your guess is as good as mine," Kathleen said, idly brushing her hand across the outside of the cubbies nearest her. "But I think everything is chronological. So, if we start at the whiskey bottles, that should be about the right period."

Juan shook his head and tsked at the layers of dirt and sediment covering every square inch in view. "Miss Kathleen, I think I can bring a vacuum in here, if I can find an extension cord long enough. I'm not sure what good it would do. But it's doable if we must come back down here again. Personally, I think it would be like trying to clean a barn," he said with a rueful shake of his head. Kathleen laughed; her houseman was such a neat freak.

Juan found several hooks designed for lanterns dispersed along the wall at even intervals and hung up each one. When enough meager light cut through the dark so that lettering on files and cubbies were visible, Kathleen and Eric began looking through the items.

A half hour passed, then an hour in the semi-darkness and the dank underground. Kathleen shivered, wishing she'd worn a more substantial sweater. Juan, Kathleen, and Eric pulled out the files, consulting the information as quickly as they could, and then returning them. Kathleen stretched, feeling a definite twinge beginning to grip her back. Eric wiped his dusty hands on his trousers over and over until there was a big, black smudge down each leg of his khakis.

I picked up one of the bottles of whiskey and wiped the thick, gray dust off the label. "Made in Canada. Hey, would your great-grandfather have been a bootlegger?"

"Yep, he sure was," she said, looking intently at me, making sure by her gaze that I understood she was serious. "We are totally legit now. No more shenanigans, no more men like Nealy besmirching the family name."

"Good to know," I said. I looked in the cubby next to the whiskey bottle. The only thing it contained was a folded newspaper. "Hey, look at this." I opened the newspaper and read the header. "Chicago Tribune, September 23, 1933, early edition. Isn't this the time period we're looking for?"

"Yes, around September or October 1933."

I carefully unfolded the paper all the way and a separate sheet fell out on the floor. I retrieved it and read carefully. "Look at this, it's a manifest, I think it's about the gold. See at the bottom, it tallies the weight in pounds, where it's going, and then the signatures with 'Federal Marshal' after it."

Kathleen looked over my shoulder at the document. She took the newspaper and examined it carefully. "What is this splattered on the paper? Look, is that blood?" Kathleen crinkled her nose in distaste and held the paper out to me at arm's length.

I took it from her and looked carefully at the splatter marks across the inside. I put the paper up to my nose and then looked at it under the lantern light.

"Yes, it looks like blood and smells like it to me. So, here's another piece of the puzzle. Why would a manifest from a load of gold that was going from Chicago to the New York Federal Reserve be here under your house? And what has a blood-spattered newspaper to do with any of it? Do you suppose Nealy stashed it here? You know those icons you were showing me in that file, do they indicate the cubby-hole in which things will be found?"

"I don't know. But now that the door has been opened to the tunnels, and we know our way around down there, Juan and I can come back another time and take a look. Let's bring the document and the newspaper up with us," Kathleen said as she wiped what I was sure was a smudge on my face. "I don't know about you, but I've breathed enough dust for one day. I'll take that bottle of Canadian whiskey and go upstairs and make us a drink. I think we deserve it."

"Sounds good to me," I said. "Juan, I'll take Kathleen's lantern and you lead the way and Kathleen can bring the document and the newspaper."

"Yes, sir."

I thought maybe I'd like it if people called me sir.

Jimmy's murder weighed heavily on my mind as we made our way through the basement and up the stairs. What if my first thought was correct, that Seamus O'Brien had Jimmy murdered because Jimmy couldn't keep the innuendo about the O'Brien's and how guilty they were out of his articles. Jimmy was an arrogant pain in the neck and felt like nothing could touch him. Maybe Seamus or one of his minions decided that just wasn't so. In all the articles and notes of Jimmy's I'd read, his writing had been acidly critical of Seamus and his Irish gang. I couldn't blame the O'Briens for wanting to do away with him. I'd probably have killed him just to shut the bastard up.

I mentally stopped for a moment; never in my life, even in jest, had the notion of killing someone remotely crossed my mind. During my adult life, I'd been part of a team that searched for new cures for many human diseases and maladies. I was used to thinking about saving lives, not taking them away. My personality was changing as I watched it like a spectator on the sidelines.

But, getting back to finding out where Jimmy was; if Seamus had rid himself of Jimmy, where had he hidden him so that no one had found him for the past eighty years? Could I, dare I, ask Kathleen something like, "Where did your great grandpa hide the bodies?" She might deck me right then and there. I'd have to feel her out. She'd been so adamant from the start that her family no longer dealt with anything illegal, and I was sure she was right. But, what about eighty years ago?

When the time was right; maybe that time was now.

"So, Kathleen, I need to fill you in on another piece of this scenario." We'd reached the kitchen by then and were washing up companionably at the kitchen sink. I glanced over my shoulder to check if Juan was around, but the two of us were alone in the kitchen. "Could we sit for a moment?"

She looked at me quizzically while she dried her hands on a towel, and then sat at the table, crossing her legs and holding her hands demurely in her lap. This woman had such an aura about her. She was self-assured, calm and beautiful. I looked at her hard, hoping this would not be the last time I'd ever see her.

"A few weeks ago, well, there was a big group of us, it was like a kid's pizza party in that we were all there to eat out and have a good time, I guess." I turned to gaze out the window over the sink, trying to collect my thoughts, trying to find a way to say this so that she didn't think I was a crackpot. "At any rate, there were about six couples, and we went to see a hypnotist in Carrboro, that's a town near Chapel Hill. The whole premise of the visit was to…" I paused and made finger quotes in the air, "discover more about ourselves through past life regression. I know this sounds completely insane; as Americans and Christians, we don't usually delve into the realm of reincarnation. But I actually went into a trance, and I saw a journalist for the Chicago Tribune, Jimmy White, run over by a car; deliberately murdered. I didn't understand any of it; I kept having nightmares of a car running me down. Clearly, I didn't know if the person I saw in the dream was me being run down or if I was watching someone else get murdered more than 80 years before. The dreams that I was having every night, over and over, were just destroying me. I went back to the hypnotist and told her what I was experiencing, and she put me into another trance. It was her contention that she didn't know if I was Jimmy White or if I had been chosen, her words, not mine, to right a terrible wrong. You know, Jimmy's body was never found. Someone ran him over with a car, that part I have seen in my dreams, but where his body was stashed, I didn't see. So, Miss Dickinson, the hypnotist, thinks it's up to me to find out why, who and where. Why was he murdered? Does it have something to do with this gold manifest? Or did he piss off your great-grandfather one too many times?"

I watched Kathleen carefully while I was speaking, sure she was going to call for Juan and have me thrown out. She shivered, and then looked at me sharply when I mentioned her great-grandfather's name. But she said nothing.

"I know this is a lot to swallow, but now that we've found this manifest signed by federal marshals, don't you think this has something to do with the murder?"

Kathleen stood and walked to the window, staring out at the backyard. She folded her arms onto the sink top and leaned forward over the sink. She said nothing for several moments. I stood and walked to the other side of the kitchen, glancing at the cookbooks stashed on top of the fridge, trying to give her a moment. I crossed my arms and leaned on the fridge, waiting for her to decide.

"Eric," she said as she turned toward me leaning back against the sink, "I don't think I've ever heard a story like this before. I don't know if my great-grandfather or one of my uncles or one of the many men who worked for him, ran Jimmy over and stashed his body so no one would ever find it. Of all the felonies I have read about that were committed by my family two and a half generations ago, none, and I mean none, was murder. *She held crossed fingers behind her back. She had no proof, but she had not found anything written about any murder, and her ancestors were fanatics about writing down and recording everything!*

"Maybe it was because they were devout Catholics, I don't know. I suppose they thought it was less of a mortal sin to extort money from someone than to have them bumped off. I know for a fact that the Aiello gang committed murder all the time to advance their position in the hierarchy around the city. And I do know there were several incidences where one of my ancestors shot someone in a fit of rage. One of my grandfathers died in prison; he was convicted of second-degree murder for shooting a member of an Italian gang. You're here to find out who murdered Jimmy and where his body was buried? This has intrigued me, my curiosity is beyond piqued. To answer your question, did my great-grandfather kill Jimmy, I feel sure he didn't."

God, at least I hope he didn't. What if he did? How can I justify this family being on the up and up if one of my ancestors bumped off a writer that pissed him off? Kathleen thought and then continued. "That was just not the way Seamus operated." Again, she crossed her fingers behind her back. "So, who did kill Jimmy? And why? I think the fact that we found a manifest for the gold that was picked up in 1933 from Chicago must have something to do with it. Let's do a little sleuthing and figure it out. You've got to find out who murdered Jimmy and why, so let's find out, and if we find the stash of gold coins and ingots in the process well then... Hurrah for our side."

Chapter Twenty-eight

September 15, 1933
Indianapolis Rail Hub
11:30 pm

Jimmy at last had caught a break. One of his informants, the one following Gillespie, had bumped into the congressman as he made his way to the railway station. The shoulder-to-shoulder nudge had dislodged the ticket the congressman held tightly in his hand. The informant reached down and picked it up for Gillespie as he read the information on it – Indianapolis – and tipped his hat with apologies. So, Gillespie was going to Indianapolis. Jimmy made sure he was on the next train.

The humidity leached under his collar, under his vest, under the belt and suspenders that held up his pants. The heat was unbearable, made more so by the humidity. Jimmy took off his suit coat, draped it over his arm, and unbuttoned his vest. Perhaps he'd just go ahead and disrobe all the way. But he was sure Carlson wouldn't bail him out of jail if he was arrested by some cop for indecency.

In Indianapolis, Jimmy made sure he'd stationed himself near the middle of the gigantic rail hub. The hub was a confusing mass of track interspersed with shacks lit by coal lanterns. In the immediate center, all of the tracks converged to one point. Belching steam engines starting and stopping, grinding metal screeching, giant couplings clasping and unclasping, men yelling in an attempt to be heard, added to Jimmy's anxiety. Then what if he was caught by Abrams and his thugs? It all sent a chill down Jimmy's spine.

Jimmy had waited in Chicago for another day, doing more digging, making more calls, and paying off more informants. Shaughnessy O'Brien was on the outs with the O'Brien's and all of the Irish mobsters, for that matter. Jimmy pieced together bits and pieces of information from the old man's ramblings and spurts of temper. It was hard to tell which, because Shaughnessy had either taken too many blows to the head or he was senile.

"And then that bastard..." Jimmy had gone to the old man's boarding house and brought a bottle of whiskey with him. "And then that bastard," Shaughnessy had already said that.

"Yeah, he said what?"

"He said that twirp Nealy was hiring..."

Jimmy shook Shaughnessy's shoulder, but ducked his head to dodge the smell of the old man and his stinking bed. "Shaughnessy, what did Nealy do?"

"He hired a bunch of men, they were gonna be Pinsherto..."

Jimmy pulled Shaughnessy up by his lapels. "Pinkertons, you mean Pinkertons? He hired men to act like Pinkertons?"

Shaughnessy nodded, once, then twice, and looked up at Jimmy through rummy eyes. "They got a load."

"A load, a load? A load of what?" Jimmy shook the old man over and over again, but Shaughnessy was out cold.

So, Nealy hired guys to impersonate Pinkertons. Pinkertons did lots of things, including protecting Federal Government people and property. So, Abrams and Gillespie were planning something that required O'Brien to bring men on board. What he'd pieced together about the operation was little to none. He might be all wrong, but he'd bet his best white shirt that he'd hit the nail right on the head. Was this all about the gold he'd heard about from the Congressional memo he'd obtained. The gold was to be collected at First Federal in downtown Chicago.

Jimmy quivered in anticipation of the headlines, the accolades, and the downfall of Abrams, Gillespie and FDR. Good riddance to bad rubbish.

God, it was so hot! He mopped his face, but his handkerchief was so wet, it did little but move the sweat around. He stepped nearer the corner of the shack, the one he'd picked because it was closest to the fence that surrounded the rail hub, and he might have to make a quick get-away. The air was still, moist and reeked of the stink of diesel fuel, oil and his own body odor. His head started to swim and he leaned back against the wall, feeling the splinters and the heads of nails driven only partway into the boards, push into his neck and back. Good, the pain would keep him alert. He reached into his vest pocket for his watch and flipped it open; it was now 1:35 am. How could it be so hot in the middle of the night?

The activity in the yard slowly wound down. There were still men about, but nearly all of the tracks leading to the center point were now occupied by locomotives, flat beds, and boxcars. And then he saw them – six men, three on each side, all in dark blue uniforms, pushed and pulled a flatbed wagon. The wagon wasn't the type that could hitch onto the back of a train, but rather one that was often used off tracks to load and unload cargo. Jimmy pulled out his small spyglass mounted on the end of a large, bulky key chain. It was only about four inches in length, but a telescoping end magnified things in the distance by up to five times. Jimmy had had the spyglass made years ago and it had paid for itself many times over. He'd even produced it when he'd testified in court against one of the Costello brothers. The testimony had put the bum in jail and had not endeared him to the shadier side of Chicago.

He wiped his sleeve across his face and gazed through the spyglass. Just on the periphery, near the far end, he saw a man move rapidly toward the wagon. Jimmy focused the glass until it sharpened and cleared. It was none other than Nealy O'Brien. He strode up to the men with his white hat pulled down on his brow and the wide lapels of his jacket pushed up around his face like Dick Tracey in the cartoon.

Jimmy pulled the glass away from his eye and watched the scene unfold. Well, well, he supposed old Shaughnessy wasn't so senile after all. Nealy approached the men, spoke to them, and then pulled the canvas back a few inches to check the load on the wagon. From his vantage point, Jimmy couldn't see what was under the canvas. He decided to watch where this particular wagon went. Maybe it had a manifest he could take a gander at. He watched and he waited.

O'Brien spoke sharply to one of the men and then backhanded him for good measure. What a creep.

Finally, the men lowered a ramp on one of the boxcars and pulled the wagon into it, and three of the men tied down and secured the wagon. One of the men asked O'Brien something and he jerked his thumb over his shoulder and the six men scattered. Within minutes, the men and O'Brien were gone and Jimmy found himself alone.

He flattened himself against the roughened wall of the outbuilding, feeling the splinters all along his shoulders poking through his shirt. The chills running up his spine escalated exponentially, and he felt the hair on the nape of his neck prickle. He took his hat off and dropped it down by his feet as he turned his head to look around the corner. There was not a soul in sight. He took a deep breath, counted to 10 and then moved around the corner and ran for the boxcar. He pulled himself up and then flattened himself, hiding behind the sliding door before he looked out again at the deserted railway. As quietly as he could, he edged toward the wagon secured into the middle of the boxcar. He pulled, pushed, and yanked until a bit of the tarp came loose. Jimmy put his hand beneath the tarp and felt around. The items were metal, cold, and… oily? Jimmy pushed and prodded the tarp until it revealed the items underneath. Farm tools: plow heads, scythes, mower blades; all bright, shiny, new, oily and ready for shipment. He wiped the oil from his hands on his trouser leg, and hurriedly jumped from the boxcar and sprinted back to the corner of the outbuilding where he'd left his hat. He bent over to retrieve his hat and jacket and get away as fast as he could. Jimmy half-walked, half-ran to the chain link fence and through the opening leading to the street. The bus station was two blocks to the west. He ran; if they caught him, he may never live to tell the tale. But if the shipment was farm tools, where was the gold? Did they have it? What had he been chasing for the past five weeks?

He failed to notice that when he'd stooped down to retrieve his hat, the notebook in his breast pocket with his latest findings, had fallen out and lay on the dirt by the outbuilding, its pages fluttering in the breeze, waiting for anyone to discover it.

The railroad security guard walked his beat in the early morning hours. Holding his lantern waist high, he shone the light in each outbuilding and dark corner, looking for hobos and derelicts. All was quiet, as quiet as a rail hub could be. He moved around the corner of a dark flimsy outbuilding and stepped on something. He raised the lantern and looked down. It was a notebook. Strange. He focused the stream of light on the inside cover.

Jimmy White
Chicago Tribune
Please return if found.

The guard picked up the notebook and put it in his front pocket. The people in the office would know what to do with it.

Chapter Twenty-nine

Chicago, one half-mile from the First Federal Bank
September 24, 1933, 03:22

O'Brien had so many irons in the fire he felt like he would at any moment, spontaneously combust. He decided that night in August that he would double cross Abrams and never think twice about it. The plan was that the document be switched at the corner near the light, and then handed over to a man in the Café. It was all very cloak and dagger stuff. Not anything like the snatch and grab beat up with a baseball bat, get your hands bloodied, enterprises that he was used to. Well, if this operation needed some finesse, he would do it on his own. He looked down at his watch, trying to see the face in the dark. If he tilted his arm, almost behind his other shoulder, he could see the time. 3:23 am. The truck should be leaving the First Federal Bank right about now. That means he had 10 minutes to stand here rocking back and forth on his heels, waiting. As soon as he saw the truck at the other end of the block, he would duck around the alley, and wait for the switch near the door of the café. He flattened himself against the garbage sitting in all its smelly glory near the back door of the coffee shop. He'd wait, might as well grab a smoke. He began to scratch the match head across the sole of his shoe when he thought better of it. Even a little flare of light from a match might be an alert.

Nealy rested his head against the brick wall behind him as thoughts swirled through his mind. His Da, a second cousin once removed from the old man Seamus, the gang boss, had not been a close enough relative to have the O'Brien's take him seriously. Why else hadn't his father been at the right hand of Patrick? His father had died drunk in some flophouse in the center of the city, and

Nealy had no intention of the same fate befalling him. He didn't drink, rarely even coffee, he wanted to keep his mind clear, and he didn't want to end up like his father.

By the time Nealy had gotten around to looking at his watch again, almost 20 minutes had passed. He looked around the corner of the building but could see nothing in the dark. Only a few scattered streetlights interspersed the darkness along the road. The city was quiet, very quiet. Nealy took a big breath and held it, listening. Yes, he heard it, the rumbling of the truck further down the road.

Within a few moments, a large truck, a logging truck with solid double back tires, rumbled up to the corner and stopped at the light.

The man inside the café with the blue tie had the doctored manifest. Nealy had seen it before it was taken away by Gillespie, complete with the federal marshal's signatures. The document stated that $20 $10, $5, and $2.50 gold coins, ingots of 400 troy ounces, and 2 ounces, and miscellaneous gold was in the shipment. The shipment would end up eventually in the New York Federal Reserve. The doctored manifest made it clear about the precise number of pounds in the shipment, about 2,500 pounds less. The shipment was neatly skimmed, and no one the wiser.

Nealy darted a glance around the corner. The man from the café pulled himself up onto the running board and switched documents with the driver. By the time the light changed, the truck was already in second gear and rumbling down the street.

Nealy heard the tinkling of the bell over the café door and hugged the wall, edged toward the big plate glass window to take a quick glance inside. The man threw a few coins onto the red and white checkered tablecloth and made his way out the door, hugging the newspaper under his arm. He left the café and walked nonchalantly down the darkened Street. Nealy followed. He was glad he had worn his soft rubber soled shoes and could not be heard. On the next corner, the man stopped and waited for the light to change. Nealy looked up and down each block and side street and turned a complete 360°, checking. Before the man stepped off the curb and walked across the street, Nealy had caught up with him. He was almost directly behind the man who sensed no danger. He grabbed him around the throat and pushed a blade up between the man's ribs, the man grunted—but made no other sound. Nealy must've struck the heart because the man went down like a sack of potatoes. Nealy grabbed the newspaper before the man hit the street. Within two heartbeats of catching up with his quarry, Nealy had the document, safely ensconced in the newspaper, and headed uptown.

Now he had to get rid of the manifest, but where?

He knew it would be several hours before the body of the courier was found, and then even longer before the men in the know would figure out the manifest was missing. The cops would get the body, send it to the coroner, then the coroner would keep all the effects to one side for the family of the man to pick up. But there would be no manifest if Abrams or Gillespie found out about the man's death and came looking for it. Well, that was their problem, because now he had it and they'd pay through the nose to get it back.

Nealy made his way to the Seamus O'Brien family home in Canaryville. He knew where he could stash the manifest. He'd just have to figure out a way to get into the house and get down to the tunnels with no one the wiser. He hadn't figured that part out yet, but he had about 45 more minutes to think about it.

The load was heavy and secured into the special boxcar traveling from Chicago to the Indianapolis rail hub. "Alright, when we get to the station, I want the six of you to load the boxes from the truck and secure them onto a boxcar." Nealy coached the men he had handpicked for the job. None of them were too bright, but all of them were loyal to a fault. "Here's the number of the train, the numbers is stenciled onto the engine, and here's the number of the boxcar. That number is on the steel girder under the sliding door. Now, Listen, if you put the boxes in the wrong boxcar, then we're up the creek, know what I mean, so pay attention. Artie here is your lead man, so do what he says. There is a nice bonus waiting for you when you finish up. You extra men, I want you to stand guard while the boxes are being loaded onto the train; each of you will carry a Colt 45 revolver, just to make sure no one gets too curious, know what I mean?

"Now you reserve guys, you have your identification, you are Pinkertons, and you'll stay with the car all the way to the New York Federal Reserve. And I hope you have a good time in the big city, but don't take too many days, get back here by the end of the week and pick up the next installment of your pay." The men milled around, speaking quietly as they picked up their fake, but very close to the real thing, uniforms.

Abrams and Gillespie made sure that no one but he, Nealy, knew what was in the heavy boxes. At the Indianapolis rail hub, the boxes of gold were moved out of the train by a completely different crew, three of which would be O'Brien's men. There were reserve Pinkertons meeting the boxcar in Indianapolis as well as at least three and maybe as many as four, Federal Marshals and other 'G' men, all legit this time, since the switching of the boxes had already taken place. No one would be the wiser about the portion that Abrams and Gillespie had skimmed off the top and left in Indianapolis.

The tricky part had been for Abrams to relinquish total and complete control of the project, to trust that someone else would accomplish what he had so carefully planned down to the last second. The 5 X 13 X 7 ½ boxes Abrams had chosen, were so similar to the different types of boxes used by the Federal government that no one would think anything about it. And each box held lots of coins. Their numismatic quality would be of no importance. After all, they were to be melted down and shaped into ingots.

Each one of St. Gauden's Standing Liberty coins, in the vernacular, a $20 double eagle, was dumped into the boxes with little care. And each box would hold just so many coins to ensure that the box's weight would not be too heavy. If each coin weighed 1.2

ounces, then a few less than 750 coins plus the weight of the box would round out to less than 50 pounds.

After the gold was retrieved each box would have to be gone through. The coins must be counted, wrapped, and then taken to a place like France or Spain or Saudi Arabia, and converted into cash. Each box would contain as much or more than $21,000.00.

Pittsburgh, the great steel manufacturer of the United States, was interspersed and crisscrossed with rail bridges and rail car, cabooses, and locomotives. Iron ore, coal, coke, and then finished steel moved across those bridges and in and out of the rail yards. Some of these rail bridges had cement abutments used as supports, and just a few were used for storing tools, and that would be the hiding place of their stolen gold until they could come and fetch it.

Chapter Thirty

8:45 AM, September 25, 1933
Chicago, Ill., neighborhood of Canaryville

Nealy had to get the manifest stashed. The manifest, still wrapped in the blood-spattered newspaper, was burning a hole in his pocket. The fact that he'd killed a man and the man's blood was splattered on the newspaper was something that concerned him little. He just cared about getting the thing out of his possession, until he needed it. Gillespie and Abrams were gonna pay through the nose. He'd make his way to Washington and meet up with them. And then he'd let them have it.

Nealy knocked on the back door and waited, half-turning and gazing out onto the yard, letting his mind wander for a blessed second. The door burst open, and the smell of ham and bread wafted out and hit him full force. Old Seamus's housekeeper, Gertrude, glared at him through the open door.

"Nealy." The word almost sounded like a curse.

She didn't like him, but he could sweet-talk her. Nealy turned on his hundred-watt smile and doffed his hat before reaching for her hand and giving it a slobbery kiss. "Gertrude, you haven't aged a day since I saw you last."

The old, iron haired woman scowled at him. The buttons of her simple, gray, house dress seemed ready to pop and her waist, much smaller than her breasts, probably from a corset. The incongruity made her look like she was wobbling and might topple over at any second.

The old lady sniffed, "and what you vant?" she asked, looking down her long nose at him.

"Well, I just wanted to come see my best girl, that's all." Gertrude clasped her hands together at her waist and sniffed again. "No, really,
I could smell that ham all the way across town."

"Well, your uncle, he won't be so pleased to see you, ja?"

"Maybe we just won't tell him," Said Nealy. How could he make his way into the basement and then the tunnels if he couldn't think of any excuse to get past Gertrude.

He took off his hat and sat accepting the offered cup of coffee. He stretched out his legs and sighed, welcoming the good smells and warmth of the kitchen as he kept a death grip on the paper that lay in his lap. He sat up quickly and snapped his fingers, "Say, you know what? Last time I was here I left a tool kit in the basement."

"You, you need a tool?"

"Yeah, my brother gave it to me. It was all put away in a nice little case when I was down there doing something for Uncle Seamus, and I left it. Think I'll meander on down and see if I can find it."

"Now, you know your Uncle Seamus, he won't like it."

"That's okay. It'll be our little secret." Nealy reached over and gave her a peck on the cheek before he quickly made his way into the basement. He had to keep the manifest away from Abrams so he could use it to blackmail the son-of-a-bitch. Abrams made him feel like a low-class scum, and now he'd pay. Ah, revenge was so sweet.

Eric ran over his notes again; things were starting to fall into place: Abrams, Gillespie, and O'Brien had somehow stolen part of the gold that was headed from Chicago to the New York Federal Reserve Vaults. Jimmy found out part or all of the plan. Abrams, et all, somehow found out that Jimmy was on to them? Did they have Jimmy killed to shut him up? After all Eric had read, after all the waking dreams, he felt secure that O'Brien, despite having cause, didn't do away with Jimmy because of the journalist's big mouth. It was much more serious than that. They had to prevent Jimmy from thwarting their plans to steal whatever portion of the gold they planned to take. He'd gotten this far, now he had to solidify his conjectures into real facts.

September 26, 1933
The Washington Hotel, DC

Joey raced down the basement hallway of the hotel pushing the trolley in front of him. The other busboy had not come to work that day and Joey was kept unbelievably busy with orders. Something must be badly wrong; folks didn't just not come to work, not in this day and age. He stopped quickly as he turned the corner, Frank the janitor, stood in the middle of the floor, just staring at him.

"Oh, hi Frank, how's it going?"

"Just okay, kid, how's it with you. Got any side work for me?"

"Uh, side work?"

"Yeah, ya know, anybody that's looking to just any old thing, like they can't get nobody else. Know what I mean?" Frank gave a gesture with his hand that could mean anything. "You know, kid, anything that ain't got to do with the hotel, extra stuff."

There were lots of rumors floating around about Frank. Someone had told him that Frank had been an enforcer for a bigtime bookie in New York City, someone else told Joey that Frank had been in Leavenworth. Now, Frank was here, maybe lying low. If he'd been an enforcer, then he hadn't killed anyone, right? You couldn't get money from a dead man. Joey had not found out anything about Frank but knew instinctively he was safer that way.

"No, Frank." This guy scared him to death. "But I'll be glad to ask around for you."

"That's good kid, you just do that." Frank stood to one side and gestured for Joey to move around him. Suddenly, he grabbed Joey's arm and squeezed tightly, staring into his eyes without blinking. "And just sos we know about each other; you remember that I can be a real nice guy. Or not." Frank let go of Joey's arm so quickly the younger man almost lost his balance.

"Uh, okay Frank. I'll see if anyone is asking."

Joey hurriedly pushed the trolley into the kitchen and leaned against the wall to catch his breath.

"Joey, go up to 10 to Senator Abrams room."

"Do you have an order for me to take up?"

"No, he just asked for you. Probably wants something other than food." The cook laughed and Joey pushed his cart out of the kitchen and back the way he had come.

Abrams paced the floor. Paced, paced, thinking, thinking; how could he get what he wanted from Gillespie when the man constantly nagged at him about 'morality', the American way, and all of that rubbish. Since the fall of the stock market and the collapse of the world economy, it was every man for himself. But that was neither here nor there; what mattered now was to get rid of White before he wrote another editorial and named names, specifically Abrams and Gillespie. He thought he knew who to ask, someone much more reliable than Nealy O'Brien. Abrams picked up the phone.

"This is senator Abrams, in suite 1005, please send the boy up, oh yes, I want Joey if he is on duty."

Abrams dabbed at his neck and forehead with his handkerchief. With the last big rainstorm, the weather had moderated a little. Regardless of the temperature or the humidity, his shirt and collar were soaked through within moments of having changed. Maybe he was just getting older. *Maybe*, a stray thought intruded, *it's your conscience*. No, he wasn't going to think about that right now. He gazed out of the window, putting his hand up to shield his eyes from the bright sun. The sky was so blue this far south, and the clouds looked so different than they did in Massachusetts. He shrugged, forcing his mind back to the project. If they pulled this off with the gold, and everything looked like it was right on target, hell, he could go buy himself an island in the Caribbean.

A few moments later a knock sounded at the door.

"Come in."

Joey pushed a trolley in front of him as he came through the door. "Did you order room service, senator?"

Abrams sized the boy up. "No, son, I just wanted to see you." Abrams gave the boy what he hoped was a smile of trust. He never took his eyes from the young man as he sat on the wing chair adjacent to his bed. Abrams knew how to play an audience. He waited for a few moments watching Joey fidget uncomfortably before he spoke.

"I know that I can help you, but can you help me?"

"Excuse me, sir?"

Joey seemed to know his way around getting any extracurricular items that the politicians in the upper suites of the hotel wanted or needed: whores, male or female, any kind of booze, and, of course, men who would do anything for a dollar. "Actually, I wanted you to hire someone for me." Abrams took a long drag on his cheroot and brushed the ash away scattering across his lap. "You'll be the middleman, and I'll make sure that both of you get paid well. You won't even have to know what the man does for me. Do you know someone that is trustworthy, and discrete?"

"Well, Senator, begging your pardon and intending no disrespect; if you need somebody, the kind that lurks around corners, if you know what I mean, I can get that kind of fella, too. Of course, I know you'll just be needing a…" And Joey stopped talking. It was especially hard to make himself understood while his foot was entrenched solidly in his mouth.

'Lurking around corners', hum.' Abrams thought he quite liked the sound of that. The senator was oblivious to the boy's embarrassment. "Yes, I think I'd like the lurking around corners type. Just tell the fellow that he will be well paid. Have him meet me in the alley behind the hotel at midnight tonight." The boy's eyes widened at the words 'alley' and 'midnight', but he made no comment.

"Right-o Senator, I'll get right on it. I'll see if I can get someone to meet you later tonight. If I can't, I'll call and let you know."

Joey backed himself and his trolley out of the room and waved to the senator before shutting the door.

At the end of the hallway, Joey ducked around the corner and fumbled in his pocket with trembling hands until he found Jimmy White's phone number in Chicago. His heart lodged in his throat. He should have kept well enough alone, he had a really creepy feeling that Mr. White needed to be warned about Abrams. When he found the card, he clutched it tightly in his fingers and felt a little braver because it was there. He should put in a long-distance call and see if he could talk to Mister White before he found someone for Abrams. But Abrams would be waiting for Joey to get someone, and if he didn't, would he complain to the hotel management?

Joey was loyal to Jimmy White because he believed Mr. White was on the side of right and of the common working man. Joey stood in the hall thinking. He'd call Jimmy, but who could he call about the Abrams job? He'd told the senator that he'd get someone. It was a tricky proposition. Joey had to fulfill the senator's request, but at the same time didn't want anyone to get hurt. Whoever he chose had to meet Abrams at midnight. That was too scary and felt too much like real life.

Or maybe he should just pass on the message and get lost as fast as he possibly could. One way or the other he would tell Mr. White and warn him.

Joey dropped his trolley off in the kitchens and made his way to the quiet bar. There were no patrons yet; it was only 3:30 in the afternoon. Just the barkeep, prepping for drinks that the upper crust clientele would order later.

A dark, elegant mahogany bar stretched across most of the room. Behind the bar, an antique mirror was old parts of it rippled as dark occlusions marred the surface. It too was framed in dark mahogany with a myriad of glass shelves holding different bottles of liquor. Each image eerily warped the reflection of the bar's patrons. Enough ambient light echoed back when Joey looked into the mirror that he saw his own reflection in the reflection many times over again. Joey thought the mirror was the prettiest thing in the whole hotel, except when it was creeping him out like it was now.

He spotted Frank mopping the hallway to the restroom.

"Hey Frank, you got a minute?"

"Yeah, what's up?"

"There's a Senator Abrams upstairs that probably has a job for you. I told him I knew somebody, and I thought of you." Joey looked at the older man's gnarled and weathered face, his gray hair grew in spurts and starts over the crown of his head, like it couldn't make up its mind whether or not it wanted to grow. But the man's body was lean and muscular under his white T-shirt and apron.

"You thought of me, huh?" Franks tone was soft, almost cheerful. He leaned nonchalantly on the mop handle and stared at Joey.

"Somebody told me you worked in New York City, and I thought maybe if you couldn't help the senator you'd know somebody who could. If you don't like what he says you can always turn around and walk out the door.

"He's in suite 1005 A, if you want to go talk, but he said he wanted you to meet him in the alleyway behind the hotel at midnight. He said there'd be good money in it; sounds all cloak and dagger, doesn't it?" Joey joked, but had no idea that just talking to Frank would make his stomach turn to water.

"Okay, kid, I'll go see what the old guy wants." Frank leaned forward on his mop, his eyes never wavering from Joey. He moved his toothpick from one side of his mouth to the next, all the while squinting at Joey. "Don't you worry about it. I'll find out what he wants and he's told you he would pay you to forget me right?"

Joey nodded.

"Okay, kid, I'll make sure he pays you one way or the other, okay?"

"Okay, Frank, that would be swell."

Joey backed away from the older man and hurriedly left the bar.

Chapter Thirty-one

Present Day
Chicago, Ill.

Eric and Kathleen had looked over each and every obscure document they could find online. If there was still a manifest of the shipment that originated in Chicago dated September 23, 1933, they didn't know where it was, exactly what it was, or more importantly, what was on it.

"You really don't think they'll, and I use the word 'they' loosely, give you information about what went to the New York Federal Reserve in 1933, before it was transported to Ft. Knox, do you?"

"Probably not." Eric stood, stretched, and yawned. He and Kathleen had worked through the afternoon on the mysterious document. There was nothing about this 80 + year old mystery anywhere.

"Um, well, I don't know. Here, let me look it up."

Kathleen tapped away on her desktop. I don't know why I didn't go here first. Listen to this This is what Wikipedia says: 'The United States Bullion Depository, often known as Fort Knox, is a fortified vault building located within the United States Army post at Fort Knox, Kentucky... used to store a large portion of United States official gold reserves and occasionally other precious items belonging to or entrusted to the federal government. The exact contents of the United States Bullion Depository are unknown as there has never been an approved full audit since the early 1930s. Since the 1930s! How can anyone run a business like this? Good Grief! 'The vault has roughly 3 percent of all the gold ever refined throughout human history. Even so, the depository is second in the United States to the Federal Reserve Bank of New York and its underground vault in Manhattan, which holds 7,000 metric tons (7,716 tons) of gold bullion (225.1 million oz. troy), most of it in trust for foreign nations, central banks and official international organizations.'"

"Again, good grief." Kathleen stared at Eric. "So, what this is saying is: that if our boys stole some gold that had to do with this manifest, it didn't go to Fort Knox because it wasn't built as yet, it supposedly was going to the Federal Reserve Building in Manhattan. The Reserve has underground vaults where gold is and has been kept for decades. The US holds gold for other countries. I read on Lew Rockwell, that Germany recently wanted their gold back that we'd been holding for them. Our government stonewalled them and didn't give it back to Germany. After the third request, they stopped asking, but Holland just got their deposit back. I really am not up on worldwide finance and how foreign countries take care of all this; I just read the stories and try to make sense of them."

Eric put his hand over hers and squeezed for a split second, liking very much how it felt. "I still have about 10 days of leave. I'll go to DC and scope this out."

"If you get stuck and need a lawyer, call me. I'm going to make you a copy of the manifest, better than the one on your phone, and if they need to see the original I can Fed-Ex it overnight to them. I know some federal lawyers, and a few of them owe me a favor, so, call here," she said as she reached into her desk drawer. She pulled out a business card and jotted a number on the back. "This is the office phone and address, but I put my cell number, my private number on the back. If you need someone to talk to, why don't you give me a call?" She smiled at him and Eric felt the heat rise in his face.

"Um, sure, that's great. Maybe if they lock me up for pissing somebody off, you can come rescue me. That would be a kick, huh? I'm flying home tomorrow. I'll check in with my mom and then drive to DC the next day. It's around four hours from Chapel Hill."

"Why don't you call ahead and see if there are PR people you can speak with. Treat it as a fact-finding trip for a paper you're writing. If you tell them you are going to give them a credit in your paper, they should be falling all over themselves to help you out." Kathleen laughed. "People can be so very transparent if you know which buttons to push. There's practically a class on that in second year law."

Eric put the business card in his wallet and stood. "Well, how about if I call after I've seen someone and gotten some cursory information. If they have a manifest of a shipment from the Chicago Federal Bank, what am I going to say? And if we do find out that some gold was missing, how can we prove that Jimmy White was murdered or Nealy was murdered for that matter, because of it."

Chapter Thirty-two

Present day, Washington, DC

Eric took the train from Raleigh to DC. It was cheap, cheaper than flying, and less wear and tear on his old Toyota Corolla. He'd called ahead to the Department of the Treasury. It took about four phone calls, but he finally found a human being to respond to his questions. The man, Mister Jenkins, told him that they would probably be able to find the old manifest from September 1933 of the gold shipment from Chicago to New York; Kathleen told him the government never threw away a piece of paper. If he could find the original or microfiche of the original, he would take a picture of that as well, and then they could use what was in the archives and compare it to what they had found in the tunnels.

He really had no illusions that he'd be able to find the original paperwork. It was so long ago, and not only had the government gone through huge upheavals, but a world war had besieged humanity for six ugly years as well. Things could get lost and never see the light of day again. He knew that.

Eric would spend a couple of nights at a Holiday Inn on the outskirts of DC; there was a great bus service in and out of the city, and he would avail himself of public transportation.

He put his head back to catch some sleep while the train rushed toward DC.

He knew he was dreaming. If he looked carefully, he could tantalizingly glimpse himself on the train. His attention drew back to the gravel road where Jimmy stood, pacing back and forth. He looked down at his shoes, noting for the first time the scuffs on the outsides. He rubbed the toe of his right shoe back and forth in the gravel. He could hear the scratching sound the gravel made against his sole. He breathed deeply, smelling the green things growing on the side of the road past the fog, the fog that hung like a curtain all around him. But this time, he looked carefully at his surroundings and used all of his senses. He inhaled sharply; diesel fuel, smoke, and — a body of water? He turned around slowly pulling in all of the sensory information he could. It was so dark, he saw only the outlines of large bulky shapes. Was that an elevated train track? He heard a train, some distance away. He turned again. He knew he smelled a body of water, he could hear the ebb and flow of the river, yes, it was a river, the Mongohela? He turned again and moved toward the sound of the water splashing the sides of the embankment. He walked several yards when he noticed a sound, somewhere off in the distance. It was an engine, a car engine. The fog was so heavy he could see little but shapes and shadows. Two pinpoints of light, leached through the fog and the darkness. The sound grew in volume, the lights grew clearer. There were two, two round lights, growing brighter and brighter. The car was coming, coming toward him, faster and faster. Like a flash of lightning on a blustery night, the realization came to him; he would be run down like a dog. He looked about frantically, trying to find somewhere to go, somewhere to hide. The sound grew almost deafening; the lights grew, blinding him...

I woke with a start and sat up with my eyes open, but unseeing. I was on the train, rushing toward DC. Sweat dripped down my face hitting my clothes with a plopping thud. I grouped for the napkins I'd used with my dinner, still on the pull out tray in front of me, and tried to wipe away the dream and the fear.

God, when would the dreams go away? But this was important. Was Jimmy at the Indianapolis Railyard? I turned on my reading light and pulled the maps, one of Pittsburgh and one of Indianapolis, from my backpack. Maybe I could pinpoint the area of my dream. Maybe that would lead me to where Jimmy was buried.

I wadded up the napkins, took the comb from my back pocket and pulled it through my hair, before laying the maps out on my table. I looked carefully, moving the maps and the transparency overlays back and forth. It couldn't have been Indianapolis. There were creeks and a river near the Railyard. But the Indianapolis trains were in a much smaller total area, and there was no river. Now, Pittsburgh, where the "Mighty Mongehela" River encircled part of the Pittsburgh Railyard, a river that a man could easily see… and smell.

There were people, people everywhere. Men and women running for the train, pushing, pulling, tugging, milling about, saying little, smiling not at all. Children cried and mothers scolded while the loudspeaker announced incoming and outgoing trains. Horns honked from the street outside. Eric turned 360° until he saw the street sign for the bus traveling to the government areas. He had decided on his return to Chapel Hill that he would leave on the earliest possible train; there were only two and get as much as he could before everyone went home for the day. He had his duffel and his computer case with him, but they were easy enough to lug around until he could make it to the motel. He found a bus that took him to the Capital Mall and the US Treasury Department. The man he'd spoken to the day before told him to come mid-morning, and he'd be able to get Eric a tour if he wanted one and show him how he could find information.

Eric had not been to DC since his senior field trip several decades before. DC, as usual, was hot and muggy. DC was miserable in the third week in April. The air conditioner in the back of the bus whirred loudly in cacophony with the automated voices announcing stops, people talking, and music leeching from nearby ear buds.

His bus stopped directly across the street from the Treasury Department. The place looked like a Greek temple with granite Doric columns running across the front of the building. A statue of Alexander Hamilton, tailcoat and knee britches, wig and waistcoat, stood directly in front of the walk leading to the entry door.

Eric made his way into the building and stood in line, while a group of security guards checked bags, IDs, and moved people through a metal detector.

"State the nature of your visit."

"I'm here to see Mister Jenkins. He and I spoke on the phone yesterday." Erik said as he showed the guard his North Carolina driver's license.

The man smiled a little as he looked at Eric's license, "Mister Jenkins, huh? Okay, go up the stairs to the next level. He's at the end of the corridor on the right. There's a little hallway past the door; go down the hallway, and you will see another door on the left. He's through that left-hand side door. Good luck to you."

Eric couldn't figure why the guard was smiling, and why he seemed to be directing him to a broom closet.

"You can leave your bag here behind the guard desk and take your briefcase with you. Your bag will be safe; you can pick it up on your way out."

Eric nodded and then made his way up the wide granite steps. He moved down to the end of the corridor and went to the right. There was indeed another hallway past that door. He walked down a little passage, dark, musty, with moldy mops, standing single file up against the wall until he saw another door. There was no nameplate announcing the occupant of the room, but Eric knocked twice and went in.

The only light in this closet of a room came from a buzzing, bare, fluorescent fixture in the ceiling. On two sides of this cubbyhole, were tall, old-fashioned filing cabinets resplendent with rust. The room was just like a walk-in closet and couldn't have measured more than 14 x 10. A rickety table used as a desk stood against the back wall. Strewn over the table were papers, pens, office paraphernalia, and folders. Some of those folders had ended up on the floor and under the table. A gray-haired, florid faced man, sat behind the table reading a computer printout. He looked up at Eric in surprise as he walked in through the door. He showed no signs of discomfort sitting and working in a room that reminded Eric of a janitor's closet in a high school. The only amenities that clued Eric believing he hadn't time traveled to an earlier century were a CPU and flat screen monitor on the table.

"Mister Jenkins, I'm Eric Douglass, I called you yesterday."

"Yes, Mister Douglass, I'm so glad to know you." Mister Jenkins got up and reached across the table to shake Eric's hand. "Won't you sit down? There is a chair behind that furthest file cabinet."

"I'm really glad you could see me," said Eric. He took out some business cards he'd made up at Vista Print. He'd designed and ordered the cards online while he'd still been in Chicago. He decided, after his faux pas with Albert, that he'd better look like what he was proclaiming he was. He'd made the business cards, stating that he was a writer, and had even made up the title of a few obscure journal articles on the back. He handed one of them to Mister Jenkins. The man read the list of articles on the back of the card, nodding as if he'd read every single one of them.

Eric pulled out the chair and discovered that three of the legs sat flat on the floor, while the fourth was about 2 inches shorter. He wobbled for a moment, but gave up and sat on the edge of the seat and pulled out his computer. "I know this sounds a little far-fetched, but I came to ask about a manifest on the gold shipment that went from Chicago to New York in 1933, and then ultimately to Fort Knox. FDR's Executive Order 6102, required that citizens turn in gold coins and ingots to be placed in the government treasury. You see, I'm writing a book about this, and I need to get as much detailed information as I can. I won't necessarily put the information into the book, but the more data I gather, the more convincing and fact filled the book will be."

"Yes, yes, very good…Maybe I can help you. I am an unofficial keeper of obscure documents." He said as he laughed and gestured about the little room, and the filing cabinets.

"I decided that if anyone could find an old gold manifest from 1933 it would probably be you", Eric enthused. He must say he was getting this charm thing down rather well. He had mountains of charisma, he'd just now tapped into. Who knew?

Mister Jenkins actually blushed with pleasure. "Well, well, we'll see what we can do to help you out. Now, tell me exactly what it is you are looking for."

"I know there was gold collected all over the country after executive order 6102, as I'm sure you're aware, and taken to the New York Federal Reserve before Fort Knox was completed, and then ultimately shipped there. What I'm trying to find out, if there are still manifests signed by the various federal marshals at the place of pickup before the shipments were put on the train and sent to New York. Are there still papers like that around?"

"Oh yes, yes. As you said, the government never throws away a piece of paper. We'll just have to see if it's actually a document or if it's been put on microfiche. And how many of these documents would you need to look at?"

"I'd like to see if there is any information about the shipments in September, October, and November 1933 to New York. There can't have been that many of them, correct?"

"Well, I'll have to look around. I do have one drawer in these filing cabinets that I have relegated to that time of history. There are so many momentous occasions in our past as a country, but as you say, few actual documents have been discarded; I don't know how many have actually been lost. The important thing for me to tell you is that over the past decades, I've been able to collect and review documents, and as a data manager, have been able to categorize them. Now let's see."

The 'data manager' got up and opened and closed drawers pulled out and then pushed in documents until he came to a huge hanging file with many manila folders inside it. "Yes, 1933; documents before WWI has been put on microfiche and I'm slowly going through the Hoover administration now."

"This seems like a big undertaking, why don't you have any help?"

All THAT GliTTeRS

Mr. Jenkins placed a huge file in Eric's lap with a 'voila' gesture before he spoke. "Budget cuts my boy, budget cuts."

Eric scanned the man's office. The place looked unfortunately like a broom closet.

Budget cuts. *I don't suppose he's on bread and water, too. He must really love what he does. I'd quit. Of course, he doesn't get peed on by mice all day long either or write down reams of boring calculations.* Eric shook his head at the irony and started to leaf through the files. He carefully laid the files he needed to look at more closely perpendicular to each section in order to keep them in order. There were a dozen or more manifests, all written in hand, notated and signed by various federal marshals. He took a few pictures with his phone for future reference.

He read many times about shipments sent from New York to Fort Knox by 1936. Nothing in the piles of documents was about the first round of shipments, the gold involuntarily taken from citizens and then sent by rail to New York. He sat back, stretched and rubbed the kinks out of his neck. Looking at his watch, he saw that he'd been working in companionable silence with Mr. Jenkins for over an hour; he hadn't once looked up from his desk.

He picked up a stack of hanging manila folders that sat haphazardly on the floor. Eric took a visual assessment of everything he could readily see from his chair that was still on the floor. There was something… he nudged the bottom of one of the piles with his foot and quickly reached down and pulled up a gray folder from under the stack. He took a quick peek at Jenkins, but the man was so engrossed, that Eric knew he hadn't seen him get the folder from the floor. Eric made sure the monitor of his computer covered him. The folder was aged and brittle. The ink on the few documents inside was faded and only a small portion of each could be read. The first document was dated 1910 and a list of names was bulleted down the page. On the next sheet were the minutes of a meeting, a meeting held at a place called Jekyll Island. Eric knew a sea island off the coast of Georgia named Jekyll. The meetings were about something that had to do with the country, banking, commerce, the Federal Reserve. Eric glanced at Jenkins making sure the man wasn't watching and carefully pushed the folder between his keyboard and monitor. The document had nothing to do with the gold, and even less wi8th finding out about Jimy's killer and his body's whereabouts. He was just intrigued. And then there was that other question…

"Mr. Jenkins," the older man looked up, startled. Perhaps he'd forgotten that Eric was in the room with him.

"Is it true that all of the gold from the confiscation in the 30s was transferred to Fort Knox in 1936?"

Well, uh, I think it did, but…"

"But who would oversee a project like that? Would the stories get into the papers; journalists reporting on the golds coming and going?"

"No, I'm sure the whole process from NY to Ft. Knox would be hushed up. I feel sure the government would not want the general public to know about it. Think how difficult it would be to guard those trains for the thousand miles they had to travel."

"You're probably right." Eric thought there had been one particular journalist who had known about the gold from the start. Jimmy knew, and Eric would bet real money Abrams knew Jimmy knew. What better way to insure their gold heist came off with no interference than to get rid of Jimmy before he plastered the story all over the Chicago Tribune's front page.

"Mister Douglass, I know what the party line is about what is actually in Fort Knox, but, I have no first-hand knowledge of it. The last time the repository was audited was about the same time-period of the documents you're looking for. The documents you want, since we didn't find them here, are probably stashed in the National Archives. I have first level documents here that I put in a database, and then send over to the archives. If you'd like me to, I'll be glad to call over and have you see someone that might be able to help you. The thing is, these documents are, some of are 70 to 80 years old. The government keeps those kinds of documents, but sometimes, things that are that old that were around long before computers or microfilm, can get lost, become fragile, and just plain disintegrate. Especially, if the documents aren't what we consider, 'upper tier'. The upper tier are documents like the Declaration of Independence and the Constitution."

Eric sat back and looked at the older man thinking about the whole mess of bureaucracy and how low-level minions like the data manager, were entrenched into 'the party line'. Mister Jenkins probably didn't know anything, but he had been around these documents for decades. He had to know something, something about the gold, something about Fort Knox, or about the Federal Reserve, ad infinitum. "Mister Jenkins, I am not a conspiracy theorist, however, since I've been doing research on these gold shipments in 1933, so many red flags have waved in my face, that it makes a person wonder."

The florid faced documentarian grew even redder. Either the man knew something about the gold, the Federal Reserve, Fort Knox, ad nauseam, or he was trying to cover up the fact that he was indeed, a glorified paper pusher. He held out his hands in a gesture of supplication.

"Mister Douglass, I have no idea what you're talking about." And the man's face suddenly became completely blank. "From what I understand, and I've seen the documents on this, gold from the 1930s was moved from the New York Federal Reserve and then moved to Fort Knox after the place was built. And that's where it still is. It stayed there, so there is no grand conspiracy. There have been a lot of folks that come to this office that are bound and determined to find out what the federal government is up to with their money. I think it's just as it seems. Take it at face value, Mister Douglass.

"I do have a friend at the national archives. He might give you more information that may help you with your book. If you would like me to, I will call him and set up an appointment for you. When can you go?"

"I'm free anytime and can go when you can set up an appointment for me."

Eric never took his gaze off the documentarian. Ever since Eric had asked about Fort Knox, Jenkins had acted nervous and jumpy. Mister Jenkins sat back in his chair and pushed it back and forth, until the thing screamed in agony. He dabbed at his forehead again, took off his glasses and wiped his face. Mister Jenkins reached for the phone and punched in a number he had on speed dial.

"Ah, Ralph, Bob Jenkins here. I have a writer in my office who would like to come and speak to you about documents from the 1930s. He has time, whenever it is convenient for you. Oh, okay. I'll let him know."

"Mister Douglass, Ralph can see you today at 12:30. I'll give you directions, the room number, and so forth. Maybe he can tell you something I can't." Mister Jenkins reached his hand out but would not look up at Eric. "I hope you find what you're looking for." Eric shook hands, gathered his things, and left the office. He shut the door quietly on his way out and braced himself against the wall.

Maybe the information in the National Archives would be more forthcoming. Eric exited the building in search of a fortifying cup of coffee. After lunch he'd go to the National Archives for another round of, 'Gee, I don't know.'

Chapter Thirty-two

Present day
Washington, DC

"Yes, documents associated with Executive Order 6102... let's see if some of that has been stored digitally." Ralph Gunderson, the man Eric had an appointment with at the National Archives was a bit of a surprise. He was a lean, but muscular young man about Eric's own age with very black hair and blue eyes. Eric supposed the man would be an old fellow and gray haired like Jenkins. Gunderson had a chip on his shoulder that Eric could see a mile away.

The National Archives was an older building, replete with granite steps and door jambs coated with decades of paint. Eric was directed down a hall to a bank of elevators for the lower level. A double glass door at the end of the hall opened in a wide room with a chest high counter, each section divided roughly by signs suspended from the ceiling: Federal Census Records NATF 81, Eastern Cherokee Applications NATF 83, Federal Land Entry Files NATF 84, and several others, the numbers and letters Eric couldn't begin to know what they meant.

Gunderson had given him a hostile glare. *Well, sorry ol' buddy if I'm making work for you; it's my right as an American citizen to see where the money is going. And for probably the first time in my life I felt my American sensibilities of freedom and the Bill of Rights get sorely out of whack.*

I sat in a bank of uncomfortable plastic chairs waiting for Ralph to find the materials and set me up in a carrel with a Microfiche viewer as I glanced through my notes. Kathleen and I had hashed over this bit, not only before I'd left Chicago, but the three times I'd spoken to her on the phone. If I had the time I thought I just might ask her out. My thoughts of Kathleen's cool blonde beauty darted through my mind clamoring for attention, like fireflies, on a North Carolina summer night. But, I didn't have time. Not till I cleared up Jimmy's murder and got back to my old boring life.

It was indeed strange that I had never thought of my life as boring until that fateful trip to the group hypnosis session with Monica.

I had seen a man murdered, and for a time, I thought, and may still find out that man was me. The dreams, so clear and precise, like watching a movie gave me so much valuable information about Jimmy's murder. But, not all.

Will I be satisfied to return to my status quo life; probably not. Certainly not the way my life in Chapel Hill had been. Maybe I'll resign at UNC and find a research job someplace exotic, exotic like Chicago. Whoa boy, one thing at a time.

Eric and Kathleen agreed that if he could see the original manifest, then they would compare it to the one they found in the tunnel, the one they were sure Nealy had stashed there on that September night in 1933. There was just no other reasonable explanation for the manifest being in the tunnels. If there was a discrepancy, then they'd know that some of the gold was gone, skimmed from the original shipment. The process then of finding where the gold was hidden would begin.

Their next move, he and Kathleen's, would be to assess each of the potential sites.

Was the information even available as to what types of structures had been in use in the 30's? Anything could have changed and not been recorded. Anything. The records of the rail abutments or trestles could have been lost or destroyed. Eric still had about a half dozen copied notebooks of Jimmy's he'd yet to decode. There'd been nothing forthcoming in the dreams he'd had lately. He had to figure out 'where and how'; there would be a better chance of finding out where Jimmy was murdered and where he'd been stashed. He would write down as detailed information as possible now, every time he recorded a dream.

"Mr. Douglass? I've found some of the documents you were looking for. The problem is, when they were copied, some of them were in pretty bad shape. There are some gaps, some holes, torn edges. But, here are the ones I've found and you can have a look. You're free to bring your computer with you." Ralph gestured to the other room crowded with microfiche and digital terminals, shelves that reached to the ceiling, trolleys filled with what looked like old bound title books. Some of those volumes had to have been around before the country had been a country, The pages exposed to the air were yellowed and the edges crinkled and broken off with decrepitude.

"Sure, thanks." Eric pulled out his notebooks and pencils, put on his glasses, and began. Ralph was right; some of the documents had holes where they'd been folded, or edges torn off. It was going to take a long time to find a glimmer of what was crucial; what made sense of the happenings in September of 1933. And that particular item that he was sure had gotten Jimmy killed.

Chapter Thirty-two

"Kathleen? Are you busy?"

"Oh, hi Eric, how goes the search? And I'm never too busy to speak to you."

Eric sighed inwardly before he spoke again. "Found lots of stuff. A few things were pertinent, most were not. And you were right; the United States Government keeps every scrap of paper that ever remotely pertained to anything. And excitingly enough, I did find a manifest from September 23 1933 with a load of seized, or confiscated, whatever you want to call it, gold leaving Chicago. The document was on microfiche, but the original had been in sad shape before it was digitized. A few elongated holes where the page had been folded left out information on $20 Liberty coins. The paper had been ripped on the side and the pounds of miscellaneous gold reported carried to New York is also missing. Now, I want you to get 'our' document out." Kathleen pulled out her center drawer and opened a manila folder.

"See on the bottom right-hand corner? This document says that the total pounds of gold ingots were 120,000. My copy of the original says 98,000. Do you concur?"

Kathleen drew her finger down the page. "Yes, that's what it says 98,000. If we don't have good figures for the rest, we have that. Make a copy and take it with you and send me one via text."

"Yes, I'm way ahead of you." Eric yawned hugely as he looked at his watch. It was 3:00 in Chicago, 4:00 in DC and he was beat. He'd stayed at the National Archives until 2:30 and took the bus to his motel. "Sorry, didn't mean to yawn in your ear. I'm going back to Chapel Hill in the morning. I have seven days left of leave plus this upcoming weekend, and then I'll have to go back to work."

Eric listened to Kathleen's reply with half an ear, thinking; *And I need to find out what happened to Jimmy. I need to 'lay his ghost to rest.' But, how am I going to do that? Kathleen has been such a trooper putting up with this bull. How can she be sure Seamus or one of his henchmen didn't bump Jimmy off. The better scenario, as Kathleen said, is Jimmy found out about the gold and who was lifting it and went in for the big front page article and got offed instead.*

"Before you go back…" Kathleen chewed on her bottom lip. What were the questions, what were they asking, how would they find out, what was imperative to know about any of this to be able to reach some kind of a solution? And whatever Eric Douglass found out, she had to make sure her family was not implicated in any of this. The O'Brien's didn't have the gold. Did Seamus have someone kill Jimmy because of his exposes and therefore completely unrelated to the gold heist? Could she deflect any blame from her family? She'd get Eric to work on finding out about the gold and maybe he wouldn't concentrate so on who killed Jimmy. She knew he was no one's fool, so maybe not.

"How about going by train to the Indianapolis rail hub? See if there is an historian that can tell you about special freights coming from Chicago and where they could have gone in September of 1933. I don't think we are barking up the wrong tree, not at all. Now we know for a fact, in black and white, that there were two manifests for the same shipment. If the one we found in the tunnels is the original, and there's no reason to think it's not, then we can assume the 'unholy three' Abrams, Gillespie, and O'Brien took what was skimmed off that shipment. I've been doing some calculations and if they stole only the 22,000 pounds of ingots or $20.00 coins and nothing else, that would amount to hundreds of thousands of dollars of stolen gold in the 1930s, and we can only try to calculate how much in today's valuation. If it was about 22,000 pounds, at what the going rate was, then that was $454,740.00 in 1933 and, wait, I'm doing the math now, all right, are you ready? If gold is around $1,300.00 an ounce and they made off with 22,000 pounds, then that would come out to approximately, $15,312,000, give or take."

"So whatever mode of transportation was used to move the gold would have to be able to move that much weight," Eric said. He did a quick calculation in his head. "I'm estimating around 6 tons. It's not just the ingots and coins, it's all the boxes the gold is packed in, then the rail cars or truck beds that the gold is packed into. Now here's another kink in the theory. What if the shipment didn't go by train?"

"Ah, Ha," Kathleen said. "I was wondering if this would come up. I've been doing a little research on trucks in the 1930's and only a logging truck could move several tons of weight. That is if it went by truck… see, too many holes in the story."

"Wow."

"Wow indeed. So we can be relatively sure they stole it. Otherwise, what's the point of making a fake manifest? With all the information we have from Jimmy White's notes and articles, there is nothing else that it could be. White was on to them, but he couldn't get the proof before his 'accident.' You told me once that you thought Jimmy was murdered to keep him quiet about what he knew. It makes sense now."

"Can we assume the gold was never picked up? I mean, wasn't Nealy murdered just a few days from the time the gold left Chicago?" "Yes, he was. The death certificate said, September 28,1933. That's five days after the gold left Chicago. Surely, the gold was in its hiding place by then," said Eric.

"I Googled both Gillespie and Abrams and this is what I found; when they were in the senate and house, all the bills both of them voted on or debated were recorded. Gillespie retired in January 1934, one year before his term was up, and if we're right about the heist, just two months after that bungled attempt 'went south'. Abrams retired in 1936 at the end of his term, and stayed at the family homestead in Wollaston Beach, Mass. He died in 1942. He rarely did anything reported on by the papers. It appears that after the gold heist, that maybe never happened at all, they just tried to fade out of the public eye. As far as I can ascertain, the two of them, for the rest of their lives, never lived outside their means and neither did the subsequent generations of both families. Matter of fact, Abrams's family died off after the 60's. An old maiden aunt lived in the family home until her death about 30 years ago. And no one has lived there since.

"And the thing about Gillespie; the family lost everything after the war. They sold the warehouse and all the land to pay debts. There had been some miss-allocation of funds from the warehouse and river boats they owned, and the IRS made them pay through the nose. Public records I could dig up from the time, report the family was forced to sell off most of their assets to pay back their creditors and the government. From there the family just kind of fades away and I haven't discovered anything else.

"I have access to a title search web site for lawyers and real estate brokers. Makes it a lot easier and faster if you can search with your finger-tips. That particular home, and I saw an image on Google, is all boarded up. If the historical society can't get the place listed as historically significant, then someday soon, it's going to be demolished. These details make me think that the gold was never retrieved. They stashed it somewhere and never picked it up. Now, why don't you use that analytical researcher's brain and figure out where they stashed it."

"I think you have a point." Eric said around another huge yawn. "Oh, sorry, I'll get on it tomorrow. Maybe I'll just drive to Indianapolis, I mean, how far can it be? There are still a few pages of the notebooks that I haven't figured out as yet. Jimmy decided to change cyphers and the new one is weird, or maybe it's just 'cause I haven't had time to really go over it. Maybe I can do that this evening and I'll let you know what I find out tomorrow."

"You really are tired, and by the way, Indianapolis is very far. It's in another time zone, remember? Take the train and sleep. Then call me when you get there, and we'll decide what to do next.

I really think going and scoping out in person what we can't find on the internet is necessary. I know you are working on the gold angle because you are fairly sure that Jimmy was killed because of it. If you can find out more or less that the gold would have to be shipped through Pittsburgh, can't we assume that Jimmy knew that too, and if he did, maybe he went to Pittsburgh to follow up?"

"Great point. If I can get these next notebooks deciphered, then I can pinpoint his whereabouts, then I can decide if he was there the day he was killed. Maybe he went to Pittsburgh and never returned to Chicago. I should have those notebooks deciphered by the time I get there and I'll look around and see what I see. It'll be a good thing to let Amtrak do the driving. Sleep tight. Call you tomorrow."

"You too, talk to you tomorrow." Kathleen clicked off and lay her phone on the desk staring at it for a moment. Why was she helping Eric Douglass with this ancient and ridiculous search? She admitted to herself that it had been a very long time since she'd met a man who intrigued her so much, and Eric Douglass was just such a man. She knew she'd never be bored around him. Men in her upper crust class, the nobility of Chicago, bored her to tears. And what if she or Eric found out that Seamus had Jimmy killed, a story like that could injure the family name. Kathleen felt a chill go up her spine. She could just hear her nemesis, District Attorney Jake, 'Mac The Knife", MacKenzie let loose on the name O'Brien. A good family name was imperative not to be sullied by murders done in the past. 'Mac The Knife', because the man would stab you in the back quicker than getting a parking ticket in downtown Chicago, could sneer better than anyone, and he never kept his sneers to himself and was happy to spread gossip around the Cook County Court House. MacKenzie had done his, oh so, subtle best to undermine her last case against a city zoning ordinance that was delaying the expansion of her business furniture warehouse. The family was losing many dollars every day. To avoid being called out by MacKenzie and mortified in front of Eric, Kathleen had to make sure that all the research pointed to the murder of Jimmy White by someone other than an O'Brien. If she had on her lawyer's hat, she could have billed a week's worth of hours doing these searches. If the two of them found White's murderer and they found the gold, how would the government treat the murder and then the find? She'd lay odds there were no precedents to research about that particular scenario.

Kathleen pulled open a drawer and took out the framed photograph she had of her mother. In the photo, Patsy O'Brien stood in front of a rose arbor at the Chicago Botanical Gardens. She wore a pink dress puffed out by many stiff petticoats, a little close-fitting hat, white lipstick, and white gloves in the style of the early sixties. Patsy was a very pretty girl; she smiled at the photographer for the photo. But her mother had never been a happy woman. Not after she'd married Kathleen's father in the early seventies and the two of them were expected to live in the family home with grandfathers, uncles, aunts, and cousins. Patsy had died in 1980 when Kathleen was four. Kathleen remembered her mother only a little, and sometimes, the memories she did have were bittersweet. She could only guess the reasons her mother wasn't happy. Patsy and Frank, and then Kathleen after her birth, were expected to live in the O'Brien's in Canaryville instead of having their own home. Kathleen could understand. Having one's own things, making a house a home; that was important to women of that generation. Hell, she decided it would have been important for her too if her life had taken a different path.

The best of the family's old clothes, dating back several generations, were stored in a closet on the third floor. The closet contained the pink dress with little capped sleeves from the photo, and was the only garment of Patsy's. When Kathleen was a pre-teen, she would go to that closet and push her face into the dress, breathing deeply, catching and holding her mother's scent. She'd refreshed her memory of her mother by digging out the family albums and seeing picture after picture of Patsy's unsmiling face. It had not occurred to Kathleen until she was a young woman herself, that her mother may have been clinically depressed. When she looked at the many pictures of her parents, her mother didn't look angry in the pictures, just melancholy.

It was evident to Kathleen that Eric's convoluted search was a way for her to search her own past and to lay her own ghosts. Finding the gold her 4th cousin twice removed, had probably stolen from the government could start that process. And what about that ephemeral gold? Did it exist? And if they found it... well she knew the Secret Service could find a way of detaining her until she handed it over to the government; to be very honest, she just didn't want to butt heads with the government.

She quickly looked through the database of lawyers and U.S. attorneys she knew in DC. She highlighted and then made bold three names of men and one woman she thought would come to her rescue if the Secret Service and the FBI got out of control. That is, if she and Eric actually found the gold's hiding place, and if they found out who killed Jimmy.

The O'Brien family fortunes had started to wane in the past three decades. The real estate she dealt in, warehouses, offices, strip malls, were now either in the wrong area of town to draw customers or had physically deteriorated so much that some were being demolished.

If there really was gold out there, she knew the procedure, the government would take it and give them a finder's fee. An infusion of cash into the family coffers would be welcome, well duh.

Chapter Thirty-two

Eric made a reservation on an Amtrak going to Indianapolis. He'd told the desk clerk at the motel that he'd be gone for about 24 hours, and could they please keep his room? A change of clothes, toiletries, and his laptop, were all the things he'd take with him. Lugging all of the notebooks, that by now had grown to almost fifteen, would be too much trouble for him to keep up with. He left them in the long drawer under the TV along with the remaining empty notebooks and some pens.

Eric made a list of questions to ask someone in the know that could not be answered in DC. First: which railroad yard would be the most likely as a final destination if the train with the gold left from Indianapolis. And if Jimmy found the hiding place in that Railyard, that was not likely, but what if Jimmy did follow the train, hot on the trail of the crooks. Was he killed in Indianapolis? Kathleen had found old maps of the areas and her 'Baker Street Irregulars' had made a transparency, an overlay of the map dated 1929 with the current one.

Eric climbed aboard the train at 10:30 pm; it would take around 16 hours to get to Chicago, then another four or so to get to Indianapolis, so he'd nap as Kathleen suggested. He settled back in the blue, full leather chair, pulled up the little footrest, and tried to get some sleep.

I arrived in Indianapolis by mid-morning. The Amtrak train station was a huge underground affair with streets above and directly opposite Lucas Oil Stadium, home of the Indianapolis Colts. I walked around the outside area trying to shake out the cobwebs. On the sidewalk, a hot dog vendor cart resplendent with striped umbrella and a guy with an Indianapolis Colts ball cap was in full swing. The smell of the man's wares enticed me to stop and order a Coney Island with the works. Onions and slaw were great for the heart muscle.

Chapter Thirty-three

Kathleen shuffled and reshuffled the papers in the file marked 1933. She'd looked through all of it several times, not sure what she was looking for. The pages were curling and becoming brittle, but she didn't know how to conserve the files, nor did she think it was important to do so, and being in the attic all this time hadn't helped the integrity of the paper. Near the back of the file was an envelope addressed to her great grandfather from a downtown lawyer.

"Dear Sir:" it began.

"I have done my part in getting your 'nephew' Nealy O'Brien acquitted of this last fiasco in the circuit court. I'm afraid that he won't go to any lengths on his own behalf. He has been accused of racketeering. There was little proof, so the judge had to throw out the case, and he was acquitted. Next time, the judge will not be so easy. I have thought about this and consulted the other partners in our firm. We have decided that we can no longer defend the younger O'Brien. His recalcitrant attitude did not help in any way our ability to defend him. Therefore, we can no longer be his attorneys. We will make inquiries as to a firm to defend any criminal complaints.

Please do know that as far as land, tax, or other commercial enterprise, we will be delighted to continue as your counselors.

Yours very sincerely,
Joseph P. Sinclair, esq."

Well, well, that makes absolute sense. Nealy was such a ne'er-do-well, I'm surprised great-grandfather didn't have him escorted to the border with an order never to come back.

Nealy was in Chicago when Abrams and Gillespie were doing their thing and from information in Jimmy's notebooks, Nealy had been up to his eyebrows in it. But Kathleen was sure Nealy had never had any of the gold. If he had, he'd have left for South America in short order. He'd gotten himself murdered in an alleyway in DC two days after the train left Indianapolis for its ultimate destination of New York. If he'd had the gold, he wouldn't have been hanging around an alleyway in DC. He'd pissed off too many people. What an idiot! The gold had already gone out of the city when he lifted the original manifest and stashed it in the tunnels.

Chapter Thirty-four

For the next half hour, Eric sat on the low concrete wall near the entrance of the station relaxing and soaking up the sun. The weather was cool and crisp, and the sun was high in a blue sky. He was relaxed, more relaxed than he'd been in a long while. Maybe he could get the information he needed and get back to Chapel Hill, rested and recovered. He took a huge breath in and held it for a second, letting the air empty out in a long stream between his lips. Now was not the time to think about what would happen next Monday when he returned to work. He had some sleuthing to do first. He went into the main lobby to the information desk.

The gray-haired man in the information booth wore a white shirt with a black string tie, and a green visor over his thicker than coke bottle glasses. The man really looked like a character out of an old Ellery Queen private eye novel. Eric glanced around quickly assuring himself that he was still in the 21st century. Weird. "Could you tell me if I can speak with someone about the railroad here in the 1930s? I'm writing a book and need some information." Eric handed the man one of his bogus business cards he'd had made up for his trip to Chicago. The clerk took the card and read it through, all the while chewing on a toothpick. It was decidedly getting easier and easier to lie with a straight face, and before this was all said and done, Eric believed he would look at his former static life in a different light.

"Hum, well now let me see here." The man sat back and moved the toothpick from one side of his mouth to the other never taking his eyes off Eric's business card. "I think you should go see our historian, Mike Betts at the train museum. He's the curator, the founder, the collector, the janitor, all rolled into one. If you go out the far stairs on the west side of the station, the museum is located in the farthest building away from the street." The man never took his eyes from Eric's card or stopped chewing on his toothpick the whole while he spoke. He looked over his glasses at Eric as he started to hand him back the card. "Go out the stairs behind this booth; make a left and keep walking. You can't miss it. Believe me, it doesn't look like any museum you've ever seen. Good luck to you."

Eric found the small building; "Indianapolis Rail Hub Museum." The curator looked about 5 feet tall, with gold, wire rim glasses, a visor, and a string tie.

"Good morning, sir. I have a few questions about the rail hub from the period around the 1930s. The man in the information booth said you might know the answers to a few questions. Might I trouble you?"

"Why sure, Mister, why don't you come on in and we'll see what we can find?"

There was glass, waist high cases all along the side of the room containing artifacts: a conductor's watch, a timetable, a comb, a collapsible tin cup, and other items that might have been carried by passengers.

"Now, what exactly are we looking for?"

"If a train left Chicago and came to the rail hub in the early 1930s, to be sent to another station, could you determine which station it might have gone to?"

"There were lots of trains back then. There weren't good roads that truckers could use to haul merchandise and produce until a quarter of a century later. Now, when exactly are we talking about?"

Eric pulled his notebooks out of his computer bag and leafed through as though he were reading. He had most of the information memorized by now; he'd seen it so many times. "Yes, if a train left on September 23, 1933, from Chicago and the cargo changed engines in Indianapolis, what are some of the other stations where it could have ended up?"

All THAT GlitTeRS

Mr. Betts settled the visor further down on his forehead and turned to the file drawers that covered much of the walls in the little museum. Each of the cabinet drawers showed a legend or schematic of what was inside. Mister Betts flipped his thumb and forefinger against several of the drawers counting under his breath as he did so. After a few seconds, he pulled open a drawer with a flourish. "Okay, here it is." He slapped a timetable on top of his desk. He leafed through the booklet until he came to the right date. "1933? September 23? Do you know what time of the day?"

"No, I don't, but I'd venture to say it was at night, probably late at night."

"Well, it says here that September 23, 1933, there were four trains that left Chicago to come to the hub: two in the early morning hours; one at 4:45 and another at 5:30, and then there was one that left at midnight."

"Can you estimate where the train would have ended up if it was the one at midnight?"

"Ah yes, if the train left at midnight, it would reach the Hub at around 4 AM. Another engine would have picked it up, probably from 6 to 7:30 the next morning. If it was the train at midnight, there are several stations where it could have gone. 1. Back to Chicago. 2. To Cincinnati. 3. To Pittsburgh, or 4. To Detroit. Do you know what was on the train? Was it perishable? If it was, it would've gone to Cincinnati. If the cargo was machine tools, it would've gone to Detroit. So, if it was neither of those two things, the train would have ended up in Pittsburgh or gone back to Chicago."

"I know the final destination of the train would have been New York City. But couldn't the train or a portion of the train go to one of these other stations?"

The Historian rattled on about couplings axles, and other 'train-language' that Eric knew would not help them, nevertheless, he jotted down everything the historian told him.

"And here's the thing, each different size car has a different coupling so heavy loads back in the 30's would be put on those different type cars. And the different types of cars would be scheduled only at certain times. A lot depended on who was hauling what, and that information could change daily, you know, like cattle, or grain, or cotton, that sort of thing."

The historian was sure the train had not gone back to Chicago. But they had to know where all of the possible trains went as well as what roads were available if the shipment went by truck. Eric slapped his forehead; it was a DUH moment.

"Gee, thanks, you've been a big help." Eric pumped Mr. Betts's hand and quickly escaped out the door before the historian could take a breath.

He hurried outside, grabbed his phone and dialed Kathleen. "Hey, Kathleen, it's me."

"Well, hi, how goes the big hunt?"

"I just had one of those 'light bulb' moments, the kind that make me slap myself for being dumb."

"Okay, give."

"I was speaking with the train historian here, he even has timetables from the end of the 19th century, but here's the thing: why are we assuming that the 'shipment', if there indeed was one, was sent by rail? We've already addressed the logging truck possibility.

"And we have to figure that the weight was measured in Troy Ounces, I forgot that, so there are 12 ounces to a troy pound, not 16. Gemstones and precious metals weigh in Troy ounces. That's about 18,000+ pounds. Six tons, right?"

"What if some guys driving a logging truck that could carry several tons were employed to drive the stuff out of Chicago. I've already discovered that Jimmy knew about the trains; it's all over his notebooks. But if the load went by truck? A great deal of the roads were horrid until the 1950s, depending on where you lived.

"Is there any chance that we could find out if there were highways and where these highways led?"

Kathleen sighed audibly. "Well, maybe I can find some old maps of Chicago and the surrounding area. I'm sure the main library downtown has some in their documents room. If we can find highways and where they connected to each other, maybe we could figure out something, I don't know… I'll Google it first, then to the library, I'll get my P.L.'s to work on it and call you back."

"Terrific."

"Eric, what's the plan for tomorrow?"

"The train leaves here at 4:45 pm heading east. You know what," Eric said, making a quick but logical decision. "I can't afford to use another 24 hours on the train. I'm going to go find a cheap flight and head back to DC to pick up my stuff, and then I'll have to head home. Monday morning at 8 sharp, I have to be back at the lab. Life goes on no matter how much you want to solve a mystery from the past."

Kathleen sighed again, something Eric knew instinctively that she didn't do often. "You're absolutely right. Why don't you call me in the middle of next week and we can compare notes. Let's video chat, then we can show documents to one another."

"Great. But ," he said, looking off past the buildings around him and up to the blue, wishing it was a Carolina blue sky. "I'm going to miss going down into tunnels with you."

"Yes, me too. You'll have to come back for a visit after all of this is figured out."

"Okay, I just might do that. In the meantime, call if you find something."

Chapter Thirty-eight

I caught a late-night flight from Indianapolis to DC and found an airport shuttle that put me within walking distance of my motel. I was so exhausted, I felt like I'd lost my edge.

Maybe I could catch a nap and check out by the cut off time of 11 to save a few bucks.

I swiped the key card into the lock and pushed it open but stopped just inside the door and stared. Someone had been in my room. I pushed through the door and it swooshed behind me shutting with a metallic thump. The mattress was half off the bed. Every drawer had been opened, the contents thrown out and then dumped on the floor.

I pulled open the long drawer under the TV. The notebooks I had thought too cumbersome to carry, were gone.

I sat on the skewed mattress, trying to remember what had been in each one and, more importantly, what had been so vital that someone had stolen it. I grabbed my pocket and was comforted to feel the thumb drive attached to my key chain.

I reached for the house phone and called the desk.

Present day
Chicago
Home of Albert James White III.

He was about to lose his mind; very slowly, and decidedly, he was going to go stark raving mad. That boy, Eric, had found a mountain of useful items that could be sold and added to the White's bank accounts. Albert was convinced there was more in the attic, squirreled away in some hide-hole his grandfather had devised. His grandfather: he hated even thinking about him. His father had never come out and said disrespectful things about the man, but Albert knew that the hurt from Jimmy's neglect had cut his father deeply and actually shaped him into the quiet, always sad man he became. He wished his father was alive now. He'd love to share with him the items he'd found under all the dust and cobwebs. The old man, as quiet as he'd been, would have smiled when he'd seen the cufflinks and the one-hundred-dollar bill, but Albert's father had been gone a long time.

Albert pushed aside an old quilt draped over more boxes revealing a trunk with a bowed lid like those of the nineteenth century. He used a paper towel from the roll he'd brought up with him and eradicated the worst of the layers of time coating the lid. The top stuck and Albert roughly handled it until it opened slowly inch by inch, letting off a screech like a wounded animal.

An old sheet carefully covered the items packed inside the trunk, and he was surprised at how relatively dust-free the interior was. An album of old sepia photographs, a gentleman's tailcoat missing a few buttons, bundles of letters tied together with various colored bits of ribbon had all been placed carefully inside the trunk. Albert put the items neatly on the floor. In the very bottom in the left-hand corner of the trunk sat a pile of notebooks with what he immediately recognized as Jimmy's self-styled cypher. The top notebook's cover had 1932 written across it. There were two more with 1932 and the one on the bottom, the one filled with that strange 'Jimmy language' in every available margin and to the very last page was titled 1933.

Something about the notebook gave Albert pause. He put it on the top of the photo album and carried them and the old clothing downstairs.

"How could anyone have gotten into my room? Who has the master keys? Could the house keeper get in?" Eric stood in the center of his motel room. The on shift supervisor had come up to his room the moment he'd called to report the break in.

"Yes, the housekeeper has a master key card and we can make one at the desk, but a key is only made if a lodger loses their key. I don't know Mister Douglass, but the police will be here in just a moment. Could you tell me again, what's missing?"

"Just notebooks. But those notebooks had some important information in them, some research for a paper I was writing. I can't understand why someone would want them, but maybe whoever did this was looking for my computer. I just can't understand it. Who would want to get into my research, anyway?"

Did anyone know what he knew, what he had found in his research, that 22,000 pounds of gold coins and ingots had been stashed somewhere, but never picked up by the guys that had stolen it, and that it was all wrapped up in who had killed Jimmy and why?

The desk clerk, a young, good-looking woman with dark wavy hair, slumped heavily in a chair near the window. "This is the first time anything like this has happened on my shift." She said as she looked up at Eric.

"It's not your fault," Eric assured her. "I'm just on a fact-finding trip. Whoever did this has got to have information about what I'm researching, although why, is beyond me." Eric sat again on the crooked mattress racking his brain. Who could have done this?

As far as he knew, there were three people who knew what he was looking for, Kathleen, Bob Jenkins, and Ralph Gunderson. And the only one of those three that knew enough to make a difference was Kathleen. Could she have had someone do this, and if so why? She had access to anything he found.

"Maybe they broke in looking for valuables?"

"Maybe, but the only thing here was the notebooks." Said Eric.

"Well, I'm going to give you my email. Please get in touch if you find anything."

During the next hour, Eric gave statements to the Metro police as well as the security people at the hotel. They dusted for fingerprints in the room and looked at the security camera footage near the front desk. Whoever had done the deed had gotten in another way, maybe through the back and climbed the service stairs. There was nothing on the camera feed.

"Whoever did this Mister Douglass was conscious of where he or she could be caught on camera and avoided those areas. If you're going to check out this morning and return to North Carolina, then I think you won't have to worry too much about this. We'll keep digging to see if there is a fingerprint match. Maybe it was another writer out to get your research," said the Metro police sergeant. "I'll call you if we get any leads, but well, I don't know," he said holding his arms out with a shrug.

Eric reminded himself that there weren't just notes about Jimmy, but that he'd recorded all of his dreams. Whoever stole the notebooks would be hard pressed to figure out what that was about.

"Thanks officer, I'll take your advice and leave mid-morning."

After he was alone in the room, Eric unpacked his computer and took everything from all the many pockets of the briefcase. He'd repack it all before he got on the train. As an afterthought, he turned the case upside down and shook it. A small spiral notebook slipped through the front opening and hung by the end of the wire where it had poked a hole in the brief case cover. He carefully untangled the notebook and opened it.

Property of Jimmy White.
If found please return to the Chicago Tribune.

Eric did not remember the book. This was not one of the notebooks that he'd decoded. Maybe it had gotten hung up by its loose wire within the mass of notebooks he'd borrowed from Albert and hadn't known of its existence. Inside the book, every page was filled in with Jimmy's old recognizable cypher and what Eric knew to be a form of rail fence code.

He'd wait to read it when he returned home. And he'd not mention the book to Kathleen until he was sure that she hadn't stolen the other notebooks.

I opened the back door of my cab, hired to take me to the train with an hour to spare. I wrestled my duffle onto the back seat when I heard tires squeal and glanced up just as a Mazda hatchback tore around the corner. As the car accelerated and headed right for me, the low, chrome grill looked like a sickening grin. Time stopped. I threw my body sideways across the cab's seat, my right arm stretching out, my left holding the handle of the left door, pulling hard with only my feet sticking out of the confines of the car. I pushed my face into the smelly, Naugahyde of the seat cover and waited as the Mazda roared past.

Déja vu, it was déja vu. I'd watched Jimmy get run down like a dog on that gravel alleyway over and over again. The scene had been so entrenched in every thought and moment it was as though the dreams were a dress rehearsal.

"Hey, mister, you okay? That guy in the Mazda almost nailed you."

"Yeah," I said, sitting up. I shuffled my belongings around as I tried to get my heart to slow down. I grasped the seatbelt and pulled, the damn thing was caught, and pulled again, causing it to catch again heightening my anxiety. I stopped, breathed deeply and fastened the seat belt. "Take me to the train station please."

"Sure, mister." The cabbie said. He looked at me quizzically for another few seconds before he put the cab into gear and pulled out into traffic.

Chapter Thirty-five

Black, and dense, the Potomac moved sluggishly beneath the bridge. The man stood against the bridge's concrete side and looked down at the inky blackness. So, someone had come. Two generations past the time of the biggest fouled heist that no one knew had even happened. And yet, someone was here asking questions.

He looked out at the red and green lights marking the channel. He forced his eyes to squint until the red and green splintered into a thousand points of light. He reached into his pocket for a cigarette. The flame from the lighter flickered in the flow of air.

The man stared for another long moment at the river, then turned and walked slowly back across the bridge.

Almost a century had gone by when things had been better, richer, for their family from the Midwest. After the Depression and the war, everyone related to the congressman had fallen on hard times. It was if the Gillespie's from Arkansas were cursed. He was just the one to turn it all around for the family. For himself at least. He didn't know who was still living in the vast network of cousins and uncles and aunts; but he was. For once, things had gone his way and he was in an advantageous place at the right time.

He knew now that the boarded up house in Wollaston had belonged to the very senator with whom his great grandfather had planned the robbery. The probability of him finding the house, although he'd looked up and mapped out the general area, was mind-boggling. The gods were at last smiling on the obscure family from Arkansas.

Abrams, the charismatic senator with the golden tongue had convinced his great granddad to be part of the screwed up burglary. Abrams had been that one that started the Gillespie's slide into obscurity and poverty. Benny, short for Benedict, had found that first bit of information in an old Bible shoved into the bottom of a box with a thousand other bits and pieces, in a dilapidated warehouse near the Mississippi. In the box, scraps of paper, parts of notebooks with writing the ink so old that it had all but disappeared from the page. Those bits and pieces of information had intrigued him. And then the note inside the Bible, still in good shape, was a confession of sorts, dated 1936.

Congressman Gillespie had written a sketchy outline of the plan for the heist in the handwritten confession, that Abrams had made sure that a reporter from the Chicago Tribune had met with an 'accident'. The reporter had enough information to write an op-ed piece and that piece would have exposed all of them. After the murder of Jimmy White, Gillespie wanted out, and resigned from the Congress.

Chapter Thirty-six

No questions Eric had asked of her or answers he'd received, pointed to Kathleen as the thief and would-be killer. He was convinced 98%, if he could put a number on it, after all numbers were something he understood. Nothing Kathleen had said in the past 36 hours, hinted at her complicity in the least. He was beginning to feel comfortable about her again, to feel that she was an ally.

He knew that he was slipping into irrational paranoia. Maybe paranoia was justified in this case.

He and Kathleen had video chatted the past two nights sharing ideas and comparing notes.

"This is what I've deduced." Eric turned toward his whiteboard and began drawing color-coded lines. "You see this," he said as he used the end of his marker.

Eric drew a huge circle in the center of the whiteboard with radiating lines pushing out. Each line labeled: Boston, Connecticut, Pittsburgh, Philadelphia, New York, Rochester, and Richmond. Eric knew more now about what had gone on in September 1933. With the last of Jimmy's notebooks decoded and the information he'd gathered at the archives, he assumed, actually it was an educated guess, that the gold had been stashed in or around the Pittsburg Railyard. Because, of all the scenarios he's sounded out for himself, that was the only one that worked. So far, he'd kept that knowledge from Kathleen. Maybe one of her paralegals would come to the same conclusion. He'd tell her soon, though.

It had been during one of the dreamlike trances he had a tendency to slip into while he watched the evening news. Everything he'd heard from these psychotic machinations reached that conclusion. He'd watched the scene the evening of Jimmy's murder through Jimmy's eyes. He'd forced himself to detach from the scene so that he could gather information about where Jimmy had been. How had he 'tuned in' to conversations between others without Jimmy's presence was a mystery. What psychic phenomenon could explain that?

But a more substantial lead had been something Nealy had said to Abrams that Jimmy overheard at the Indianapolis rail hub. Then Jimmy, and now Eric, had filled in more details. Something that Jimmy had dismissed, but then revisited, something he'd written down, something that Nealy had said about a truck, a truck with a hidden compartment. Eric glanced again at the whiteboard and then looked at Kathleen. Stay on topic!

"According to the train historian, the status quo would have been for all the trains to leave from the Indianapolis hub, anything that came from Chicago. We've already ruled out Boston and Connecticut. We know what was left of the shipment did go to New York, and I'm really convinced that they would have made sure it didn't go to Richmond; too close to DC. And Rochester makes no sense, not as easily accessible. So, this is a total assumption based on facts; even if a truck had taken what was left of the shipment in Chicago, remember, the shipment had been weighed again by the federal marshals with the new doctored manifest before it even left for Indianapolis. Somehow, Nealy's men made sure the Feds had seen and recognized all the boxes tied down in that boxcar. Then they either put it on a different train or put it on a truck. So we know it didn't go to New York and it didn't go to Richmond. It didn't go to Boston, 100% sure of that, nor would it have gone to Connecticut. So what's left? You searched through maps from the early 1930's, right? So, what do you think; Pittsburgh or Philly?" He asked her this all though he knew it wasn't Philly. Inside his gut and even if he ignored this intuitive feeling, he knew it was Pittsburgh because of his damn dreams.

"But this has to be a fool's errand." Eric said, rubbing his hands over his face thinking backward, forward, and sideways about everything they'd come up with so far. "Suppose we do figure it out through a process of elimination or any facts we may find. I saw how big the rail hub was in Indianapolis. It is a mass of track and lights and noise and lots and lots of it obviously brand new. So we discover where it was stashed and we get there and the place was renovated after the Second World War, what then?"

"Very good point. Maybe somebody else lifted it from the crooks that put it there. Or it was buried under a mound of rubble when they demolished something to make way for something else. The variables are eeeennnnnddddlllleeeessss." Kathleen groaned. "Tell me again why we are doing this? I haven't had a good night's sleep since we went down in those tunnels. I probably picked up some horrible microbe of some sort, and it's making me very anxious."

"Kathleen, take my word for it, you did not pick up a microbe, it was all the excitement of perhaps seeing many millions of dollars' worth of gold coins and ingots reappear after 80 years. And… figure out who murdered Nealy and Jimmy and why." He stopped again, rubbing his hands over his face, and then looking fully into the webcam. He took a deep breath. Maybe he'd gone too far, but he said it anyway, the thing that was about to bust out of his brain.

"We need to know if Jimmy White was murdered for the same reason and by the same man, or ordered by the same man.

"I'll lay you odds Abrams hired some hit man to do it. And we may find the gold the Feds had no idea was even taken. And we need to know," said Eric. He snapped his fingers as he thought of another reason they were on the case. "First, we're going to figure out where they stashed the gold. Second, we're going to figure out who killed Nealy O'Brien, Jimmy White and why. Third, we just may give a news conference and spill the beans to the average citizen. An announcement like that would get people talking; we'll go viral." Eric wiggled his eyebrows into the web camera. "Gold taken from average citizens and then stolen by crooked politicians."

"We have the information about the gold. Whoever killed Jimmy is dead and in hell by now, don't you think? His death, who killed him, and the death of Nealy are a moot point. Think about it. Eric it's not important who killed whom. Not now, not in 2017, just knowing that they were murdered and why should be some closure. I know you think it's important, but even if we discovered who it was, we can't prosecute a dead man. I don't know how doing anything but assimilating the information we have and to somehow find a resolution. I just don't think who killed Jimmy is important, not in the bigger scheme of things. Don't you think we'd be better served if we figured out how all of this ties together, track down what we can, and then go on. See, in that way, the bi-product would be that we'd find out why Jimmy was murdered."

"But," Eric said, closing his eyes. *'The hell you say.'* But— Maybe she was right and finding out who killed Jimmy almost 80 years ago was a fool's errand. He struggled with that thought, that idea. If she was right could he stop obsessing on Jimmy's murder? Knowing who had done it was going to get him—them nowhere with this search. If he focused on the murder and not the thieves that defrauded the government so many years before, he'd be no better off. They had to follow the facts that they had. If they did, then maybe they would find Jimmy's killer, if they knew 'why', it would be easier to figure out 'who'. He pushed his hands through his hair in resignation. "Look," he said finally, staring at her hard. "I would just like to get this all resolved. You know his body was never found. If we find the gold can't we just as well see if we can find him too? I'd like to go back to work on Monday and not be the rube that makes a colossal foul up because I keep seeing that car run me, or Jimmy, down." Eric pushed his hand through his hair again and turned toward the window staring out at the cracked surface of the parking lot behind his apartment building.

"We'll figure it out. I know we will. Maybe you aren't supposed to have a boring life after all." And then Eric knew Kathleen had nothing to do with any of it, she was as puzzled as he was and just as blameless.

Eric laughed and then continued. "In Jimmy's notebooks I got from Albert III, a little spiral one was in the front pocket of the computer case and was with me the whole time. Whoever took my other notebooks missed this one.

"So, who do you think broke into your room?"

"I don't know," he said. "I entertained the idea that it might be you. But I have revised my thinking," he said quickly seeing the shock on her face. "Don't take offense, please. I've come to realize that one gets a bit paranoid after escaping being run over, which happened when I was leaving DC."

"What? Tell me what happened?" Kathleen's warm green gaze coming through cyber space registered nothing but concern. If she was the culprit, she had an academy award winning acting skills.

"When I returned from Indianapolis, I discovered that someone had been in the motel room. All my research, gone." he said as he made a raspberry. "Then, as I left the motel, I was half in, half out of the cab when someone in a Mazda hatchback tore around the corner and almost nailed me."

Kathleen breathed in sharply and her eyes widened. Eric knew that her surprise of the news was genuine.

"Well, I'm here to tell the tale, and no one has tried to do me in since I got back home."

"We're going to Pittsburgh. I'll set it up, and pick you up at RDU. I know a man who owns a private 6 place plane for hire; we'll fly there. I'll bring my two paralegals, and I'll make a reservation at the airport Ramada. Stay tuned for when and where."

"Hi, Janine, it's Kathleen O'Brien, how are you?"

"I'm great, so what's up calling me all the way from Chicago?"

"I need a U.S. attorney, but I need one just to throw ideas too; to pick your brain, so to speak. Are you game?"

Kathleen heard an almost imperceptible intake of breath on the other end of the phone. Silently, she counted to 10 before she spoke. "There's a man I know who started doing research on a reporter from the 30's. The reporter was doing a series of articles about F.D.R.'s executive order 6102, the one that ordered citizens to turn over any gold they had to the federal government. To make a long story short, it seems my very distantly related cousin Nealy, was working for a senator, and a congressman. Those three were out to do one thing; to steal gold that was in transit, from Chicago to New York.

"There were two manifests on one particular shipment. We found the real one and a fake." Janine did not make a comment; Kathleen could almost hear her wheels turning. "The fake was the one that has been in the National Archive's for the past eighty years. The real one, that I just found, shows that 22,000 pounds of gold never reached its final destination. The 22,000 pounds I think is stashed somewhere in the Midwest."

Her friend, Janine, the hard as nails US Attorney, still had not made a comment. Usually, US attorneys were never at a lose for words.

"So is there any precedent for the average citizen that might stumble on 22,000 pounds of gold stashed somewhere that had originally belonged to the government? And what would the government's stand be on a problem of this kind?" Silence, just silence, then Kathleen heard Janine take a huge breath.

"Huh?"

Chapter Thirty-seven

Albert White III scanned his grandfather's notes into his computer. He had some software that just might help him figure some things out. He plugged the scanned pages into an encryption program he'd found from a recommended government site, but to no avail. He diddled around and tried to decide how best to decipher the notes. If he could just get one letter to make up one word, then the rest would be easier to figure out. In some of the notebooks, the message was straightforward, a kind of transposition code that should be easy to decode. He worked through lunch, and then again through dinner, to the complete disgust and annoyance of his wife. At around 9:00 that evening the cypher began to coagulate, and thoughts of what his grandfather had written appeared slowly across the screen.

In the notebooks marked August–September 1933, the cypher changed and those notes were stretched across a graph like a fence rail:

> T . . . E . . . C . I . . . P . . S . . I. T. T.
> E . H . . I . H . E . D .. I. S . . . . G . . A .
> . . E .. S . . T. . . . N . . P. B. U. R.

From the information he found, the message was read up to down and sometimes across. But extra letters were thrown in obviously to exacerbate the message. He could read *The Ship ends* … Okay, but what is the shipment or is it an actual ship? He had no idea. Maybe it was time to read through Jimmy's newspaper articles to see what, if anything, the arrogant SOB was working on.

At 10 PM, Albert made himself a cup of coffee and ate a sandwich at the kitchen table. His chewing reverberated inside his head as his mind raced with the information he'd found. And what about Eric Douglass? Was he really a writer doing research for a book or had he somehow found out what Jimmy had discovered.

By midnight, Albert knew what Jimmy knew all those years ago, that three men had stolen millions of dollars in gold by diverting part of a shipment bound for the New York Federal Reserve and hid it in the Railyard in Pittsburg? Could that really be it? The whole idea was absurd.

Albert left the kitchen and returned to his office. He pulled up Wikipedia and typed in gold, 1933 in the search bar, settled back, and started reading.

Chapter Forty-one

Washington, DC
September 24, 1933
1:30 pm EDT

"Ah, gee, can't you put me through to him? Will he get a message? This is really important, lady. I just gotta speak to Mr. White."

"Now listen to me, young man. I've already told you that Mr. White is not here, he is on assignment. Now, as I've said before, I will give him the message as soon as he comes in. You'll have to accept that for what it is. I will tell him, I have your number, now that's all I can do."

"Aw, all right, I guess if he's not there, he's not there. Thanks lady."

Joey hung up the phone and let out a breath and felt the bottom fall out of his stomach. He'd heard the group of men grousing and belly aching about Jimmy. Surely, they wouldn't do anything, would they? Not really.

1:45 pm the Chicago Tribune
The News Desk

"Oh, Mr. Carlson, have you seen Jimmy White?" Mrs. Rogers, the switchboard operator stuck her head around the corner to hale the editor. Mr. Carlson did not look up; he waved his hand behind him in the direction of the operator and waved with the other hand toward the elevator signaling it to stop.

"Later," he gesticulated and stepped onto the elevator just as the doors closed.

"Oh, well, I suppose that young man from Washington, DC will have to get through to Mr. White tomorrow."

Chapter Forty-two

Raleigh Durham International Airport
Durham, NC
Present Day

The setting sun threw fingers of pink and white across the blue sky, slowly changing to black as Eric arrived at the airport to meet Kathleen. The area was west of the RDU international airport with its many terminals. Eric pulled the Toyota into a spot at the edge of the small lot near the hangar.

The doors stood completely opened, revealing the two small planes anchored inside near the open mouth of the hangar.

A larger plane, a Cessna Caravan, was anchored by a cleat and wheel blocks. The plane was a six-place turbo prop. The pilot was doing a 'walk around' as Eric walked up to Kathleen and the plane.

"You have so many people in all kinds of places doing your bidding. It reminds me of Sherlock Holmes and the Baker Street Irregulars; all those little urchins doing Holmes's bidding. I don't suppose any of your paralegals wear rags and have dirty fingernails, do they?

Kathleen laughed as she pulled him up the small ladder inside the plane. At the front of the cabin, a man and a woman sat together looking over some documents. The man saw Kathleen and stood.

"Hi, Ms. O'Brien. The pilot says we'll get there late, 10:30 or so. Jim is going to pick us up and take us to the Airport Ramada. We have rooms for what's left of the night, and then he'll drive us to the train area the next morning. The problem is there is a large amount of territory in this one area. We're going over the old maps and we have maybe three different areas that are still used as trestles and abutments. That's all, in the whole Railyard, just about three."

Kathleen looked at Eric. "Maybe that's a good thing. Everyone, this is our intrepid 'gum shoe', Eric Douglass." Eric nodded his head to the chorus of hellos. "Great, have you heard from Janine Reynold's?"

"Yes ma'am, she said, she'll meet you in the lobby of the Ramada at 5 am."

"God, she always was a glutton for punishment. I guess we'd better get to Pittsburgh and try to get some rest before all hell breaks loose tomorrow morning."

"Well, the breaking news is, the FBI has sent out their local people. I heard it from my contact. He told me the agency thinks we're nuts and they hold no view that we have found anything, nor will we find anything with any credence. Everyone is getting to the site, the area we narrowed in our search down near the river at around 6 am. I know the FBI has already talked to the administrative folks at the Railyard. They think we're nuts, too."

"We have to stay out of their way, and then we won't cause too much heartburn for them," said Kathleen.

"It's a VERY busy place," added the paralegal, holding up a schematic chart for the Railyard of the Bessemer line as well as the CSX rails. Drawn on the page were lines intersecting each other making the page resemble a complex spider's web. "We'll be lucky if we can hear ourselves think, let alone communicate. There are so many trains coming in and out being loaded and off loaded, the place is controlled mayhem.

"Spoke to the Railyard officer myself. He'll have one of his folks take us to the three different areas. Here's the thing, Ms. O'Brien," and he looked hard at Eric before he turned again to Kathleen. "We don't know exactly what we're looking for, just an educated guess that gold was stolen in transit in 1933. We're not sure how to find it. We're just up against a whole raft of unknowns. No wonder the FBI thinks we're nuts." "Yeah, I know," said Kathleen as she squeezed his shoulder. "We'll get

there and see the lay of the land. We'll know tomorrow what we can and can't do. The two of you have done a wonderful job.
Talk to you in a bit," she said as she sat down.

"Ms. O'Brien? We're ready for takeoff," the pilot said.

"Okay, let's get going." "Yeah, I know," said Kathleen as she squeezed his shoulder. "We'll get there and see the lay of the land. We'll know tomorrow what we can and can't do. The two of you have done a wonderful job.
Talk to you in a bit," she said as she sat down.

"Ms. O'Brien? We're ready for takeoff," the pilot said.

"Okay, let's get going."

Chapter forty-three

The plane banked passing through a clutch of clouds revealing the black edge of the oncoming night. The setting sun glowed on the wings of the plane and reflected mightily back in through the window. Eric pulled the window shade down and rubbed his eyes. He looked around the small cabin of the plane, taking in the alien surroundings. He was a fish out of water with this legal brain trust. Kathleen and her two paralegals were poring over documents an inch thick while they animatedly discussed what would be a very interesting day to come. Kathleen answered her cell and spoke animatedly before giving instructions again to her 'minions.' He stared at the scene for a few minutes ruminating about the merry-go-round he'd accidentally stepped on almost five weeks ago. All his attempts to climb off the damned thing had accomplished nothing but encouraging the damn thing to go faster. He was a 'stranger in a strange land', and no matter how many times he had attempted to regain his old and comfortable life, the exercise had been futile. Maybe he'd be stuck in overdrive forever. The trouble with that particular scenario was that he wasn't sure if he really wanted to make it off that merrygo-round. His mind was layered in a fog and only pinpoints of light could escape to keep him from tumbling through that abyss.

"Eric." Suddenly, Kathleen stood near him successfully holding back that fog. Her face lit up, every thought parading across it. "Here's what's happening; the FBI is coming to the Railyard; I have retained my old friend Janine Reynolds as our legal go between. I've already told her about the manifest we found in the tunnels, and I gave her most of the story you started out with when you came to the house that first time. She doesn't think we have to tell anyone why we had a hunch about Jimmy's murder, and as I said, I've only told her the first part, about your research, and look," she said as she sat down and gave him a fierce hug for just a moment. He hugged her back, pressing down that beautiful blonde head.

"After we try to get the gold heist resolved, I think we should sit down and really hammer out all the information we have about the two murders; just like we did with the gold. The more we talk, the more I think you'll be able to put it into perspective and perhaps that will be all you need to get your derailed life back on track. We can always go visit the hypnotist in Carrboro. I'm sure she'll have some trick to get this ironed out." Just one side of her mouth quirked up in a smile and he knew she was being a little sarcastic. He'd learned a lot about her, just watching and being attentive, so he nodded, and smiled and pulled her hand up and kissed the palm, lingering a moment breathing in her scent and feeling her hand tremble a little.

"And here," she said as she reached into her bag. "I had Juan buy two 'burn phones'. These are untraceable. If we have to call someone while we are rooting around a train yard, and don't want them to know who we are, we use these." She shrugged her shoulders a little. "It's just a precaution."

He nodded and put away the phone. "Yep, that makes sense. Must stay incognito," he said. He smiled at her. He'd figure out how to put his 'murder' into perspective.

"I'm glad it happened, otherwise I'd never have known you."

Kathleen stared at him hard. She was glad too. Her life had been as static as Eric's had, and despite all of the trials they'd gone through and would go through, they'd found each other and that was worth… well she'd think about that later.

Chapter Forty-four

Albert White III deplaned in Pittsburgh during the early afternoon. He carried a briefcase and a hang up bag, stood on the sidewalk outside of the terminal making a 360° turn. The automatic doors behind him whooshed open and closed regurgitating passengers getting into cars and making for the taxi stand. He had to get to the train station, not the passenger station, but the many trains and trestles at the industrial area. First, he'd check in at the Airport Ramada Inn. He'd decide the best place to look after he had made a few phone calls and poured over the maps he'd printed off the internet.

He stood a moment longer and then grabbed a cab to put his plan into motion.

Benedict Gillespie stood outside the Amtrak station in Pittsburgh looking, and smelling, like the homeless person he was. But he liked it that way. No one bothered a homeless person; maybe they thought they'd catch it. He smiled to himself; he had no illusions that his life would change from what he found or didn't find, or whom he found or didn't find, at the Pittsburgh Railyard.

He was going, maybe just to lay the ghost of his great grandfather, Congressman Gillespie, the man that had so screwed up the family who had never recovered either their good standing, or even a small part of their fortune. The thought crossed Benedict's mind that he was blaming his failure at life on a man that had been dead a quarter century before he was even born; then he buried that thought. He quashed it and focused again on the ruination of the Gillespie family. He knew the old man had been a pathetic 'nervous nelly'. Attempting, but then not following through on schemes that would have made him and ultimately, the family rich for generations to come. His morality always got in the way. Benedict had never been one to stand on the possibility of moral or immoral behavior. He did what he had to do to survive, and if someone was hurt… or killed, that possibility made no difference to him one way or another.

Chapter Forty-five

10:45 pm
Pittsburgh
Ramada Airport Hotel

Kathleen lay on the bed and used the remote to flip through 101 channels that had nothing worth watching. She was bored out of her gourd, wishing something would just *happen!* She had to wind down, that was, just wind down. She kept the volume on the TV very low while Eric slept in the other bed; he looked exhausted. Her eye drew back to the inane infomercial, as she mulled over their 'project'. Maybe the gold was still in the railyard. If that happened, then they could leave this place, and she could shore up the dwindling O'Brien fortunes. If she took that thought, of recouping some of the family's wealth, just a little further, who was she going to leave it too? That was just too depressing to think about.

Suddenly, Eric shot up in the bed. His eyes darted around the room, trying to reconcile where he was. He saw Kathleen and took another big breath, breaking into a smile.

"Hey," he said.

"Hey yourself. You okay?"

"Yeah," he said and threw the covers back. He stood quickly and made for the bathroom. Seconds later Kathleen heard the water running. After a few minutes, Eric returned, his hair damp and his T-shirt wet around the collar and upper torso. He was so well built for a guy that worked in a lab and herded mice. Eric sat on the bed and glanced at the TV.

"What's on?"

"Infomercials, Gawd spare me." Kathleen held up the remote and, with a flourish, turned off the set. "So, you want to talk about it?"

"Same–old, same-old. Nothing changes – no, that's not true. Many times, I get new information, not this time though. I will admit the severity of the fear and anxiety has lessened. I assume this will all run its course at some point. I think you're right about one thing, the more we talk about it, the less the anxiety plagues me. I really believe this whole escapade started because, well, maybe that's just too inane, thinking Jimmy was reaching across the great abyss calling to me. It's like slowing down the speed of a horror movie, and seeing frame-by-frame what was so terrifying, and then it's not so scary seeing it again."

"Yeah. Inch by inch… The events of tomorrow will surely have a big impact on your nightmares."

"So, what if we don't find anything?"

"I'm prepared for that. It's been 80 years, anything, anything could have happened, the most obvious being that the gold never got there in the first place. It was in Chicago, we know that. We know the shipment went through, anyway you know the drill. Let's get some sleep. We have to meet our counselor at 5 am. Groan." Kathleen stood and gave Eric a kiss on the cheek. For a moment, she touched his face gently and looked into his eyes. His arms encircled her waist, bringing her close. "We'll figure it out, I know we will. See you in the morning," Kathleen said.

Eric stood and wrapped Kathleen in a bear hug, and a grin spread across his face. "Are you kidding me? Sleep when I am about to put an end to all this mess of the past five plus weeks. Hell, I'll sleep when I'm dead. I'm going to go over to the railyard. I've had my little 'combat nap.' If you're too tired, stay here. I'll be back in a few hours."

"What? You think you're going over there without me? Not a chance, boy-o. Just wait," she said. She popped off the bed and scrambled to put on a pair of hiking boots. "Wait, we don't have a car."

"Uh, yes, we do. Sorry I didn't tell you. I rented a car in Chapel Hill before I left, and the keys should be at the desk waiting for me. So how about it? Are you game?"

"Are you kidding, I am wide awake. Let's go."

Albert White zipped up his windbreaker, pulling the collar high up and around his ears. He'd left his room at the Ramada at midnight, driving in his rental through rain-splashed streets. He'd tried consulting the GPS on his phone, pushing on buttons, swiping back and forth, even using voice recognition. But nothing he did resulted in the maps of the city he needed to locate the Bessemer and CSX Railroad located somewhere in the midst of the gigantic railyard. He pulled the rental into an all-night convenience/gas station and hurried into the store.

The convenience store's harsh florescent lighting at the back flashed rhythmically: on, off, dim, bright, on, off, dim… it was enough to make him seasick. The partially stocked, dirty shelves were revolting, and Albert decided that eating food from a place like this could give one ptomaine. He sidestepped the debris in the aisle, concentrating on making it to the clerk, a young black kid, sloppily dressed and wearing a dirty ball cap, slanted sideways across his plentiful dreads. He wore ear buds, but, nevertheless, hip hop poured through them and into the store.

"Yes, uh, do you have a city map?"

"Huh," the young man said, as he slipped one ear bud out. "Whadya say?"

"Do you have a city map?"

"Map? Man, nobody uses no map, no more. Where you wanna go?"

Albert let out a disgusted breath. It wasn't the kid's fault everyone had a smart phone …and knew how to use the damn thing. "I need to get to the railyard. Not Amtrak, the other one, where all the containers get shipped out."

"Oh, I gotcha. Now, just go out the parking lot, turn left and keep going down that road. Then when you get to the light, you go…" the boy paused and started counting on his fingers. "Oh, yeah, you go to the fifth light and then turn right. After a while, you'll begin to see the trestles and trains and stuff. Just keep going. There is an entrance and to get in you gotta tell them why you're there. See?"

"Uh, yeah. Gee, thanks."

Albert left the convenience store looking up the street, scanning the area before getting into his car. He rehearsed the trip in his mind the way the man had explained it and was confident he could make it with little trouble.

12:45 am
Near the CSX Pittsburgh Railyard

As Eric said, the keys to a rental car were at the desk and the car itself was conveniently waiting under the awning of the motel. Eric had memorized the route to the CSX line and railyard. They traveled down Interstate 376, going southeast in the rainy dark. As a backup, Kathleen had a city map lying in her lap that they'd downloaded and printed, along with the document from her paralegals that she'd scanned with the help of a very un-Kathleen-like 'blingy' lavender flashlight on the end of her key chain. There were several hours before dawn, the weather was miserable, and the road was heavily traveled. They crossed the Monongahela River over the Fort Pitt Bridge and entered the industrial part of the city. The city's streets were laid out in grids, with elevated tracks, huge water tanks, and other large containers hovering over the streets and endless warehouses.

Eric worked through the steps in his mind; find the three areas of possibility and see if anything was evident, and make sure the FBI wasn't already there.

They drove on, saying nothing, looking out at the wet, drab streets. Rooster tails of water from the downpour flowed from the rear of the car.

"There is so much rain."

Out of the corner of his eye, Eric saw a flash of white on the street corner. He took his foot off the accelerator, applied the brake and turned his head to look at the street corner where... had he seen?

"Jeez"

"Eric, what's wrong?"

Eric looked straight out the windshield and applied his foot to the accelerator. "Nothing, nothing." No, he had not seen the ghost of Nealy O'Brien; that spirit would have to be conspicuously absent. Within a split second, he again turned all his attention to Kathleen. "So, what are you going to tell your US attorney friend?"

"Shit, I forgot momentarily about that damn 5 am meeting. Well, just momentarily. If we aren't back, I'll call her. She will be put out, but good that we didn't wait for her; I've known her since law school. She is determined to keep the two of us out of federal jails, I'm glad to say. But we'll be back, no worries."

"No worries, and 'mums the word'. We can go and check out the areas before the morning. I'm sure the place will be lit up from top to bottom. Railyards, airports, and train and bus stations... they never turn off their lights, but we'll bring the big flashlights; there are bound to be lots of shadowed areas."

They traveled the next few miles in rainy silence. Soon, they saw the marks on the industrial side of Pittsburgh; elevated tracks that stacked up like terraced vineyards, huge, corrugated buildings, dump trucks, cargo containers, cranes and rusted trestles and train bridges. The place was massive. Illumination from hundreds of lights rose up like soldiers at a parade rest, brightening the black, rain drenched night. On one side of the highway, the beginnings of the Pittsburgh skyline rose up past the river, and the railyard opened like a deep gash butted up against the river. They stopped to get their bearings.

Eric was very glad that the 'Baker Street Irregulars' had accomplished so much in narrowing down the areas that needed to be searched.

"Okay, let's go east about a half mile from here," he said, pointing past what seemed to be a fleet of dump trucks. The street crossed about a half dozen tracks, spread out like the fingers of an opened hand.

They moved slowly, aware that there was no real entrance, or guardhouse or anything like that, just open tracks and trestles, garages, workshops, offices and other outbuildings. The closer to the center they traveled, the more it became evident that the area contained sheds, offices, buildings, and elevated areas where operators could direct trains on the tracks and the equipment that was loaded and unloaded.

Kathleen's paralegals had pinpointed three areas of primary interest. Their assessments were based on when the buildings and tracks were built and how frequently the areas were used over the past eighty years. Not only was it a monstrous task, but at any moment some official-looking guard could escort them from the premises telling them not to come back until the Feds got there. Eric pulled over to the right and stopped the car, killing the lights.

"Here, let me look at the map."

He scanned the map, looking up often for recognizable landmarks.

"Look, if we drive down to the right, we're going away from the river, we head for the center of the yard. I just need to find something that looks like a road. This place is a helluva lot bigger than I thought it was, way bigger. I'm going to keep the lights off. I think there's enough ambient light to help us navigate. Please look dead ahead and warn me if I'm about to run into something." He patted her hand and gave her a quick peck on the cheek.

They drove along in silence, seeing the signs posted at intervals: "No unauthorized entry, you must have a permit to enter this area." After 9-11, American companies took the possibility of terrorism seriously. A huge railyard that connected many, many railroads around the eastern half of the country could be a vulnerable target.

Albert drove slowly down the rain-slicked streets, staring into the darkness, trying to find the beginning of the giant railyard complex. He knew the river was going to be on his left, and he knew approximately where the area was that he needed to search. But the place seemed to go on forever. He knew that this yard could process more than 150 engines an hour; loading and unloading; the place was massive, larger even than the Chicago Port of Entry on Lake Michigan.

It had taken him hours to decipher his grandfather's writings. Perhaps he had some of his grandfather's purported savvy, because it came to him in a flash what the old man had been trying to communicate. It was all about how Jimmy White had found out this most vital piece of information, a mystery no one even knew about. His grandfather had had a finger in every pie, and an ear around every corner, from the late 1920s until his death in 1933.

Jimmy had heard something, a piece of news about a location and about something valuable that had been stolen by a congressman and a senator. It all had to do with the confiscation of gold by the Federal Government in September of 1933. The loot was then hidden, taken off a train or maybe put on a truck, and then the only logical place it could be was Pittsburgh. Albert could only surmise that the loot, if he could find it, would make him very rich.

He patted his front coat pocket. The small .22 caliber handgun he'd bought that afternoon after reaching Pittsburgh, bulged comfortingly against his shirt. He'd found a pawn shop in the industrial area on the outskirts of what folks would call a 'nice area' of town. The proprietor hadn't wanted to sell it to him. There were papers that needed filling out, fees to be paid, and on and on. Finally, Albert had pushed a $100 bill across the counter and promised the man that he would fill out and mail the documents himself. The information did not appease the man, but the Ben Franklin did.

"If you are buying the gun to protect yourself, the .22 won't be a lot of help, not unless you're a dead-eye-dick," the man had said.

"Oh, yeah, I sure am," Albert had said. He'd earned a merit badge for proficiency with air rifle in the Boy Scouts, but he hadn't touched a weapon of any kind in the past 50 years. Still, this man didn't need to know how good he was with a handgun – or wasn't. He did understand that a .22 could be inconsequential against someone bent on hurting him, unless, like the man said, he was "a deadeye-dick." But the thought of using a *real* gun that could put a real *hole* in another person made him a bit queasy.

Chapter Forty-six

Benedict Gillespie moved rapidly across the massive tracks. He knew the river was on his left, so he was headed to the center of the yard.

At an outbuilding near the huge office complex, he stopped to get his bearings. He took a 360-degree turn, looking quickly, cataloging everything into neat compartments in his mind. No, he was still in the newer section of the yard. He had to move further into the center and then analyze the trestles and abutments he saw. He took out a cigarette, and glancing around to make sure he was unobserved, lit it. As he took the first drag, his eyes never settled on one thing, but looked, assessed, and then moved on. He pulled the papers, the ancient fragile papers and map from the inside pocket of his coat. Through a haze of cigarette smoke, he tried to figure out where he was. He was headed to the older part of the area and he had to make sure that no one was looking at him… or for him.

His route was slow and methodical. He traveled as far as one of the Bessemer Rail's buildings, a windowless edifice made of concrete blocks. The door was shut and probably locked; he didn't need to get inside anyway. He leaned against the corner of the building, looking again at the map. The string of letters and numbers across the top of the second page had confused him from the start. The string had no spaces, just letters and numbers. He looked at the area over the door where a line of numbers and letters was stenciled above the doorjamb. Could this be it, the letters and numbers designating a building? Damn, it did look like a code, but maybe it was something far simpler than that. Perhaps the ingenuity was in the simplicity of the thing. Alpha 712739.

"No, idiot!" he screamed at himself. It had to be like letters and numbers similar to designations on a ship; each bulkhead, passage, ladder, every place a sailor could pass through, was acknowledged by specific letters and numbers.

Benedict hurried to the next building; again, a string of letters and numbers were stenciled above the door. He hurried to the next building to confirm his findings. *Yes, that's it!*

Benedict moved toward the center, always keeping the river on his left, looking for buildings with a stenciled 'A' above the door, being careful not to pass any in his haste. An hour passed, and then another as he made his way to the older buildings. His coat was soaked through, and his greasy hair, stuffed under a hoodie, hung in clumps over his forehead. But he couldn't care less how he looked, he had to find the building.

He worked his way past buildings made of corrugated steel, hangar-like garages with trucks equipped with cherry picker extensions and smaller pickups left at the railyard for the night. Looking up, he saw a two-story trestle. A train, engine, boxcars and passenger cars sat on the track above him; darkened, still, and looking like it had been there forever, just waiting.

Everything around him was massive and frightening. He braced himself against the corner of one of the buildings and breathed deeply. He reached for another soggy cigarette. It took some time to light it only after he'd found an overhang, a tiny shelter of the building. He wished he had a drink, that would calm him, but he didn't, so he decided to press on. For the sake of his family name, he'd press on. He knew he was a little obsessed; a little, okay, a lot, but by damn, he'd get this figured out. He'd get the gold and then he'd be in control. They would all squirm.

He knew now… he knew the location. If the building was still here, he'd find it.

Chapter Forty-seven

Ralph Gunderson had spent the day looking through his grandfather's cluttered closets, the attic, and then the sheds; there were two in the yard. Soon, Ralph had gone to the nearest convenience store to buy leather gloves because ho knew what kinds of spiders and other unsavory critters had taken up residence in the old out-buildings? Better safe than sorry.

It had been well into the afternoon when he'd looked up and seen several boxes perched on the cross-trees of one of the sheds. He'd managed to get them down and started to go through them. The first three boxes were filled with pieces of old tools, rags and letters that were so old and had been exposed to the elements for so long, that the paper had reverted back to pulp. Ralph had shuffled through the debris, separating the trash. At one point, his grandfather had ventured out to the sheds only to put the garbage in the trash bags back into the boxes.

"No, you can't..."

Ralph turned to see his grandfather staring at him, anxious, overwhelmed, and with his hands trembling.

"Grandpa, we've got to get this sorted." Ralph put his arm around his grandfather's shoulder. "We have to go through it and find whatever is important and ditch the rest."

Grandpa stood still for a moment, but then his eyes lit up. He stood up straight and snapped his fingers. "I know! Weren't you looking for that man's articles? You know that fella from the Tribune?" "Yes, and I..."

"No, wait, I know, I mean I remember. I found a whole box of that stuff. That fella from Miss O'Brien's came over and I showed it to him. But then, where... Okay, yeah, now I remember, I put it in my closet. Maybe you can make something of it, but I sure can't. Come on."

Ralph took off the gloves and threw them into the garbage bag before following his grandfather into the house.

At the bottom of the small, musty closet were two ancient cardboard boxes. Ralph hesitated to put his hands inside, but reached down and opened the flap of the box. It was sagging and wet-stained and only partially filled. Several newspapers lay inside, along with old spiral notebooks, their metal spirals now rusted; the paper disintegrated as he picked up a notebook.

"That young fella from Ms. Kathleen's found these in the back shed. I didn't know they was there. Then he brought them in here and I ain't looked at 'em. Forgot they was here."

"It's okay, grandpa. Why don't you put the coffee on and I'll meet you in the kitchen while I get this sorted?"

An hour later, Ralph had some answers, answers he'd found in the soggy and faded bits from the two boxes. He'd copied everything he figured worth copying and left the whole mildewed mess in his grandfather's closet, before moving to the kitchen.

"Hey, Ralph, I didn't know you was here."

Ralph shook his head. Noting that the old man had not made coffee, he pulled open the refrigerator to grab a soda. No soda, so instead Ralph pulled out the terrarium where the old man kept his pet turtles. Ralph looked at the cold, hopefully not dead, little box turtles. He took the terrarium to the screen porch and put the turtles in the sun. Maybe they'd survive, but the turtles were the least of his worries.

He'd have to go through all of these notes and bits of paper at least once more. Maybe, just maybe, something would click.

Ralph used his forearm to clear the kitchen table, setting down the notebooks and scraps of paper. It struck him that whoever had written the notes, had done so in such a hodge-podge manner that, to figure out what the messages were, they would also have used the files that Eric Douglass had accessed at the archives. Ralph continued working; reading, taking notes, trying to decipher what had been so important in September of 1933. After several hours of myopic study, he leaned back in the chair and rubbed his hands over his face. He'd go tonight to Pittsburgh, and lay odds that Douglass and the O'Brien woman were already there, looking and profiting, while he was stuck here with his senile old grandfather.

Ralph moved into the den of the house. It was a dreary little room with curtains so infused with dust that little clouds puffed out when he touched them. They'd soon disintegrate, like everything else in this God forsaken keepsake from a mobster. He looked around, noting that he felt more disgusted with himself than with his grandfather. There was no one left in the family, so wasn't the old man his responsibility? After… after he came back, he'd see about putting the old guy in a home and closing up the house.

He remembered that it had always been in the bottom right drawer of the desk. Gingerly, he grasped the handle and pulled. Damn, the drawer was stuck firm. He pulled, tugged, hit the thing with his hip, jostled it up and down, until at last with an ear-deafening screech, the drawer opened crookedly from the top, exposing an inch or so of the interior. He put his eye to it and saw the butt of the Colt 45. Crap! Ralph went to the garage and grabbed the biggest claw hammer he could find. He drove the claw into the top of the drawer and pried until he'd exposed a gap large enough to see the items inside. He raised the hammer above his head and hammered at the drawer until the face came off in two pieces.

He grabbed the Colt; it had probably not been oiled or cleaned in the last millennium. The rust showed in the barrel at the end of the hammer and on the cylinder and that was frozen in place with rust. *Well, fuck me!* He closed his eyes, trying to decide what to do. He'd clean up the outside of the revolver and get it shiny enough so that if he had to aim it at someone, they'd think it would fire.

With or without the revolver, he'd go to Pittsburgh, to the railyard and just maybe get to the goods before 'they' did. And then… Then, he thought as his gaze encompassed the cluttered dilapidated den, then he'd have to come back here and see about his grandfather.

Chapter Forty-eight

The rain dripped from his forehead into his eyes. He dashed it away again and again, convinced that his promise to himself to never wear a ball cap because it was just too 'demode', had been one of his dumber ideas. He stooped behind a wall near an older part of the yard that offered some protection. Seconds of abject, soggy misery passed by. He tried to decide where he was, reconciling with the area on his map. He moved again, a few hundred feet away, stumbling, but righting himself and ducking behind another corrugated steel wall. He saw someone, just an impression of lighter gray against the black. He couldn't identify who, but it was a man, and the man moved further away from him and into the blackness.

"Your paralegals found three areas, and I'm sure this is one of them, the largest to comb through."

Surely, that was Douglass speaking; he'd know that southern accent anywhere.

"I understand," answered a young female voice. "But what are the coordinates from here to the next possible area?"

He didn't recognize the voice. Did Douglass have an ally, someone he'd found in Chicago, and who was she? Albert eased around the edge of the wall. The rain sheeted down in front of his eyes so effectively, he could see absolutely nothing.

He pulled back under the overhang, dashed the wetness from his face, and then grabbed his binoculars, turning his upper body, trying to catch a glimpse of the two. He saw instead a tall shadow, skirting around the perimeter of light cast by the lamps affixed to the corners of the corrugated building. Who was that? How many people knew about the gold, and how did they all manage to get here on the same night?

He looked back at the woman and Douglass who were stumbling around like two drunks. They knew less than he did. He trained his binoculars again on the figure across the boundary of light cast by the lamps. It was a man... tall... lanky, dressed in a blue windbreaker and a ball cap.

The man had binoculars and he'd trained them on the woman and Douglass. Albert could see the glint of reflected light against the glass in the eyepieces. He pulled his binoculars down, afraid that the man would spot him. What was he doing? The man took out something that looked like a smart phone and clicked on it a few times. He looked for a long moment at the screen before putting the device away. Again, the man looked at the two, while leaning against the side of the building. He was leaning, relaxed, waiting.

Douglass and the woman were using a flashlight and searching through a document that could be a map. He caught a look at it through his binoculars, seeing that the margins were filled with notes and figures. Douglass rattled a rusted door under the closest trestle and gave up after a minute. The two consulted the document once again and then looked up at the other massive structures around them and moved away from Albert past the illuminations cast by intermittent yard lights.

Albert watched as the man, almost nonchalantly, followed Douglass and the girl.

He glanced down at Jimmy's notes, a carefully compiled list of items, but there were no diagrams, no maps, just words, translated from an old overused cypher. He heard gravel crunch behind him. Someone was coming and he shrank down as small as he could. A rock knocked by a shoe skittered past him.

The man – he was sure it was a man now – passed within feet of him. His shadow grew dimmer until it faded away completely. There were two men following Douglass. Maybe everyone knew more than he did, but he had his grandfather's notes. That had to count for something.

Chapter Forty-nine

Eric heard the quick snap of gravel from a shoe and turned quickly, grasping the flashlight, aiming it over the path. He held his hand out to Kathleen, staying her movement.

"What is it? What's the matter?"

"Someone's following us."

Kathleen moved to his side as he trained the little LED beam of her flashlight over the path.

The rain sheeted down, puddling in the indentations left by shoe prints. Then they moved away from them toward one of the dump truck garages.

"See here," he said. "I'm no Daniel Boone, but I'll bet there's a big man and a smaller one, see." he said as he pointed to the prints.

Kathleen stooped down to get a better view. *Crap, two men, but why?* She stood again, dashing the rain from her face, and stared into the darkness.

"This is insane. Even if we find the gold, we can't just pick it up and take it with us. It's raining so hard I can't see anything. Look, let's get back in the car and go get a cup of coffee and wait for the sun to come up."

"Kathleen, when the sun comes up, this place is going to be crawling with Feds. Look," he said as he dashed a hand across his face. "Let's get back in the car and dry off a little, re-group, you know, so we won't walk around in wet circles. I don't want to leave until we have to go see the US attorney. If there is someone following us, then she and our FBI friends need to know about it and figure out how they are going to deal with it."

"So you say, but how could anyone know?"

"Let's go back to the car and we'll talk out of the rain."

They turned around and began walking, using the footprints they'd just discovered to minimize wet feet. The car was parked, not nearby, but adjacent to the first trestle they'd searched. They walked in silence, their heads down, making sure of their footing, hearing the far-off noise of the busy railyard and the rain hitting buildings, trucks and them.

"Eric!" Kathleen shrieked. "Help!"

Eric jerked around and his heart almost stopped when he saw a man holding Kathleen, his forearm held tight around her throat and squeezing so hard that her feet swung free of the road. Eric trained the beam of his flashlight into the man's eyes. "Put her down!" Kathleen wheezed and gasped for air

The man's eyes squinted against the light while his forearm perceptively tightened around Kathleen's throat. "Put the light down mister, or I'll snap her neck."

Slowly, Eric lowered the flashlight to the ground. "Let her go." A lump of ice had lodged in his throat. Nothing was worth Kathleen losing her life. Nothing.

"Sure, mister, I'll let her go. Just show me the way to the gold." The man's arm loosened, enough for Kathleen to pull in a great gulp of air and hack and cough.

"Now, where is it?"

Eric gave a laugh. "Hey buddy, do you think we're half frozen and soaked to the skin because we know where it is? Come on! We don't even know if it's real." Man, he could bullshit with the best. "So, who are you anyway?"

"Just never mind who I am. Now, what have you got there?" The man's elbow pointed to the documents Eric held.

"Just some ideas, just some educated guesses. We don't know any more than you do. You can have them, just let her go." Eric held out the pages. The man grabbed them with his free hand as he pushed Kathleen violently away. With his right hand, he pulled a small handgun from his front pocket. Kathleen stumbled into Eric's arms, leaning into him and struggling for air.

"Okay, mister, you've got what you want, so get lost, go find Eldorado." Eric walked slowly away backward, keeping Kathleen clasped tightly to him while he watched the man. Eric was pissed, but the guy could pull the trigger and no one would hear, not now, not in this place. He had to think fast and out-think this lunatic. The man looked down at the pages and then jerked his gaze up to Eric. For a minute, the man looked like he was undecided. Then he made a jerking motion with his head, waving the gun, signaling them to leave. Eric stared for a heartbeat, and then another. Grasping Kathleen tightly, he walked, never taking his eyes from the man. Then he turned and jogged away clutching Kathleen against him until they reached the perimeter, the limit of the well-lit paths cast by the lights. Eric took another quick glance before he made a sharp right and moved quickly for a dozen yards. He pulled Kathleen down next to him and crouched behind the wall of a garage. He saw a side door that was ajar. He put his shoulder to it, shoving until it opened enough for them to squeeze through.

The garage smelled of diesel fuel, oil and garbage. They stood quietly, not moving for a minute, hearing their own breathing and the sound of the rain pounding on the corrugated roof. Eric pointed toward the back and they moved in single file until they stooped behind a dump truck between them and the door. They crouched down, leaning against the huge tire, their butts on the concrete floor.

Five minutes passed, then ten. The man hadn't followed them. Whoever the crazy man was, he'd let them go.

Eric nudged Kathleen. "You okay?" he whispered. She trembled so intensely, he could feel it through his parka. He held her tightly to him, trying to ease her shivering.

She nodded, afraid to speak. Her larynx felt mangled. If she cleared her throat to get past the mess, she'd make a lot of noise. She tried to mumble, but nothing came out. She tried again and croaked.

"Who the hell was that?"

"I don't know. That was the most terrified I've ever been. When I saw your feet dangling off the ground…" he shivered.

She could barely speak, croaking and sputtering, but Eric understood every word. He held on to Kathleen's arm as they made their way to the door. No one was in sight as they squeezed through the opening.

They sprinted through the rain toward the car, turned to the right moving toward the river and the first trestle they'd searched. They were almost there; the outline of the car was a blob against the night sky. Kathleen pitched forward and cried out. Eric grabbed for her, holding her solidly in his arms.

"What?" she croaked. "What did I trip on?"

They looked down. The prone body of a man lay sprawled on the road, a gash from his head bleeding sluggishly in the cold rain.

"Looks like you tripped over a body."

Chapter Fifty

Eric called 911 on the 'burn phone' as Kathleen fished a handkerchief from her jacket pocket. She gingerly raised the man's head to press the handkerchief on his wound. He groaned.

"I need to stop the bleeding." The man groaned again and his eyes fluttered open.

"Who are you?" His speech was slurred and stilted.

"He needs an ambulance," Kathleen said.

"Working on it. Hello, I'm at the railyard, near the Bessemer Line. My friend and I just found an injured man. Looks like he's been knocked out… yes, head injury. My location… well, let's see. I'm at the one, two, three… okay, I'm at the fourth trestle from the opening on the west side, oh and the number above the trestle is A 45-768. That's the best I can tell you." Kathleen pulled on his pant leg pointing to the letters on the man's ball cap. "The man has an FBI ball cap and windbreaker on; maybe you should call those guys. Someone for sure has attacked him. He's conscious, but pretty out of it. Who, me? No, I can't tell you my name."

Eric shook his head at Kathleen. They were not going to stay here for hours and hours at the local precinct and go through all that fol-de-rol. He'd make sure the cops were on their way, and that the guy was out of the rain and comfortable. But he could not, would not, stand around and go through the questions and never-ending shit thrown at him by Pittsburgh's finest. "So how long? This guy needs medical attention. No, I won't tell you my name… how long?

Okay, I'll make sure you see him."

Eric clicked off and then half dragged, half carried the man to the doorway of one of the locked offices. He checked the wound on the man's head. It wasn't too bad, but he would have one hell of a headache and would probably need a dozen stitches. The door was locked, but the agent was sheltered under the door jamb.

"Maybe we should call the FBI, too."

"Good idea, I'm way ahead…" Kathleen cleared her throat and handed Eric the phone; she'd just dialed the local FBI office. "Here; you'd better talk to them."

Eric checked the phone; the number of the local FBI office appeared on the screen.

"Okay, ma'am, if you want to report…"

"One of your agents is at the railyard, he's been hurt. I've called 911 and they are sending an ambulance." Eric said into the phone. "No, I won't tell you my name… no I don't have to. I'm giving you a courtesy call, the ambulance is on the way, so if you want to check on him, better come here. Building A 45-768. Bye, gotta go, I hear the ambulance, they'll be here in 30 seconds."

Eric clicked off the phone, and grabbed Kathleen's hand. "Come on." He knew that leaving an injured man hoping someone else would find him was not the way he was programmed. He was the one always helping, always caring; well he did care, he just didn't have the time to mess with the situation.

He had changed since that fateful night in Carrboro, changed so much he hardly recognized himself. He hadn't second guessed any decision he'd made since he was in DC.

Eric led the way toward the river, weaving around trucks and buildings. They saw the ambulance, the cop cars, 'all the king's horses and all the king's men'…. the guy was damn lucky they'd found him. If they hadn't, he might not have survived till the next morning.

Kathleen tugged at his sleeve. "How come?" she could barely talk, and she rubbed at her throat, already reddened and looking like it would bruise badly by the morning.

"Like I said, we've got the next half dozen hours all sewn up. If we'd waited to give a statement, we'd miss out on meeting with our attorney and a myriad of other things. Let's get out of here and back to the hotel. Besides, we heard the ambulance, we saw the police cars. I don't want to be heartless, but we did our Good Samaritan thing, and now we have all kinds of matters breathing down our necks. Yeah, I know I sound heartless." Eric shook his head. God! Maybe he was turning into Jimmy. "Look, I have to get you out of the rain and get that throat of yours looked at."

Kathleen shrugged. It was apparent that it was just too painful for her to speak.

Chapter Fifty-one

Eric drove through the rain, avoiding the major roads and using his better than average sense of direction to get them to the hotel. It was a quiet, uneventful twenty minutes, enough time for Eric to try and figure out who the madman that attacked Kathleen had been. When they pulled in under the covered area, it was 3:32 am.

"You okay waiting for a few minutes in the lobby?" Eric asked. She nodded. "I'll be there in a minute, please see if they have some complimentary coffee in the lobby and then sit until I get there. Don't get it. Just sit near the coffee pot. I need something hot to drink, and you do too." Kathleen nodded and walked in.

Eric looked around for a place to park near the back row. He had to be incognito, even though logically he knew it was too late to be coy. Someone had their number. Maybe two someones.

He pulled the car into the spot facing a chain link fence and killed the engine. He glanced through the back window, retrieved his computer case, got out and locked the door.

Kathleen met him at the lobby entrance, and cleared her throat. "Are you okay?"

"We're going to get this finished and get back south where it's warm." He shivered.

Eric fixed himself a coffee, keeping his eyes on the cup, not looking up at Kathleen, as the adrenaline ebbed slowly away. He glanced at his watch; 3:45 am. "Let's go to the room and get into something dry." He punched in the floor of the elevator.

As the elevator started, Kathleen put her hand on his arm.

"Who do you think it was?"

"I have no idea, and I have a notion that we will never find out."

They went into the room and pulled dry clothes from their suitcases. After changing, Eric lay on the bed, putting his arm over his eyes.

"Nudge me when it's 4:30."

He knew he was dreaming. If he looked carefully, he could see himself standing behind Jimmy as the journalist scribbled something in one of his many notebooks. He was so close, he could almost smell Jimmy's aftershave and the ink in the fountain pen. He waited quietly, reading everything Jimmy wrote. He felt his quick intake of breath.

And then he knew where it was.

Chapter Fifty-two

5:00 am
Ramada Inn coffee shop

Eric and Kathleen sat in a booth across from Janine Reynolds, US attorney. She was a tall woman, professionally dressed in a dark business suit. Her long blonde hair lay provocatively across her face, just on the right side, reminding Eric of Veronica Lake, the 40s film star. She seemed to be unaffected by the early hour. She looked focused, intense and ready to go.

Kathleen wore a turtleneck; the bruises on her neck from their encounter with the crazy man at the railyard, were already darkening and turning purple. She could barely use her voice and kept her talking to a minimum.

Janine took out her legal pad and a handheld recorder. She pushed the button and looked up. "Do you mind?" Kathleen shook her head.

"Mr. Douglass, will you start? I want you to be aware that since I am a US attorney, the government is my client, but Kathleen and I go way back, so I am more than willing to give you my advice, but I can't represent you."

They both nodded.

"I was doing some research in Chicago about three weeks ago and I came across some information about FDR's Executive Order 6102, which required all Americans to turn in their gold coins and ingots, and that gold would be sent to the NY Federal Reserve vaults." "Your research about that?"

"I wanted to find out about a journalist for the Chicago Tribune in the thirties. He was murdered and his body was never found. Kathleen and I have figured out he was most likely murdered because he was going to expose some men who were in very high places. These men, one a US Senator, planned to pull off a heist of the gold that was being collected, bound for NY." Janine's gaze shot up in surprise at the mention of gold. "White gathered information for an exposé on FDR, a congressman named Gillespie, and the senator named Abrams. He knew they planned to make off with a portion of the gold. I got some old notebooks from White's grandson who lives in the same family home in Chicago. After looking through the notebooks, I found out that White discovered these politicians were staging a heist of the gold to be collected in Chicago. From what I can figure, that was around 1% of all the gold collected around the country. It was a clever, clever robbery. They got a small-time mobster, one Nealy O'Brien, a distant relation to Kathleen, to get some of his bad guys to pose as the Pinkertons guarding the gold. Then they only took a portion and hid it somewhere. We think it was here in Pittsburgh. The original manifest said the gold weighed in at 120,000 pounds. Through a process of elimination, Kathleen and I decided Nealy was the one that stashed that document, the original manifest. We looked for it in Kathleen's house and found it squirreled away in the basement. That was just dumb luck, finding the original manifest, that's how we knew there had been a robbery. I really don't know how we managed, but the doctored manifest, the one that's been sitting in the National Archives for 80 years, says that the gold that went to the New York Federal vaults was 22,000 pounds lighter. Here are the manifests, side by side." Eric pushed over his laptop and Janine studied the monitor as she jotted notes, and took a picture of the two documents with her phone. She showed no outward reaction to any of the information.

"We don't have any definitive proof of who killed Jimmy, but we can make an educated guess that Abrams and Gillespie had someone do it to shut him up. There is definitive information in his notebooks: names, dates and places that would have been enough evidence to prosecute the men. Kathleen tells me the information can be cross referenced and verified. I've ruled out anyone from the O'Briens." Eric reached out and squeezed Kathleen's hand and was rewarded by her sweet smile. "I'm eighty years too late to find Jimmy's murderer and have them prosecuted, but I can find out who did it." Eric mumbled under his breath. "At any rate, Janine, what we really need from you is to make sure we stay clear of any trouble from the FBI."

"Yes, I think that's highly recommended, and I'll do what I can. Do you have attorneys on retainer?"

"No, not in Pennsylvania."

"That's okay, I'll call a man I know in Philadelphia. Here is his name and number," she said as she scribbled on the back of her business card. "You get your attorney from Chicago to call him to be on the lookout, just in case. As far as the murder case, with what you've told me and the documents you've shared, someone must have been trying to shut White up before he exposed them and what they were about to do; it has to be related. If you do find this 'phantom gold,' if you find out it's real, if it's actually in your hand, will that tell us who killed White?"

"I don't know." Eric thought for a moment, *could finding out about the gold be enough to find closure and ultimately stop the nightmares and waking dreams?* He turned his mind back to the here and now. "So, Janine, what's the plan for today?"

"The FBI is overseeing the project, and the railyard is not happy about any of this. They have about a half dozen hand-picked men that are following everyone around to make sure no trestles or abutments are damaged, and that the work of railyard personnel is not disrupted in any way."

She looked up at them and quirked a smile at Kathleen.

"So, did you bring a shovel?"

Chapter Fifty-three

The sun would be up in another 45 minutes and he'd found exactly nothing. The documents and the maps that he'd taken from Douglass had not helped; they'd only raised more questions. He was in the right area, but my God, the place was massive. Benedict Gillespie sat down heavily on a wall, so close to the river, he could smell it over the diesel fuel, oil and machinery. The tall, bright lights interspersed around the perimeter cast massive shadows of both people and equipment. He knew he was in the general area. Nothing within his immediate line of sight was newer than 50 years. He couldn't give up, not now, not after he'd figured all of this…

Sirens, there were sirens screaming, tearing around the curve off the tarmac and onto the gravel roadway toward him. Cops, ambulance, fire truck, the whole damn menagerie was headed right down his throat. Gillespie folded the map and stuck it in his pants. He looked toward the sirens for a split second and snuck around the corner and away from the lights. That idiot Douglass had mocked him, just like Abrams had mocked his great-grandfather. He'd gotten the hand full of documents from him and that O'Brien woman, but there was nothing, nothing. They'd tricked him, and now they'd pay.

Benedict slowly moved just on the edge of the lights, well away from the approaching ambulance and more law enforcement that he'd seen in one place since… well, he wouldn't think about that.

Now, the only thing he could think about was revenge. Douglass would pay.

Albert III's head snapped back, his heart rate pumped up painfully. Sirens roared toward him. He moved backward toward the nearest building and peeked around the corner. An ambulance, fire truck, police cars, and good grief! The FBI? What in hell were they doing here?

Albert stood up straight, his jaw slackened in disbelief. The FBI? Great Scott. Albert looked down at his hands still holding the notebooks, each page dog eared, poorly folded maps crammed in between the pages making a nasty looking, soggy sandwich mess. He glanced up again. The ambulance had stopped and paramedics pulled a gurney from the back, and hustled over to a building to his right. Three men from the FBI car rushed forward. The lights flashed and men shouted to one another. A few of the men were moving his way.

Nope, he was outta here.

He walked stealthily backward, never taking his eyes from the men swarming around that building.

His nerves couldn't take it. Adventure with a vision of riches worthy of Midas were one thing. Thinking about what he'd do in a holding cell with a guy weighing 300 pounds was another thing all together. He watched TV. He knew what went on.

Chapter Fifty-four

5:22 am
CSX Railyard, Pittsburgh, PA

The sun had yet to make the slightest difference to the dark rain clouds. It was miserable, dank, the air chilled like a fine dry dirty martini.

"We're here just as a presence, you understand," said the FBI agent in charge, Mike Abernathy to Janine Reynolds. He watched Eric Douglass and a woman, who stood quietly on the perimeter of the group. Douglass's eyes moved slowly from one side of the group to the other, taking in every word and every movement made, with an eerie detachment. The man ought to be a 'spook', he'd do a damn good job. "My director wants to make sure you know we're here just in case."

The rumors were that digital copies of two manifests of the gold confiscated in 1933 had surfaced. The computer forensics guys had done their bit in assessing that the newly found documents could be authentic, but there was no proof.

Mike watched as one of Kathleen O'Brien's paralegals spoke to one of the agents, gesticulating wildly at the concrete abutments under several of the older trestles. Abernathy had heard that Ms. O'Brien was an attorney; she had hordes of minions doing her beck and call, one of them was gesturing for them to move one hundred yards to an old rusted trestle nearest the river.

"Listen," the paralegal was saying, "this is one of the only structures still standing since 1928. That's the map we used, the one from 1928. It can't be anywhere else, nothing else was standing then."

"I understand that," replied the agent, "but is there a certainty that anything is here? It's been 82 years since this all happened. A lot can happen in 82 years, including a crippling depression, a world war, and frankly kid, this is complete bullshit."

Kathleen's paralegal looked at her, his glance pleading.

Jeez, Abernathy thought, *the kid had swallowed the tale; hook, line, and sinker.*

"Sir," said Janine, "Ms. O'Brien has the manpower, and as you said, you are just here as a presence. Would you consent to let them take a crack at it? We've cleared it with the railyard people, so how about it? I'm just here as a presence, myself, making sure the government is represented."

Mike Abernathy, hands on hips, shook his head, turned and walked away a few yards.

"Okay, go ahead, but I'm not lifting a shovel, and neither are any of my men."

Kathleen smiled at her six paralegals, nodded and gave them a thumbs up. They looked like kids about to see what Santa had brought on Christmas morning.

Crowbars, shovels, and pitchforks came out of the back of two SUVs parked near the perimeter of the trestle. Auxiliary lights shone, illuminating the area. Railyard employees were there to ensure that any load-bearing walls didn't come down along with trestles, trucks and trains. No high-tech gear: no x-rays, no metal detectors, and no geophysical machines to measure solid masses under the dirt had been brought. The players of this strange tale couldn't commit to such an expense for a wild goose chase.

"Look!" said Tom, Kathleen's paralegal, as he stood up holding a box. He was the farthest away from the group, just on the periphery of the lighted area. He swung the box over his head as he ran to Kathleen and Eric. "See, it's made of wood. It had a place where a clasp could have been and portions of the hinges have rotted away."

Eric took the box and turned it over a few times. It was well over a foot long and more than eight inches deep. He pried at the top, which was shut tightly, despite the rotten hinges. At last the top came open and a velvet drawstring bag fell to his feet. He picked it up, turning it over and looking at it carefully.

"Isn't this the kind of bag you put silver in to keep it from tarnishing?"

"Yes," Kathleen said. "Perhaps it's used to keep the contents cushioned as well. Do you suppose the gold was in this?"

Eric shrugged his shoulders. "Okay, Tom, see what else you can find." Tom hurried back to continue his digging.

A shadow moved, and Mike Abernathy's trained eye honed in on the figure of a man moving around the edge of the lighted expanse. He was tall, and even from where he stood, Abernathy could see that the man was unkempt and scraggly. The man looked menacing, even from this distance. Abernathy watched for a few seconds as the man snuck behind the abutment, stopped and was very still. Slowly, he moved behind the crowd. Abernathy placed his hand, ever so lightly on the butt of his 9 mm weapon, and moved closer, perpendicular to the man, never taking his eyes from him.

The man tensed, moved forward, and leaned his upper body as he slowly took something out of his inside pocket. The man held the object up and aimed it at Douglass.

Time slowed and Mike Abernathy watched the man and his gun as if in tableaux; he could see a sneer spread across the man's face as he took aim.

"Gun," Mike screamed.

Abernathy launched himself at the man, his body hung in midair, sailing, defying gravity. He saw Douglass's head snap up and around. Kathleen O'Brien crouched, her hands covering her head. The paralegal with the pickaxe turned as he hoisted his tool like a weapon; he saw all of this, his body hovering in mid-air, coming down to fend off the attack. Mike heard the report of the revolver and felt a staggering blow, like a sledgehammer, as the bullet hit his chest, taking his breath away. He fell, hitting the gravel and tarmac below. He heard a scream, someone running, a weapon discharging, and then saw Douglass's face hovering above his. He heard him speak, but he was far away. He shook his head, and squinted, but Douglass's voice had slowed, and he sounded like a tape player rapidly losing its battery power. Mike couldn't hear or understand him; then everything stopped.

Chapter Fifty-five

Kathleen cleared her throat. She tried to make her voice work past its injuries of the night before. They were in the hotel coffee shop and still reeling from Mike Abernathy's death. I had had seen each painful second when Mike had jumped in. If he hadn't, I would be the one lying on a slab at Mercy Hospital. How can an act like that ever be repaid?

Kathleen and Eric had been staring into cold cups of coffee, trying to come to terms with all that had happened earlier.

I shook my head, thinking about sending Mike Abernathy's wife a card, maybe some flowers. The overwhelming feelings like nothing I'd ever felt before, relentlessly washed over me.

Neither spoke again for a long while. Then Kathleen cleared her throat again and spoke.

"We just have to get all these loose ends tied up. Our Pennsylvania attorney, the one Janine retained for us, anything that we have to tell the FBI will go through him, thank God! Thank God for most attorneys." She cleared her throat again and sipped her coffee. "And oh, I wanted to tell you, Tom found something, he just texted me. The abutment was solid, one of the load bearing walls to that trestle, but on the side, a space about twenty by twenty, looked like it had been a structure of some sort under the ground, attached to the abutment made with planks of wood for the sides and bottom. But the opening was mostly caved in and empty except for…"

"Except for what?"

"Except for the wooden box that Tom found. We measured and it is four inches deep, and 13 x 7 1/2 inches. As you know, nothing was in it, except for type of velveteen cloth used for protecting precious metals."

I shook my head. "I can't believe... well, I can. Trying to find the gold was what got Nealy and Jimmy killed."

"I think we've done enough for FDR's executive order and whoever stole it. We'll write up a report, make copies of all the documents, not mentioning, of course, how you got into this, and file the damn thing. Then we'll be done with it."

"But..."

"I know, I know, you want to find the murderer, I know that. But like I said before, whoever did it is long dead. You have to put it where it belongs, not in your dreams, but in your past. Maybe this psychic phenomenon was to help you get this far, to figure out this much."

I nodded. "Yeah, maybe you're right. So, we know who the man following us was last night, Benedict Gillespie, great-grandson of the congressman. God, he was the one that hurt you, I would have liked to clean his clock."

"Eric, you have changed so much. Two weeks ago, you'd never have talked about cleaning someone's clock. I hope Jimmy hasn't taken up residence." Her brows pulled down in a frown.

The last thing I wanted to do was upset her. She'd put up with enough grief in the past month just knowing me, so I put my arms around her and hugged her tightly. When we went back to the hotel room, I'd write down everything and see if I could make some sense out of it.

"No, it's okay." I reached down and kissed her. Thinking about nothing more than how good she felt.

"This is Rebecca Thompson of KUBD Channel 2 with breaking news. Early this morning a shooting occurred in the old CSX Railyard. Mike Abernathy, a special agent for the FBI, was shot and killed. There is no further information. The FBI was investigating rumors of missing government property at the site. More on this
breaking story when it becomes available."

Chapter Fifty-six

Pittsburgh Railyard, PA
01:02 September 24, 1933

The fog, thick and gray, seemed to wrap around his legs and body like a live thing. He shivered despite the hot, humid night. A kernel of fear slithered like a serpent down his backbone. Jimmy stopped and listened. Something was coming. He tried to recognize the rumbling off in the distance. He held his breath and focused on the sound. It was the hum of an engine.

The sound of the engine grew louder, and very quickly, two lights, the two headlights of a car, moved like a ghost with a lantern through the fog. Jimmy leaned forward, squinting, trying to make out where the car was and how fast it was traveling. He straightened, quickly. The car was moving, charging right toward him. Jimmy stared, mesmerized at the glare of the headlights. Time slowed, slowed, slowed, until it seemed to not move at all. He was frozen with fear, and like fighting against the swell of the tide, he couldn't get his feet moving. A quarter of a second ticked by as his heart knocked loudly in his ears. His eyes cut to the right and saw a strip of grass away from the car rushing toward him. He dove to the side, just as the car struck him with a blow that knocked him back several feet. For a split second he felt pain, and then darkness pushed mercifully toward him.

Frank looked in the rear-view mirror and saw the body half on, half off the path. He stopped the car and set the brake, his eyes never straying from Jimmy White. He opened the door and walked slowly, almost casually toward the body and looked down. White's eyes were open and staring, as a trickle of blood meandered out of the corner of his mouth. Frank nudged the body with his foot. Nothing. He lifted the wallet from Jimmy's breast pocket and saw his watch. It was bloodied, the crystal broken, the second hand stopped on its sweep toward 12. He'd just take the cash. Frank opened the billfold, pulled out the money and dropped the wallet, watching for a moment as it fluttered down to plop next to the body. Unhurriedly, he picked up Jimmy's body and slung it over his shoulder and walked toward the place he'd already scoped out.

Frank turned toward the elevated line that lay close to the river. To his left were a series of abutments, all the numbers stenciled neatly above each door. There was a large area, a depression, between two of them almost completely under the elevated line, a natural dip in the landscape. Frank let the body slip to the ground and retrieved a shovel he had stashed in the back of the car.

It took an hour of sweat and dirt before Frank made a hole deep enough. He took the lap robe from the back seat of the car and wrapped Jimmy's body in it. He laid the body of the reporter in the hole and covered it before looking around one last time. This place was as remote as an inlet off Sheepshead Bay in Brooklyn. No one would find this guy for a long, long time.

4:15 pm
Ramada Inn Airport
Pittsburgh, PA

He shot up in bed, his gaze darting around the darkened room. He was in Pittsburgh near the airport with Kathleen.

He leaned over the gap that separated the two beds and gently shook her arm.

"Wha..." she croaked. She cleared her throat roughly before sitting up to drink some water. "What is it Eric?"

"I want you to call the airport and tell our pilot that there will be a delay. Tell him we'll leave after 10 tomorrow, and dismiss your

'Baker Street Irregulars'; they can go back home. What I have to do,
I have to do alone."

"But Eric…"

"Just do it, I have to go. I'll make some calls for you, I know your throat is still a problem."

Kathleen sighed and gestured to her tablet on the desk.

"I'll do this downstairs. I'll call everyone except the pilot and Janine. Can you do that?"

She nodded.

"Good. Go back to sleep, sorry I woke you." He reached over and gave her a kiss before slamming out of the door.

Eric stood by the elevator and glanced at his watch. The time change wouldn't happen until next week, so it would be dark enough very soon. When he went back, it would have to be dark.

"Hey, wait for me." Kathleen stopped the closing elevator doors and slipped quietly inside next to Eric.

"Honey, you should go back to sleep."

Kathleen gave him a look. "Not, likely, boy-o."

It was 5:15 as Eric and Kathleen headed for the railyard. They'd be there in a half hour and by 6:00. The overcast sky, thick with clouds would hasten the oncoming darkness. He glanced over at Kathleen; it would have been obvious to a blind man that she was troubled about this turn of events.

"Eric," she said, as she turned in her seat to face him. "You aren't going to solve Jimmy's murder by going back to the railyard. Isn't that why all of this started?"

He squeezed her hand, but kept his eyes on the road. With the theft of government gold and the murder of a journalist two generations before, it seemed like Abrams and O'Brien were thumbing their collective noses at him.

"Yes, I know that now. If I can wrap up this mystery at the railyard then, as you said that will be closure. I'm sorry I'm dragging you around. Would you like me to take you back to the hotel?"

"No! No way, I'm still in this, whatever this ends up being. But what has prompted this early evening excursion?"

"I'm just following a hunch."

Eric parked the car in almost the same spot as the night before. He turned to her and gave her a quick kiss, and then fiddled around in the glove box for the flashlight. "This won't take long, please stay in the car."

It was past dusk now and the wind began to pick up. Eric looked up at the huge white stratocumulus clouds scuttling across the sky, their underbellies illuminated by the city lights. The wind, high and steady off the river, blew grit in his eyes and mouth, and bits of paper, twigs and leaves scattered across the gravel road and against his pants and shoes.

The wind moaned around the edges of the buildings. Eric heard nothing but that lonely, chilling sound, not even the beating of his heart. He followed the same path he'd used in the early morning and reached the edge of the area. The trestle, abutment and the big damn hole in the ground were cordoned off by yellow crime tape. There was no one there, no guard, but then again, what would they be guarding? Eric glanced around before stepping under the tape. He knelt down in the two by six-foot cavity that had been made from vertical planks set in a semi- circle. Jimmy had made a guess as to where the gold was hidden and recorded this in one of the last notebooks that Eric had deciphered. It was a solid guess and made sense to Eric, and he was going to check it out. He took the handle of a discarded shovel and thumped on the vertical planks that formed the interior of the cavity. He hit each plank with a gentle tap. Thump, thump, thud; a hollow sound like an elusive echo sounded behind the plank that faced away from the river and near the end of the semicircle. Eric wedged the blade of the shovel between the two boards and pulled. The board on the left loosened enough for him to put his hand behind the plank. He jimmied and wiggled the board back and forth until it came loose.

He looked past the edge of the board and shone the beam of his flashlight into the cavity. The light shone on another round of planks, some twelve inches further in. An entire side of the closest plank had rotted away, and Eric could see another cavity hidden behind that second round of boards, almost as big as the one he was sitting in. The entire hole, as big as a horizontal shower stall, was filled with boxes like the one Kathleen's paralegal had found earlier. Eric pushed his hand and arm in past his elbow and could barely touch the nearest box.

He strained to reach the box, just past the beam of his flashlight when the wind whipped up and blew grit and debris against his body, stinging his eyes. He put his hand up to ward off the grit, and the flashlight bounced out of his grip. It wasn't important now; what was important was to find out what was in there. He wedged his right hand into the cavity, lying down inside the first hole. He felt around for the flashlight with his foot, as he pushed forward with sheer force of will to reach one of the boxes. Suddenly, a beam of light struck past his shoulder, flooding the hole. Eric froze

"Okay, Mr. Douglass, you can come on up with your hands raised."

Chilled and shaking, adrenaline coursed through him. Eric slowly pulled his hand from behind the planks, pushed up until he was on his knees, stood and raised his hands over his head. His heart thumped wildly in his ears as he stepped over the lip of the hole and turned.

The florid-faced data manager from the Treasury Department trained a revolver right at Eric's chest. "Mr. Jenkins? What the hell..."

"Mr. Douglass, you've done a wonderful job finding the gold for me, and I wish to thank you for that. Unfortunately, you'll have to go. No one can know that I absconded with the treasure... and the one who killed you."

The clouds, dense and thick, scudded past the illumination of the perimeter lights to reveal Jenkins's maniacal grin. Eric shivered;

Jenkins looked like one of the patients on the 10th floor of the medical university, the patients that orderlies were forced to sedate when the moon was full.

Eric took a step back, his first thought of Kathleen. What if this maniac had seen her?

"No, don't move. I will decide what to do with you in a moment. I hadn't really thought you'd be here, but now, since you are, well…" Jenkins's voice was devoid of emotion, like a man giving his order to a waiter.

A gust of wind tore around the building, scattering grit and dust in its wake. Jenkins brushed the back of his hand across his face; and Eric saw the man's eyes tear madly as he looked down and away from Eric. At that split second, Eric dove for the gun. His hand found the barrel and pulled up and away, but his hands were slick and the gun slipped out of his grasp. He turned and ran for all he was worth.

"You! Come back here! Stand Still!"

Jenkins couldn't see him in the dark, but he could hear him. Eric stopped. One heartbeat, two, then the wind rose again and the clouds parted, lighting the area.

Eric abruptly changed course and ran as fast as he could toward the car and Kathleen. He skimmed across the gravel, abruptly changing course yet again, zig zagging away from the pounding feet behind him. He glanced over his shoulder. If he could see Jenkins, Jenkins could see him. A flash from the muzzle of Jenkins's gun. The bullet sped past Eric's ear and ricocheted off a building just ahead. Eric changed direction, moving to the right toward the sound of a truck. Gravel from the path shot up, cutting into his jeans bruising his shins. A rock flew up hitting his forehead, and warm, sticky blood flowed into his eye. Looming ahead was a dim shadow, a dump truck. He ducked behind the massive back wheel, leaning heavily on the tire, trying to catch his breath. He peeked around the wheel and watched Jenkins's shadow move to his right. Eric shot out from his hiding place and ran to his left, putting distance between him and Jenkins. Ahead, he made out the gray outline of a building and poured on the speed as he darted to the right. The gravel smoothed out to tarmac and only yards from where he'd left Kathleen.

Another report from Jenkins's gun barreled into him, the sound so deafening it encompassed him entirely. There was a sting at his temple and a sluggish trail of blood trickled into his ear. Jenkins was close, but a terrible shot. The revolver belched out again and Eric felt the projectile so close, it touched the hair on the other side of his head. Within the next few yards, the tarmac narrowed and the perimeter lights were few. He moved to the left, heading for the river.

He saw no one about, no one. Where were the lights, the sounds of machinery, people talking; he had to go there. He had to find workers, anybody; there was safety in numbers.

He heard a train on one of the two elevated tracks on the left and the shouts of workmen. They were close to the river; if he could get there, he would lead Jenkins as far away from Kathleen as he possibly could. He heard nothing but his own labored breathing and the pounding of Jenkins's running feet, moving too fast.

A bit of scrub, an inconsequential weed stood in the way of freedom. His arms flailed out churning, trying to regain his balance, but he went down hard on his left side and his body slid for a few feet before it stopped. Gravel shot up around him, pelting his face, head and chest. He shook his head and in one movement, put his hands down to push himself up. The business end of a revolver was an inch from his nose.

"Mr. Douglass, get up, steady… now turn around slowly. We're going to walk down to the river. A good place to get rid of you." Jenkins was breathing hard and was almost doubled over, but he had the gun and held it steady right at Eric's head. "It may be some time before they find you, if they find you, but soon I'll be in South America."

Eric stood with his hands on his head, blood rushed in his ears so fast he could hear little around him. He had to think of a way. He had to…

He heard the report, so loud it deafened him. Had he been shot? Something heavy fell in the gravel behind him. He turned; Jenkins was face down in the road, his arms splayed out on either side, the revolver lying a few feet from his head.

A wisp of smoke curled from the muzzle of a gun Kathleen held steady with two hands.

"Oh God. What…"

She walked to the body and kicked the gun away from where it lay on the ground near Jenkins's hand and bent forward to feel for a pulse. "He's gone."

"Kathleen." Words failed him, completely failed him.

She walked to his side and hugged him fiercely. "I heard Jenkins talk about killing you, so I ran over here as fast as I could." She hugged him even tighter, then stepped away, but still held onto Eric's hand as though she was loath to let him go. "Before I left the car, I called the FBI. I knew something was up."

"Yeah. Well, how he knew, I can't guess. Maybe he's been following us the whole time."

"That's what I think." Her head came up, listening. "Sirens." They stood quietly, waiting.

"Girl, you rock my world. God, I'm sure glad you didn't stay in the damn car."

KATHRYN SCARBOROUGH

Epilogue

It took another two days for the FBI, the Secret Service and Treasury to dig and pull allthe gold from its long and dusty hiding place. The questioning was endless, tedious and on the afternoon of day two, Eric told the special agent in charge that he'd had enough.

"You have my phone, my email, my address, and those of Ms. O'Brien; we have a life to get back to. If you need anything further of us, just get in touch, we are at your disposal."

It was a perfectly reasonable request, so reasonable that the special agent told them to go with his blessing.

Of course, there was an investigation into Bob Jenkins. It hadn't been difficult to figure out what he'd known, and where he'd gotten the information to follow them to Pittsburgh.

Jenkins followed Ralph Gunderson, his colleague at the National Archives, to Chicago. He'd tailed Ralph and waited. He watched while Gunderson went through the sheds, watched as he'd thrown out the boxes from the old man's house and gone through the rubbish himself.

Ralph had gathered all the notebooks he'd found and disseminated all of the information. When he left the house to follow his hunch to Pittsburgh, Jenkins shot him, returned to the house, killed the old man, and took everything. Jenkins's DNA was all over Ralph and the old man, and his fingerprints were found in the house and on the boxes. They found the notebooks, with Gunderson's blood all over them in Jenkins's car. Bob Jenkins had been a sloppy killer. He'd thought he was too good or his state of mind was such that he believed he wouldn't be caught; crazed maniacs often thought that way.

The government, in all its infinite wisdom, gave Kathleen and Eric a finder's fee; 10% of the valuation of the gold. After Christmas that year, they'd received their checks from Uncle Sam. The finder's fee netted them each a cool $1.25 million after taxes. A stunning amount, something Eric never thought he'd see.

Kathleen snuggled in Eric's arms in front of the roaring fire in her Canaryville home. In the months since their momentous find, she'd restructured her business and felt once again secure about the financial prospects of her family. Meeting Eric Douglass had had more than one terrific benefit. She watched the firelight play across the planes of Eric's, now so endearing face, letting her thoughts drift. She sat up quickly and shook Eric's shoulder.

"But, what about Jimmy."

Eric didn't speak for a long moment.

"I know, somehow," he said as he shrugged his shoulders, "that Jimmy is in the Pittsburgh railyard near the river. He didn't know exactly where he was; he was snooping around and made an educated guess as to where Abrams and Gillespie would stash the gold. So, he isn't buried with the gold; if he had been, they'd have found him. Remember, they used a backhoe around the area where the gold was buried, and no Jimmy. Someday soon, someone will find him and he'll get a decent burial."

Eric was quiet for a moment as he stared into the flames. He'd thought about this long and hard for more than six months. Had he been Jimmy? At this point he didn't think knowing, one way or the other, was important, just that he'd found out the why: because Jimmy was closing in on the Abrams/Gillespie/O'Brien triumvirate and was about to expose them. Nealy O'Brien had not been in Pittsburgh when Jimmy was killed, so it had to have been some thug hired by Abrams to kill Jimmy.

Eric had written a letter to the CEO of the railyard. He had explained Jimmy's murder and where he might be. He asked if there was ever any excavation around the river near the elevated tracks, and of course there were miles of those, to be aware of a possible grave and who may have been buried there. It was obvious by the curt, but courteous reply, what the man thought of Eric, but he was too polite to say. He told Eric that gangsters had probably buried their enemies around the railyard since it had opened in 1894.

Eric sighed and snuggled back and gently pulled Kathleen's head down on his shoulder. "Someday soon, we'll find him. The best part of our adventure was the dreams that had plagued me for weeks are gone. I don't dream about Jimmy or your cousin anymore. I have laid those ghosts to rest, thank God! I can still remember things about Jimmy, about the family that really wasn't mine, about being a journalist. But the rest of it, the exhaustion and the terror are gone, hopefully gone forever."

"What are you going to do with your share?"

"I've thought about that, I'm going to give Albert III $50,000. I told him it's money he earned for letting me go through his attic and helping me research my 'book'. He was so blown away when I called, he was speechless. I decided that's the least Jimmy could do for his descendants, the bastard. I suppose acting irresponsibly is a byproduct of what happens when you're convinced you're a rock star.

"I'm giving $50,000 to the University Medical School. That's just chicken feed to them, but maybe it will buy a few beakers and lab trays. Dr. Lu was ecstatic and forgave me for missing two days of work, then I took an indefinite leave of absence and I still haven't decided if I'm going back. They've done without me for six months now. Maybe I'll find someplace exotic to work, like Chicago," he said as he squeezed her hand.

"Then I'm giving about $50,000 to the Boys and Girls Club. Kids with no-account or missing fathers need all the help they can get. It took me until the age of 36 to figure out that my father dying when I was 12 had been so detrimental, that I wasn't engaging in life; I was just being pulled along. That's a hell of a note."

Kathleen kissed him and smiled, then asked. "So, are you giving it all away?"

"Give it all away? What, do you think I'm nuts?" he said with a grin.

Author Notes

I researched how precious stones and metals are measured, how much weight of said gold could be transported in separate boxes, and what type of transport would be needed to carry such a load.

FDR (the only real person I mentioned in this book), did write an executive order in 1933 that compelled American citizens turn over their gold coins and ingots. In return, each citizen received a $29.00 certificate for each ounce of gold they relinquished. In a too short period of time, gold jumped to $33.00 per ounce. There was spotty outrage from the public about the order. Several citizens took the government to court in a bid to retain their gold, but they lost.

Ft. Knox was completed in 1936 and supposedly, the gold reserves from the NY vaults were transferred there for safe keeping. There was an audit of the contents of Ft. Knox more than a generation ago, and since then, no one has reported on what is inside the huge vault.

For the rest: the characters, places, incidents, in this novel are all figments of my overactive imagination.

Thanks for reading! Any questions, comments, REVIEWS PLEASE on the books' Amazon page.

https:www.scarboroughbooks.com
kathryn@scarboroughbooks.com

Your Next Great Read!

Try <u>Deception</u> Book 1 of my 3 book series, of family secrets in the midst of tragedy and turmoil!

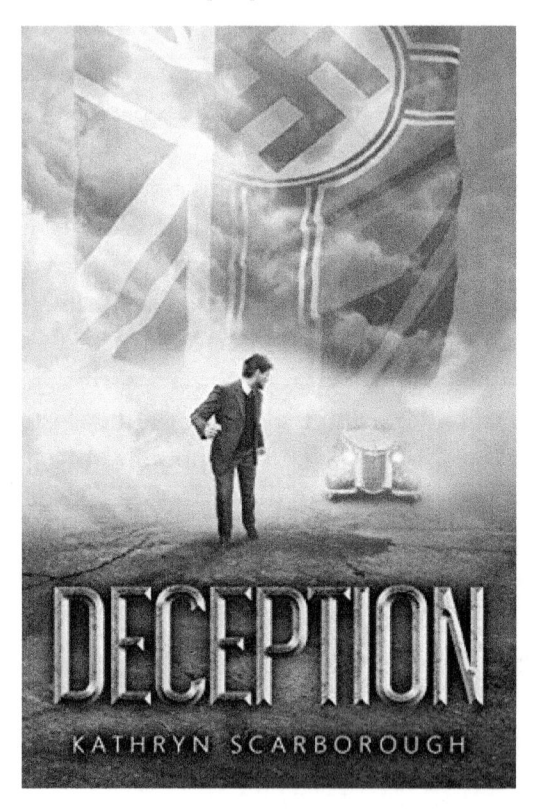

https://www.amazon.com/dp/B08VRQTF6S

Deception

Lovers, Elsbet, a propagandist working for Germany, and Ian, an intelligence analyst and 'spy master' for the British MI5, are torn apart by a war Ian saw coming but Elsbet refused to acknowledge. Covertly, Ian travels to Germany to compel Elsbet's return, and in November 1939, after England has declared war on Germany, their daughter

Margaret is born. Elsbet begins a cat and mouse game with a splinter group of the S.S. and discovers their dark secret. She tries an escape for her daughter and herself, but it is too late, and she is trapped until the end.

"**Deception** " **The world is balanced on a precipice; the slippery slope leading right into Hell, and all it will take for the world to topple is for Hitler to sneeze." Will Elsbet return? Will Ian finally be caught as a spy? Get Deception today to find out!**

https://www.amazon.com/dp/B08VRQTF6S